To my family,
who doesn't understand my obsession with romance novels,
but loves and supports me anyway.

Please Note

TRIGGER WARNINGS ARE AT the back of the book to avoid spoilers for those who don't require them. There is gun violence and issues related to pregnancy. Be sure to check the full list under Author's Note.

READY
to Risk

SHEFALI PREM

ISBN: 979-8-9922335-3-7 (paperback)

ISBN: 979-8-9922335-4-4 (ebook)

Previously published as Free to Risk by Bella d'Amour

Published by WIP Media LLC

wipmediallc.com

1

Stevie

*G*OD, *I MISS HOME.*

I blow out a breath, tired and dejected, as I roll to a stop at a rural intersection somewhere in Nebraska. Miles of farmland await me in every direction—endless and lonely.

Somewhere along the deserted back roads between the Badlands of South Dakota and the rolling grasslands of northern Nebraska, I was hit with a crushing wave of loneliness. My nomadic life feels so empty. *I* feel empty.

Of course, it didn't help that I played Springsteen's *Nebraska* album as a tribute to the state and to my father, who had loved The Boss. The songs were as dark as I felt. Talk about mood music.

What was the name of the town that prompted me to take the last turn? Doughboy? Valentine? There's no point in checking Google Maps. My phone has been searching for a signal for a while. I unfold my paper map and spread it out over the steering wheel, trying to figure out where I am. There's nothing around me for reference so I haven't a clue. I've been driving aimlessly, my thoughts on home.

It doesn't matter where I am or which direction I go. I am at a literal crossroads in my life. I want to go home, but to what? That is the question that has kept me on the road, searching for an answer.

I try to recall the feeling of freedom and exhilaration I experienced when I got on a plane for the first time, heading to Jamaica. Back then, I'd been eager to see the world outside my small, rural Connecticut town. I'd been trapped by the never-ending responsibility of taking care of my mother and younger sisters. When I'd finally been set free, I felt like a tightly wound spring exploding away from its casing.

Looking back, I shake my head at my naïveté. I'd pictured a carefree, endless spring break filled with parties and nonstop fun to make up for the ones I'd missed out on with my friends. But when I eventually got my chance, I'd been neither eighteen nor on spring break. The endless partying felt empty without friends. They had moved on with their lives with college, jobs, and families. Wanting something more to fill the void in my soul, I stopped island-hopping and broadened my horizons to the rest of the world.

Over three years later, it's all beginning to blur together. If it wasn't for the meticulous labeling of the thousands of photos I've taken around the world, from South America to Asia and just about everywhere in between, I honestly wouldn't remember where many of them were shot.

I glance at the camera bag on the floor of the passenger seat, realizing I haven't taken any photographs since this morning. Peering out the Jeep window at the gray skies and muddy, harvested fields of the Heartland, I feel uninspired. The emptiness around me reflects my current mood, but I force myself out of the car with my camera. I adjust the settings to shoot black and white photos that will capture the stark desolation I feel.

I start with several shots of the wide-open space with trees sparsely scattered along the road. Switching to a long-range zoom lens, I shoot closeups of nearly naked branches, a few leaves clinging to them. I imagine them as survivors, holding on for dear life during the wind and rain of the night before.

Adjusting my view, I see what appear to be rooftops in the distance. I can't tell if they're houses or storefronts, but at least they're a sign of life. I'm hungry and getting low on gas, so I pack up my camera and get back in the car to follow the gravel and dirt road toward the structures.

By the time the gravel turns to asphalt, I can see that the squat buildings are a tiny town, if one could call it that. It's nothing more than a short, wide street with angled parking in front of shops that appear deserted. After filling up the Jeep's tank at a gas station that still has old-fashioned fuel pumps, I scan the street until I see the ubiquitous CAFE sign. I pull into a parking spot in front and consider taking a few photos of the quaint town until I remember I have hundreds of photos of similar places already.

As soon as I enter the mostly empty establishment, a female voice calls out, "Grab a seat anywhere. I'll be right with you."

Looking around for the owner of the voice, I don't see anyone but three older men sitting at one end of the counter. They are all dressed in flannel shirts and denim overalls, with baseball caps over their gray hair—and all of them have turned to look at me.

"Thank you," I say in the direction of the kitchen window behind the counter. The diner appears to be straight out of a movie set in the '70s, with teal and orange décor and chrome accents. It goes with the old fuel pumps at the gas station. It's as if time has stood still here.

Spying the restroom sign, I head to it, smiling politely at the men whose heads swivel to watch me as I walk past. After using the facilities, I settle into a booth overlooking the street. I take a quick scan of the laminated menu, then unfold my map and fish out a red marker from my battered leather backpack.

"If you're lost, no wonder. Haven't seen one of those in forever," the voice from before says.

I look up at the waitress, a pretty but tired-looking woman in a knee-length dress that's almost the same shade as the teal blue vinyl seat I'm sitting on. She's gesturing to the map with her pen, a notepad in the other hand, ready to take my order.

I give her a rueful smile. "I keep it in case I don't have internet, but it wasn't much use earlier. I took a wrong turn somewhere and ended up lost."

"Sounds like the story of my life," the waitress sighs. She leans over and taps the end of her pen on the map. "Here we are. We're too small for most maps to label our little village." Standing straight again, she asks, "What can I get you, honey?"

"I'll have the chicken Caesar salad and a Diet Coke."

"Sure thing."

Just as she's about to turn away, I add, "And fries with a side of ranch, please?" It's my go-to comfort food and I'm in desperate need of some comfort right now.

"You got it, honey."

When she leaves, I mark my giant paper map with the red marker, adding the route I've taken since starting out this morning. When I can't remember a particular turn, I take my best guess.

My gaze wanders over the lines I've drawn to mark this particular trip. They crisscross several times since I left Connecticut with no planned itinerary. I'd recently come home from my last trip abroad with the decision to stay close to home. Yet when my sister Charlie revealed her pregnancy, I packed my bags again and got back on the road. I needed to get away from the buried feelings that threatened to emerge.

I used the excuse of visiting Georgie, Charlie's twin, whom I hadn't seen in a couple of years. She's been living in Missouri since her sudden marriage to a politician, the last place I expected my sister to end up. But when I called Georgie, she had been busy with campaign events and unable to see me.

In the ten weeks since, I've meandered through upstate New York, then hugged the shores of the Great Lakes with occasional detours. I continued to wander around to the northern Great Plains, through Native American reservations and national parks. With less than three weeks until Thanksgiving, I'm hoping to follow through on my promise to see Georgie before I head home.

The waitress brings my meal, and I engage her in conversation. The traveling may have gotten old, but listening to people's life experiences never will.

"What did you mean when you said 'the story of my life' earlier?" I pry after asking about the area and what it's like living here.

"Oh, I followed a boyfriend, way back when, to Nashville. My parents warned me against it, tellin' me I should finish school, but I was afraid he'd find someone else by then. 'Course, he found a new girl anyway and dumped me as soon's he did. I came home pregnant, tail tucked 'tween my legs. I've been at this diner ever since. My kid is grown and gone, but here I am." She sighs in resignation. "Such is life. Let me know if you need anythin' else, honey."

Feeling more dejected than ever, I wonder if I'll be telling a similar story one day, minus the kid. Unwilling to dwell on that depressing thought, I concentrate on the map while eating instead of the past or the future.

With little enthusiasm, I try to decide which direction to go next from my current location in central Nebraska. I'm not sure I have the energy to zig-zag around the Midwest for the next couple of weeks while I wait for Georgie's schedule to free up for my visit. Wandering around with no destination and no plan will not help me find my way in life at this point. So why am I still doing it?

Because you're trying to avoid what's waiting for you at home.

The voice I've been ignoring finally cuts through the bullshit I've been telling myself.

Are you going to live out of a suitcase for the rest of your life? Enough is enough. Go home. Face him and move on.

"Okay, okay. I hear you," I mutter, silencing the voice that sounds too much like my mother's. But before I can go home, I need to try one last time to visit Georgie. Pulling out my phone, I look up the distance to her address, just south of St. Louis. Ten hours. I call her but get her voicemail as usual, so I text her.

I'm driving in your direction again. Can be there tomorrow. Would love to see you before I go back home.

By the time I finish eating, look for a good place to stop for the night in a few hours, and pay my check, she replies.

Sorry, I'm away. Connor's upset about losing the election, so we're taking some time away. I'll call you when I get back. Promise. Love you.

Well, hell. No more excuses for me. Looks like I'm going home. But rather than dread weighing me down, my step is lighter than it's been for far too long.

My cell phone rings just as I reach for the car's onscreen menu to call home before I get back on the road.

Smiling at the name flashing on the screen, I answer.

"Hi, sweetie. It must be a blue moon to have you actually call instead of text," I say to my baby sister Bobbie. "I was just about to call Mom."

"Mom's with Charlie."

I frown, my heart jumping at Bobbie's serious tone. Trying not to jump to conclusions, I ask, "Why? What's going on? Is Mom okay?"

"She's fine. It's Charlie. She's been in an accident."

"Oh, God. Is she hurt? What happened? What about the baby?"

"Geez, slow down," Bobbie huffs. "She's okay but banged up a little and might have a concussion. Joey was talking to her on the phone when she heard Charlie crash. Sounds like some jerk was tailing her too closely and the roads were bad from the snow.

Brent says Luc's father might be responsible, so Gabe is sending bodyguards to the hospital."

My brain is spinning, trying to keep up with everything Bobbie is telling me, but it screeches to a halt at the mention of Gabe. My heart squeezes painfully.

"Stevie? You still there?"

Bobbie's voice pulls me back from the edge. I suck in a deep breath and bring myself to the matter at hand. Charlie. Accident. Home. I have to go home.

Where Gabe is.

I shake my head. Not now. "I'm here. Just thinking of how to get home. I—"

"Mom said you don't need to. She just wanted to let you know in case you hear about it."

"Hear about it?"

"Yeah, because, you know. It's Luc."

"Who's Luke?"

"Lucien Saint? The Firebirds quarterback? *The* Lucien Saint! Charlie has been secretly dating him and she's having his baby! Can you believe it? And he's *here*! He came with Brent to the hospital."

Bobbie's squealing excitement filling the Jeep reminds me of her age. Because of her genius brains, I forget sometimes she's still a teenager.

Her words slowly sink in. Charlie's mystery baby daddy is the star quarterback of the New York Firebirds and our brother's teammate. Is that why Charlie wouldn't tell us who the father is?

Mom was right about the possibility I'd hear about the accident. Luc's fame outside of New York City and football is such that if his involvement with Charlie and the accident leaked, I'd hear about it even if I didn't follow the Firebirds news.

But why would Luc's father want to hurt Charlie if she was carrying his grandchild? I shake my head, deciding it's better to get the details from the grownups later.

"I know. Shocking, right?" Bobbie's voice cuts into the silence.

"Calm down, Bobbie. He's just a man, not Superman, even if Charlie sees herself as some TV version of Lois Lane. Is Mom okay?"

"She's fine, just worried. She's sitting with Charlie. Joey's here too," she adds, referring to Charlie's best friend and an honorary member of our family. And possibly our future sister-in-law now that she and Brent are together.

"Where are you guys now?"

"We're at the hospital in Danbury."

"Okay, I'll be there just as soon as I can."

"I told you, Mom said you don't need to come home right away."

"Of course, I'm coming home."

"Okay, fine," Bobbie huffs at my unintentionally sharp tone. "I'm just the messenger. Geez."

I can't help but smile at the sound of teenage angst in her voice. I can clearly picture the eye roll that accompanied her words. I helped raise Bobbie after our mother had a stroke, but I've seen only glimpses of the transition from adolescent to teenager while I've been away.

"I'm sorry. Didn't mean to snap at you. I was literally about to call Mom to let her know I was heading back home. Keep me updated, sweetie. Love you."

After hanging up, I switch over to the GPS. Fifteen hundred miles. Twenty-four hours if I drive straight through, which I cannot without getting into an accident of my own. I woke up early to catch the sunrise at Badlands National Park. Checking flights out of the nearest airport, I see I'll miss the last one by the time I reach Omaha. I book the first flight out, as well as a hotel room near the airport. I'll return the rented Jeep in the morning.

Finally pulling out of the parking space in front of the diner, I get back on the road again, one last time.

2

Gabe

"**L**UC, EVERYTHING'S ALL SET. Team's in place," I say as I enter the living area of Lucien Saint's massive West Village home where everyone is gathered. As stretched thin as my staff is, I'm thankful the star quarterback has asked his pregnant girlfriend to move in with him while we protect them from his father. A row house with limited points of entry is a lot easier to secure than the sprawling Hutchinson family home in Connecticut where Charlie lives with her mother and little sister.

Glancing around, my eye catches Charlie's. She looks a lot better today than she did in the hospital yesterday. A bandage still covers the gash she got when her car hit a tree—No. When a lunatic, Luc's father, rammed her car off the road and into a tree. Not wanting to think how much worse it could have been, I turn toward Luc.

"I'm going to take off, and I'll check—" I stop abruptly when my brain registers who is standing next to him. "Oh."

Stevie.

My initial shock at seeing her turns into joy for one quick flash before my entire body stiffens against the flood of painful memories.

I force my jaw to unhinge enough to say, "Hey, Stevie."

She turns to fully face me. "Hello, Gabe."

More than ten years may have passed, but I know that smile on her is as forced as my greeting was.

Stevie fucking Hutchinson. The girl I thought I was going to spend the rest of my life with the moment I first saw her as more than Brent's little sister.

"Thanks, man, for everything."

Luc's voice breaks the awkward silence in the room. I blink, popping the bubble Stevie and I were in, memories of all the love and hurt and regret vibrating between us.

I pull myself together to focus on the moment. It appears Stevie only just arrived, because she turns away to greet her mother and other siblings. Forcing a grin, I tell Luc, "Remember that when I send you the bill." I glance over the gathering in Luc's family room that includes most of Charlie's family as well as Luc's baby sister Daphne.

"See you around, ladies," I tell them. Giving a casual salute to the oldest of the Hutchinson siblings, I add, "Brent."

He tilts his chin at me, most of his attention on his girlfriend Joey, who's wrapped in his arms. Having recently gotten back together after their breakup, the two are practically glued to each other's side when they're in the same room.

An image of Stevie and I doing the same after an argument tries to break through. I push the memory and all thoughts of her out of my head—something I had a lot of practice doing when we first broke up. I leave the house and slide into the passenger seat of the waiting SUV.

Rafe, my twin and the person who knows me best, takes one look at my face and states, "You saw Stevie."

"Briefly." I give him a look that he should know means I don't want to talk about it. But Rafe being Rafe, he keeps yapping.

"Shocked the hell out of me when I saw her go downstairs. I tried to find you and warn you. You okay?"

Avoiding his concerned gaze, I slip on my aviators. "Why wouldn't I be? We went our separate ways a long time ago. A lot has happened since then."

"It has. You're different people now."

As twins, we're able to communicate by what's not said as much as we do by spoken words. Despite the flicker of hope that flares to life at the suggestion Stevie and I might be able to overcome what we couldn't back then, I snuff it out with a heap of common sense.

"Like you said, a lot's happened. Two of those happenings are waiting for me at home, so let's get moving. And tell me when the new hires are going to be ready."

Rafe is finishing up the training of several men we recently hired to join our personal security business. He and I founded Guardian Angels Personal Protection Services when I made the decision to move back to my hometown three years ago. Between my military experience and Rafe's as a mixed martial arts champion, we were up and running in no time. We'd grown enough to expand our services as well as buy land for a training facility in Connecticut and move our office to the exclusive Anastasios Towers.

It helped that Rafe had celebrity status from his time competing and, unfortunately, even more so after his last fight. But his notoriety and my background as a Navy SEAL helped us get clients quickly. It also helped that he and I work together in sync, allowing us to share the responsibility of recruiting and training new hires, bringing in new clients, and overseeing the administrative work that comes with running a business—one that grew faster than we anticipated. But with growth came the money to hire employees to take over some of the administrative tasks.

"I was hoping for a few more days," Rafe answers, pulling away from Luc's. "But we can switch some of the guys around and put the newbies with the experienced guys on the low-risk jobs."

"I'd prefer to have them fully trained before they start, but let's take a look at the roster when we get to the office. With the last-minute coverage at Luc's, we're likely going to lose two prospective clients we have waiting in the wings."

"That's pretty much a sure thing," Rafe says with a grimace. "But family first, and Charlie's practically family."

We've known the Hutchinsons since we were little, our fathers having worked in the same firehouse. Our mothers' fondest wish was for our families to be joined by marriage. They thought it would come true when Stevie and I started dating.

I shake off the memory when Rafe continues. "Luc pulled me aside earlier. He intends to keep Charlie and his sister at his place, but asked if we can have a couple of guys at the Hutchinson house when Sandra and Bobbie—and now Stevie—go back home. At least until Victor is caught and behind bars. Luc doesn't want to take any chances that his father will go after someone in the family if he can't get to Charlie or Daphne."

"I'm surprised Luc's not asking us to put someone on Brent and Joey too," I mutter.

Rafe laughs despite the situation. "He did. Since Joey was planning on staying at Luc's to help Charlie while she's on bed rest, Brent agreed to stay too. But probably because he doesn't want to spend a night away from her, not because of the danger." His lips quirk with humor again. "Hard to believe Luc was a bachelor living alone a couple of weeks ago. Now his house is filled with his twelve-year-old sister, his pregnant girlfriend and her mother, two of her sisters, an overprotective big brother and *his* girlfriend." He uncurls a finger at a time as he lists everyone until he's steering with only his palms and two fingers.

"As Charlie's BFF, Joey would be there even if she wasn't dating Brent," I point out.

"True. Blows my mind how happy that player looks."

"More like sappy. I don't think he left her side the whole time we were there."

Rafe chuckles, then turns serious as he steers the conversation back to business. "Luc's guy Reggie will drive him and Brent to the Firebirds facility with one of our guys. But you and I will have to pick up more shifts until we put the newbies into the rotation."

Shit. I had hoped to start cutting back so I could spend more time at home. I don't spend enough time with Arianna and Leo as it is.

Sighing, I say, "We might want to think about hiring an operations manager if we're going to be in the field on duty. In the meantime, I'll reach out to a few Navy buddies who were thinking about joining us and see if I can persuade them."

"Great. If they're already trained SEALs, even better. We can get them up to speed faster if we can waive some of the licensing requirements. And make sure your boys are good-looking," he suggests with a grin as we approach the towering black and red building where our office is located. "The ladies are more amenable to hiring us when we have bodyguards that look like the cast of *Magic Mike*."

I snort. "Getting tired of being specifically requested?" We may be identical, but our female clients prefer Rafe. Might have something to do with his charm and my lack thereof. "And they know we supply bodyguards, right? Not male escorts?"

He enters the underground garage and swipes the entry card before giving me a fake indignant look. "Hey, those *Magic Mike* guys are dancers, not escorts." Waiting for the barrier arm to rise, he continues, "Besides, the ladies find out soon enough that personal stud is not part of a bodyguard's duties—*after* the contract's been signed." He grins, driving toward the spaces reserved for our company.

I shake my head in exasperation at my brother, who finds humor in almost everything. "Why don't you recruit some good-looking fighters *before* they get their teeth knocked out and faces smashed in?"

He reverses into a parking space. "My well has run dry there for the moment. You do the recruiting and I'll keep bringing in the clients with their beautiful, overflowing...bank accounts."

I smile as I exit the car. His easygoing personality is the reason he's the face of the company. We joke that I'm the brains and he's the beauty, though most people couldn't tell us apart if it wasn't for his slightly longer hair and pretty boy scruff.

The elevator glides swiftly and smoothly up to the fifty-fifth floor, and we step out to face the door leading to the Guardian Angels offices. When not in the field, I spend most of my time at the training compound near home, which we consider our headquarters, but we agreed having an office in Midtown was an expensive necessity and convenience for our wealthy clients.

Whenever I walk into the space, I'm glad I agreed with my brother's suggestion to keep the view of Central Park visible from the entrance. It makes quite an impression when it's the first thing a prospective client sees as they step into our office.

I take a moment to appreciate how different my life is from a few short years ago. Abruptly, an image of Stevie bursts my moment of gratitude, making me wonder if I'll ever feel more than content again. Or satisfied with "content" instead of reaching for more.

"You coming?" Rafe calls out as he heads into his office.

Shaking off thoughts of the girl who broke my heart, I follow my brother into our office and focus my attention for the next hour on adjusting our roster.

Summer – 10 years ago

"What's this?"

I flinch when I see the letter Stevie is holding. I left my room in a rush earlier and forgot to put it away.

"You're going to the police academy?"

Her voice rises in shock and I brace myself for the argument I knew would come when she found out.

"When were you going to tell me?" Her shock is quickly to turning to anger.

"I just got the letter today," I say, becoming defensive.

"What? The academy pulled your name out of a fucking hat and decided to send you a letter out of the blue?"

Okay, not an argument. It was going to be a full-on fight. A blow-out of epic proportions. I keep my voice calm in an effort to keep her from erupting.

"Babe, I didn't see any point in telling you if my name never came up. It was a long shot, with the budget being cut and all."

"No point? You didn't think I needed to know that my boyfriend of three years is joining the police academy? Especially when you know how I feel about it?"

"I can't sit behind a desk all day, Stevie. Just going to classes every day is driving me crazy. If this academy thing didn't work out, I wasn't planning on going back to college in the fall anyway." I need to be doing something, not just sitting and listening to some boring professor drone on about some subject I'll never use in real life.

"There are a lot of other things you can do that don't involve sitting at a desk. Why do you have to pick one of the most dangerous jobs out there?"

My own temper begins to rise. We've had this argument so often and it always ends with her crying and me giving in. I capitulated to the point of enrolling at the community college and not bringing it up for the past year. But I've never forgotten my dream. Now that she's eighteen, I'd hoped she'd matured enough to understand and be able to handle her fear.

"Being a police officer may be risky, but it doesn't mean I'm more likely to die on the job than a...construction worker. Look at Pop and Nonno. They're still alive and kicking."

"Yeah, well, not everyone is that lucky."

My usual compassion for what she's been through thins at the bitterness in her voice. "Jesus, Stevie. Am I supposed to feel bad that my father survived and yours didn't? I'm sorry your dad and RJ died, but you are so fucking irrational about this." I pull at my hair in frustration.

"I can't help how I feel. You should have said how you felt."

"I told you I wanted to follow in my grandfather's footsteps, but when you told me you'd never marry anyone who had a dangerous job, I thought I could do something else. I tried college for you, but I can't do it anymore."

I pause. This isn't how I planned to say the next words, but it seems the time has come. I need her to understand how much she means to me.

I stand in front of her and hold her face in my hands so she looks at me. "Stevie, I love you. I have since the moment I looked across the pool at our first swim practice together and our eyes met. I knew you were the girl I was going to marry. That first time we went out, just the two of us, and really talked, you told me your fears, which made my biggest fear losing you. So if that meant I had to pick a different job, then I was willing to do that."

"Oh, Gabe."

She looks at me with eyes full of hope that I'll continue to do that.

"But I don't think I'd be whole if I didn't follow my dream," I say with profound regret, dimming her light. "I sent in the application, figuring if I got in, I'd apply for the dive team. Less dangerous." I smile wryly. "Because of course I know how you feel. And I hope you still love me and want to fulfill all the dreams we talked about." I take her hands in mine and drop to one knee. "I had planned on doing this later this summer with a little more romance, but..."

"What are you doing?"

"I think that's pretty obvious." I smile up at her. "Stephanie Anne Hutchinson, I love you with all of my heart. My life would not be complete if you weren't standing by my side every day. Will you make me the happiest man alive and marry me?"

Tears overflow her soft blue eyes. I stand to wipe them away with my thumbs. "Marry me, Stevie. I promise I'll take care of you and cherish and love you forever."

3

Stevie

"Now that Charlie is up and about, I'd really like to go home," I tell Mom as we add finishing touches to the dinner we're making.

While Luc has made our family feel welcome at his house during Charlie's recovery, it's been almost a week, and I want to go home. After the hundreds of strange beds I've slept in over the last few years, I'm ready to sleep in my own for longer than a couple of weeks.

And I hate to admit it, but it's difficult to see Charlie glowing with pregnancy and Luc's tender care of her. I'm happy for them, I really am, but it's a painful reminder of what I'll most likely never have. Seeing Gabe again makes it so much worse.

"We'll have to check with Gabe or Rafe," Mom answers. She peeks through the glass door of the top wall oven to check on the lasagna.

"We have a security system at home," I argue, stirring pieces of yesterday's sourdough bread into the ribollita.

"Do you think it's safe?" Bobbie asks from the family room.

Luc's entire downstairs is one big space. Even though the row house has several levels, most of our time is spent on the ground floor where the kitchen is. Like our house in Connecticut, it's where the heart of the home is.

Daphne, who is a couple of years younger than Bobbie, also looks up from the show they are watching on the big-screen TV, anxiously waiting for an answer.

"I don't understand why it wouldn't be," I huff, then quietly add for my mother's ears only. "It's Charlie and Daphne that need protection from Victor. It's highly unlikely the man would come after one of us to get to them."

Mom faces me, her eyes narrowed. "Unlikely but still a risk that I'm not willing to take."

The anxiety in her voice surprises me. She is not one to let fear rule her life. But then, she didn't have time for fear when tragedy first struck. After the warehouse fire that claimed the lives of her husband and eldest son fifteen years ago, she still had four remaining children with another on the way who were depending on her to remain strong. Charlie's accident must have shaken her up more than she let on.

I'm saved from having to reply when Mom turns toward the sound of footsteps coming down the stairs.

"Hello, ladies."

My heart thuds even as my body stiffens in self-preservation at the sight of Gabe. His tall, powerful body is casually dressed in jeans and a T-shirt with a sport coat over it, likely to hide his gun holster. My gaze is drawn to him despite my effort to avoid even looking in his direction. I meet his eyes, a deep blue ocean that I find myself drowning in. I've stared into them so often that I still remember every speck and striation in each iris. And the way they darkened to midnight when we—

I look away before he can guess my thoughts, going to the oven to turn it off. Mom passes me to greet Gabe, who gives her a kiss on the cheek.

"Where are the others?" he asks.

"They'll be down soon," Mom answers. "Joey is giving Brent a treatment."

Yeah, right. Brent had rushed Joey upstairs as soon as he came home from practice, saying he needed her to "stretch out his tight muscles."

"And Luc went up to drag Charlie away from the computer," Mom continues.

Out of the corner of my eye, I catch Gabe shaking his head. "He should be thankful she agreed to work from home. I know I am, otherwise I'd have to follow her around."

"Luc has almost convinced her to give her notice," Mom says, moving to stand next to me. "Come taste this. Tell me what you think."

I casually round the island to put space between us as Gabe walks to the stove. He lowers his head to the spoon she holds out. His eyes close in pleasure and he licks his lips after tasting the soup. My own mouth salivates as I watch him.

It's been more than ten years since our breakup, but I remember that look as if it were yesterday. He had a similar look when we shared an ice cream only hours before we made love for the last time. I'd teased him that it was his Italian heritage that made everything he did, even eating, look so sensual. The memory of him licking his lips again later, after feasting on me, makes me bite my lip.

His lips form a smirk and my gaze flies up to his. Embarrassed to be caught staring, I angle away to put my back to him and pretend to watch TV. Unfortunately, I can still hear his deep, sexy voice.

"Mm-mm. Delicious. Ma would disown me if I said your ribollita is as good as hers, Sandra, so I'll only admit it comes in a nanobeat behind hers."

"Well, it is her recipe, but I didn't make it. Stevie did."

I'm tempted to face him to see his reaction. Instead, I turn to the sound of the elevator doors sliding open. Luc steps out with Charlie tucked against his side. Brent and Joey follow behind, also pressed against each other from shoulder to hip. Gabe and I used to be the same when we were dating, unable to bear being an inch apart. My heart clenches at the memory.

"Hey, Gabe," Luc says. "You're here. Good. I wanted to—"

"Before you boys start talking business," Mom interrupts, "let's sit down for dinner. I'm sure you're both hungry and Charlie needs to eat. Gabe, you too. Girls," she calls to Daphne and Bobbie, "please set the table."

"Thanks for the invite, Sandra, but I—"

"No buts. Sit." Mom's voice brooks no argument.

I smile at Gabe's consternation as she points to a chair. When he moves to the table, I round the other end of the island to hand the dinner and bread plates to the girls. I grab the basket of ciabatta I made and hand it to Mom. It's light enough for her to hold it against her side with the arm weakened by the stroke, while holding the forks and soup spoons in her stronger hand. Charlie takes the basket from her and places it on the table.

The kitchen is busy as we sidle around each other to take what's needed to the table while Gabe talks to Luc and Brent about their security for the upcoming away game. I ladle the soup into bowls and place them on a tray. Joey takes it and distributes the soup, then refills the tray with the remaining bowls. I pour the rest of the soup into a tureen and bring it with me, stopping short when I see the only remaining empty seat is between Gabe and Bobbie.

The table is meant for eight people. Gabe is sitting in Daphne's usual spot so she's sitting on a bar stool on the other side of Bobbie. Four of us on one side of the table means a tight fit. I want to demand Bobbie move over, but how can I without making things awkward? For me, if no one else.

Gabe stands to make room for me to get to my chair, waiting for me to sit before he settles back in his seat. As soon as he does, his leg and shoulder press against me. I almost jump at the contact, dropping the spoon I'd just picked up, the clattering loud against my plate.

I'd hoped that the years had extinguished the special spark that had always been between us, since our very first date. As much as it would hurt to know that he no longer feels that way for me, it would make it so much easier to move on and to be around him. Especially now that the chance of seeing him has increased significantly. I should have known better when just the sight of him gets my heart pumping and my blood flowing.

I shimmy closer to Bobbie, who frowns at me, but there's not a lot of room to spare. Thankfully, several conversations are flowing around me, and no one pays attention. Except Gabe. He presses his thigh more firmly against mine. I whip my head to him even as I try to cross my legs in the cramped space under the table. His face is toward me as he looks to Brent, who's sitting at the opposite angle from him. He lowers his gaze to me briefly, his eyes burning with blue fire before he ducks his head for a spoonful of soup.

I can barely breathe, never mind eat, but I force myself to lift my own spoon. My body feels overly warm, but it's not from the hot soup. I hardly taste the meal I made, my entire being focused on the smell and touch of Gabe. He took off his sport coat before sitting down, leaving him in a form-fitting T-shirt that hugs his biceps. In the brief glance I gave them, I noticed they were a lot bulkier than when he was twenty. My fingers itch to run over the hard muscles, to see how different he feels.

The skin of his forearm feels the same as he brushes mine every time he takes a bite. The sprinkling of hair makes me shiver despite the heated flush infusing my body. The more I try to fold my arm closer to me, the more space he takes up between us.

"Stevie made it all."

The sound of my name pulls my attention back to the others. Unfortunately, not a single word of conversation has made it through the turmoil in my mind and body.

"Huh?" I glance around the table. Everyone is looking at me, giving me no clue as to who was talking to me.

"You feeling okay?" Charlie asks.

"What? Yeah, I'm fine. Just tired," I add, realizing I haven't said a word since I sat down.

"No wonder," Luc says with an empathetic smile. "Thank you for making dinner. The soup and bread are delicious."

"Oh. You're welcome. And thank you."

"Wait until you try the lasagna," Joey says, bringing it over and setting it in the middle of the table. I vaguely recall Bobbie taking my soup bowl, but I have no idea how much I had eaten.

"I'm surprised you still remember how to cook, Mermaid," Brent teases, using my childhood nickname.

"How could I forget? I think I made this lasagna recipe at least once a week for years," I say.

Since there was nothing else to do while being stuck in Luc's home, cooking and baking was the only way to pass the time. If I'm honest, I've missed spending time in the kitchen. After all the meals I had to make for my family since I was thirteen years old, I never thought I'd enjoy cooking again.

"You've finally mastered it," jokes Brent.

"Says the man who can barely make toast."

"That's a lie," he says, taking Joey's hand and kissing the back of it. "Josie's taught me a few things." He pauses, then looks at Joey and adds, "So to speak." He winks at her and she blushes.

"Gross, dude," Charlie protests. "We're trying to eat here." She wrinkles her nose, and Daphne giggles, though I'm not sure she understood the double entendre. "Stevie used to do all the cooking," she explains for Luc and Daphne's benefit. "Brent did the yard work and fixed things around the house, and Georgie and I—and Joey when she came to live with us—did all the cleaning and laundry."

With Mom busy taking care of Bobbie, who was born with a heart defect that required multiple surgeries, the four of us had split the chores. Brent was busy with sports—his ticket to college and the NFL—which meant cooking fell to me as the next oldest.

"Why do you all have boy names?" Daphne asks, looking at Bobbie.

"My father's name was Robert and my oldest brother was Robert Junior. I was named after them. Roberta. Bobbie for short."

Daphne nods and looks at Joey, who says, "Josefina is my actual name."

Brent takes her hand and kisses the back of it, giving her a compassionate look. There's a story there, but neither of them say more.

"But you call her Josie," Bobbie points out.

"And only he's allowed to call her that," Luc says, shaking his head at Brent.

"That's not true. I'm the only *man* who's allowed to call her that."

"Caveman," Charlie accuses, pointing her fork at him.

"What about your name, Charlie? You don't like Charlotte?" Daphne asks.

"Charlie was too much of a tomboy," Gabe says. "She would try to start fights with anyone who called her Charlotte."

"And we would do that anytime she tried to tag along when we didn't want her to," Brent adds. "Which was all the time."

"Only when RJ wasn't around, because he would yell at you if you were mean to me." Charlie sticks her tongue out at him before turning back to Daphne. "I'll let my mom explain how she let two little boys pick names for me and Georgie."

Mom smiles. She loves to tell this story. "When we learned we were having twins, we let RJ and Brent each pick a name." She pats Brent's arm. "They refused to consider girls' names, convinced the babies would be boys. RJ loved to watch *Curious George*, so that was his choice. George. This one," she says, gesturing to Brent, "decided to also choose his favorite animal character, Snoopy."

Everyone at the table erupts in laughter, even though most us have heard the story several times. Gabe catches my eye, his face creased in a grin. I smile back and almost lean into his shoulder, his arm slung over the back of my chair. I stiffen as I remember we're not that couple anymore. He's forgotten he hates me, but I can't allow myself to forget. It'll be a stab to the heart when he remembers and looks at me with ice again instead of heat.

"I was four and RJ was barely six," Brent defends himself and our big brother, who is no longer here to do it for himself.

"When we finally convinced Brent to choose a different name, he chose Charlie—as in Charlie Brown," Mom continues. "RJ updated his choice to Georgie. We liked that it matched with Stevie—" She looks at Daphne. "Short for Stephanie, though she was named after our favorite singer, Stevie Nicks."

At Daphne's blank look, Bobby tells her, "I bet you've heard some of her songs in movies. I'll send you a link to my playlist of old songs."

"Or you can ask Brent to make you a playlist," Charlie interjects with a teasing look at our brother. "He's good at those, right, Joey?"

Brent glowers at Charlie and Joey blushes. For the first time, I realize how many inside jokes I'm not a part of and all the behind-the-scenes stories I've missed out on by being away for so long. My short breaks home for major holidays were not enough to catch up on everything—and the long absences created more than a physical distance. That knowledge reaffirms my decision to stay home for good. Staying away to avoid dealing with Gabe meant I missed out on everything else.

"Anyway," Mom continues, "they would talk to them in my belly, calling them Charlie and Georgie. We debated how to revise them to girls' names and decided to make them sort of similar since they were twins. We came up with Charlotte and Georgette."

"Charlie should have been named for Curious George," Luc says, smiling softly at Charlie. "It's that trait that makes her good at her job." He leans in to kiss her before grinning. "She is very good at digging for information."

"You mean *snoop*ing?" Brent asks. "Then I stand by the name I picked."

Charlie pouts at Luc. "Hey! If it wasn't for either of those things, we wouldn't be sitting here right now."

Her eyes widen, as if realizing what she said, and her smile disappears as her eyes tear up. What the hell? She is not one to cry so easily, but Luc appears to know what she's thinking.

He takes her hand and cups her cheek. "Charlie, darling," he says in his Louisiana drawl. "This is not your fault. Victor is the one to blame. We shouldn't have to hide and defend ourselves from him. Understand? If you blame yourself, then you have to blame me too, for not being honest with you from the beginning."

Charlie sniffles. "Being honest with a stranger who wanted to put your life story on TV as entertainment for other strangers?"

He smiles and whispers something in her ears that makes her giggle. Ugh. What happened to her? She was never one to giggle over a boy either.

"Speaking of Victor," Bobbie says. "Stevie asked about going home. What do you think, Gabe? Can we go home now?"

"Don't you want to stay here, Bobbie?" Daphne asks quietly.

Bobbie gives Daphne a smile and a one-armed hug. "I love hanging out with you, but I miss home and my bed."

Me too.

"There is a chance that Victor may look for Charlie at home, though it's likely he knows by now that she's staying here," Gabe said.

"Not that Luc needs help being in the entertainment news, but his publicist has been making sure news items mention me as his girlfriend and that I've moved in with him."

"And your family," I add. "So he would have no reason to go our house if he thinks we're all here."

"I can't guarantee that it's a hundred percent safe," Gabe warns. "Victor is unpredictable, and right now, he's also desperate. There's no telling what he'll do."

"We can't stay here forever. Why haven't you found out where he's hiding yet?" I meet Gabe's gaze, irrationally angry at him for the situation.

He returns my gaze with some hostility of his own. "What's the rush? You haven't lived at home for years."

I inhale sharply at the barb. "Not that it's any of your business, but that's exactly why," I reply. "I was on my way home for good and looking forward to it."

His eyes widen and eyebrows rise at my response. "You're staying put?"

Tearing my gaze from the sudden intensity, I look around to see everyone following our back and forth with varying degrees of curiosity. I include them when I answer, "Yes, I'm staying. I'm done with traveling and want to move on with my life."

The rest of my family voice their surprise and happiness. I already told Mom when I came home, yet her eyes glisten with happy tears. Remembering the anxiety I heard in her voice before, I realize what my traveling must have done to her peace of mind. Yet she never said a word, allowing me to have my freedom without burdening me with guilt for taking it. My mouth twists in silent apology and reassurance. She smiles in return, accepting both.

"Fine," Gabe says. "I can't spare anyone to stay with you at the house, but if you really want to go back to Connecticut, you can stay at my place."

4

Gabe

T HE SHOCK ON HER face has me silently repeating my words
to myself. *Fucking hell.* That's not what I meant. Well,
maybe my subconscious did. My house is where she always belonged. With me.

But I don't currently have a house of my own. I've been staying
with my parents since I moved back from San Diego. A temporary
situation had become long-term with no plans to change the very
convenient arrangement anytime soon. Leo and Arianna need the
stability and I need the freedom to travel and work long hours,
knowing they're safe and well-cared for. My parents love having
their only grandchildren living with them, so it's a win for everyone.

But my kids are the reason I can't bring Stevie home, even if it
was mine. Not only for their physical safety, but their emotional
well-being. It would be too confusing for them.

"What?" Stevie's shocked question brings me back to Luc's
dining table. Looking at the faces around me, she's not the only
one surprised by my misspoken offer.

"I mean, if you really want to be close to home, you can stay at
the Guardian compound," I clarify. The compound is where we do

the training of new recruits as well as clients who want to learn how to defend themselves. Eventually, it will include comfortable living quarters for our clientele who are training or need a temporary safehouse. But right now, it only has basic housing with shared quarters for our new hires or our staff who live too far to go home on their days off.

I shrug and continue. "Sorry. It's the only option right now until we onboard more personnel."

"Why don't you stay at our place instead?" she asks.

It's my turn to stare at her in surprise. "What?"

"Since you probably won't let me leave the compound anyway, what difference does it make if I'm close to home...if I'm not actually home? But if you came over after work and stayed with us, we could all go home."

"Except Charlie," Luc interjects, standing with his plate and Charlie's. "She's not going anywhere."

The others also get up, finished with dinner. I am too but remain seated since Stevie doesn't move.

I shake my head. "Sorry, that won't work. I don't have the manpower for someone to stay with you during the day while I work."

I watch as she chews the skin inside the corner of her mouth in consternation, a habit I remember well. It causes her lips to pucker, almost as if she's waiting for a kiss. I used to oblige her often, and I fight the urge to do so now, as I did earlier when I saw her staring at me. There was no mistaking what she'd been thinking then, giving rise to desire that continues to simmer.

I look away before memories of kissing her make me forget that any thought of rekindling our relationship is insane. During dinner, I did temporarily lose my mind, trying to maintain physical contact with her as we ate.

What was I thinking? Oh yeah. That it had been too fucking long since I touched her and was desperate to have her naked in my arms again.

Seeing her at the stove, making dinner, as I walked in after working all day, had been surreal. For a brief moment, it almost felt like I'd dropped into the dream of the future we'd once had. Except she'd turned away instead of greeting me with a welcoming, passionate kiss. Some of the hurt and anger had bubbled to the surface again. She'd thrown away not only the dream we'd shared, but the love we'd pledged to each other daily, sometimes hourly. Catching her staring at my mouth when I tasted the soup, her pretty blue eyes heavy with desire, made me want to goad her into feeling it again.

"How about if I stay at the compound during the day and we come home together—back to my house, I mean—when you're done for the day?"

An ache blooms in my heart at her words, reminiscent of the dream I thought I'd stepped into earlier. But the tone was not quite right. Instead of excitement and love, I hear frustration, a hint of desperation, and maybe even a tinge of sadness. Except for the one big obstacle that had always stood between us and caused the ultimate demise of our relationship, I'd never been able to see her unhappy or upset.

Before I can stop myself, "Fine" escapes my lips.

"Really?"

She can't be more shocked than I am. What am I thinking? Seeing her smile and feeling her fingers grip my forearm in excitement, I know exactly what I'm thinking. And it has everything to do with feeling more of her skin than just her hand on my arm.

"Yes, but only you. For liability reasons, I can't have Bobbie at the compound." She may be a mature teenager, but she's still a kid. We have evasive driving drills and target practice as part of the training. "And it's not the most comfortable place to hang out all day, especially for your mother."

I stand with my plate before turning back to Stevie. We're too close and she has to look up at me from her sitting position, giving me all sorts of fantasies that are mixed with memories. "You want to go back tonight or when Rafe or I can come back to get you in a day or two?"

She stares at me, chewing the inside of her lip again. Wondering at her hesitation, I ask, "Unless you've changed your mind and—"

"No," she replies quickly. "No. Tonight's fine. I just need to help clean up and pack up my things."

"The girls and I will clean up, Stevie. You cooked, remember?" Charlie smiles at us as she cleans the table.

Stevie stands and picks up her plate, her food mostly uneaten. I can't see the look she gives her sister, but Charlie returns it with a smirk. We drop off our plates at the sink where Bobbie and Daphne are loading the dishwasher. Stevie goes up to pack, and I step out onto the patio to call my mother to let her know I won't be home tonight.

It's not the first time and it won't be my last. My family is used to my frequent travels for work. The tougher job will be to break the news to my mother that Stevie's back for good.

Ma still holds a grudge against Stevie, blaming her for not only breaking my heart, but what I'd done as a result. Instead of going to the police academy, I'd enlisted with the Navy and left town to wait for boot camp to start. I'd barely been back home after that. There had been very little time for visits between SEAL training, several deployments, and being based in San Diego.

"I wish you'd stay away from that girl, Gabe," Ma says when I tell her where I'll be tonight. "She broke your heart once and I'm afraid she'll do it again. Asking you to stay with her in her house? Alone? She's toying with your heart. I know it."

"Stop worrying, Ma. Nothing like that is going to happen again. I won't let it."

A part of me might want to be with her again—in bed—but I have no intention of opening my heart to her ever again.

5

Stevie

WHY DID I INSIST on going home right away? Gabe was right. What's my rush after staying away for so long? But once the thought of going home had taken root, I didn't want to delay another moment.

An hour after we leave Luc's, we're driving on the dark and winding highway of the Merritt Parkway in Connecticut. Gabe and I have barely spoken a word. I was never tongue-tied and awkward with him when we were younger, even when I first realized I liked him as more than my brother's friend. Yet I can't think of anything to say to him. What his reasons are for staying quiet, I don't know. Regretting doing this for me? Remembering why he hates me?

How on earth am I going to handle it if he really does still hate me? We live in the same small town. I'm surprised we never ran into each other during my brief visits home. I don't know if I'll be able to cope running into him. And his kids...

The thought of his two children, created with another woman, brings a sharp ache to my heart. I've heard about them over the years through my family, but I'm not ready to ask him about them. It's too painful.

Despite my effort to avoid keeping tabs on Gabe, I've seen the occasional social media post by mutual friends. I knew when he got married in San Diego, when each of his kids were born, when he divorced, and when he'd moved back home.

I should probably ask about his parents or his business, if only to fill the silence.

"How are—"

"So, you're done with—"

I let out a nervous laugh when we both speak at once.

"Sorry. Go ahead," he prompts me.

"I was just going to ask about your parents."

"They're both well."

More silence.

"What were you going to say before?" I ask.

"You said earlier that you were done traveling."

Since there wasn't a question there, I nod, then realize he can't see me in the dark and his attention is on the road. "Yes, I am."

I watch him drive, both hands resting lightly on the steering wheel. His profile is in shadows, exposed briefly every few seconds by lights from a passing car. He looks so much more mature. I suppose it's to be expected since he's thirty years old. His jawline is more defined, even with the heavy five o'clock shadow on it. He has the finest of lines near his eyes when he squints at a passing headlight. And his dark hair is shorter than it was back then. My fingers itch to run through the thickness the way I used to. The way I probably never will again.

"You don't look too happy about your decision to stop traveling."

I startle at his voice and quickly wipe my face clear of any expression. I have to be more careful around him. He'd always been able to read me.

Shaking my head, I say, "No. I really am tired of the travel." I give a short laugh. "Never thought I'd say that, considering how I couldn't wait to leave after being stuck at home."

"Everything gets old after a while. You've been on the road for...what—three or four years?"

"Three and a half. I left as soon as Charlie moved back home to be with Mom and Bobbie after she graduated from college."

"Where did you go first?"

"Jamaica. I wanted nothing more than to sit on the beach, drink mai tais, and do whatever I felt like."

"And what did you feel like doing?"

"Absolutely nothing."

"I can't picture you doing nothing for very long. You were never one to sit around."

I scoff. "I didn't have much choice back then. There was always so much to do at home that there wasn't time to sit around and do nothing." I pause before adding, "But you're right. It didn't last very long. I started getting antsy, so I went to different islands. Turned out, they were almost all the same."

"And yet, you stayed away for years."

I shrug and drop a truth bomb without thinking. "What was there for me at home?"

"Stevie—"

Not ready to talk about what happened, I keep talking. "I moved on from the Caribbean and discovered a great big world out there. And now I'm ready to come home and move on with my life."

Neither of us speak after that. I want to ask him about what he did when he left after we broke up, but I'm not sure I want to hear the details of his life as a SEAL...a husband...a father...of his life without me.

Bitter resentment wells within me when I remember learning he'd gotten married two years after our breakup. I hadn't even gone on a date during that time. When I heard the news, I went to a bar, got drunk, and had my first one-night stand. I'd cried during and after, thinking of Gabe, the only person I'd been with until then.

Summer – 10 years ago

Tears overflow my eyes at Gabe's proposal. He stands to wipe them away with his thumbs and cups my face with so much loving tenderness, it physically hurts. "Marry me, Stevie. I promise I'll take care of you and cherish and love you forever."

My heart breaks at his words. I can't marry him, not now that he's shown how much it means to him to be a police officer. I know he wanted to follow in his grandfather's footsteps, but I thought he gave up on that when he went to college instead.

"I didn't know that being a cop was still important to you since you haven't said anything for a while."

Gabe shrugs. "I thought I'd be able to give it up, try something else."

In other words, he tried to give it up for me, but I'm not enough of a reason for him to sacrifice his life's dream. I can't completely blame him for feeling that way. I have no right to ask him to give up something so important to him. Just as he can't ask me to live with fear every day when he walks out the door in his uniform.

I can't go through what my family and I went through when Dad and RJ died. Time is supposed to heal all wounds or some bullshit like that, but the pain of losing them hasn't lessened in the five years since their deaths. I wouldn't survive if something happened to Gabe too.

I disengage our hands and take a step back. "I'll always love you, Gabe. But you can't make promises you have no control over. And I can't ask you to give up your dream."

"My dream includes having a life with you. And you know, better than I do, there aren't any guarantees in life."

Yes, I do know that, which is why I can't accept his proposal. As usual, he reads my thoughts.

"You'll only marry me if I become an accountant or something? I could die in a car accident or have a heart attack or get cancer. No one can promise you they'll live forever, babe."

I hear his voice edge into frustration.

"I can't help how I feel, Gabe."

"Fuck that! Stevie, I love you and I want to marry you. We can live nearby so you can still help your mom every day. I'll—"

"Stop. Please." *Every word is an arrow to my heart. I know he loves me. But it is his actions that are putting an end to our relationship. And he's the one to do it without consulting me, even though he's been thinking about it for a while. I reach behind me to pick up the letter from the police academy. I hold it out to him.* "You need to do this. So go do it. Because we can't go back to pretending I'm enough for you. You're going to hate me one day for it and I couldn't bear that."

"So that's it? You're just going to give up on us?"

"I'm sorry, Gabe. You should follow your dream, but you need to understand it's not mine." *In fact, it's my nightmare.* "I hope we can go back to being friends." *I try to be mature, though the thought of being friends with him while he goes on with his life is unbearably painful.*

"Get out."

I blink, unsure I heard his words correctly. All love and tenderness are gone. His face is hard as stone and as unfeeling. "What?"

"I said, get the fuck out. I don't want to hear your fucking calm rationalizations when you can't be fucking rational about your own hang-ups. So...Get. Out." *The last two words are bit out between clenched teeth.*

"Gabe—"

"Fine. I'll leave." *He spins away and storms out of his room, out of his house, and out of my life.*

6

Gabe

I CAN'T DO IT. There is no way I can sleep under the same roof as Stevie. All the old feelings are resurfacing—love, desire, anger, bitterness...I can't decide which one worries me the most at the moment.

Love? I just have to remember my anger at her rejection of my proposal to get over that one pretty quickly.

Desire? We'll be in the same house together, all night. Alone. But as much as I want to get her into bed again, the thought feels a little empty without the love we once had for each other.

So anger and bitterness prevail at the moment, guiding my decision to go directly to the compound. Stevie has fallen asleep—or pretended to?—and doesn't open her eyes until we pull up to the gate at HQ. She blinks at me in confusion.

"What are we doing here?"

"I need to talk to Rafe for a few minutes."

After making sure the gate closes behind me, I drive up the gravel road to the trailer that houses our temporary administrative space and park the car. "Stay here," I order before getting out of the car. I ignore the glare she throws my way.

Rafe is sitting at one of the desks in the open area of the trailer, leaning back in the chair, his feet crossed on the desk as he reads a file.

"What are you doing here?" he asks, glancing at his wristwatch. "Aren't you supposed to be tucking my niece and nephew in bed by now?"

"I called home to let them know I wouldn't be there." I rake my fingers through my hair, pacing in front of the desk, feeling like a caged lion in the enclosed space. I can't remember the last time I was this worked up over someone.

That's a lie. The last time was when I'd proposed to the same person turning my insides into knots now.

Rafe watches me, waiting in silence, eyebrow raised.

I exhale sharply and stand still to face him across the desk. "Stevie's here. In the car."

He drops his feet to the ground and sits up straight. "What the fuck? What is she doing here?"

I start pacing again. "Because I'm an idiot. She wanted to come home, and I agreed to bring her back."

"We don't have anyone to watch them at the house, remember? That's why they're all staying at Luc's."

"I know. I told her she could hang out here during the day and I'd stay with her at night."

"Again, what the fuck?" Rafe stands.

I hold up a hand, palm out. "Again, I'm an idiot. I know, but I need you to take my place, to stay with her. I can't do it."

"Okay, I need to break all that down. You want me to stay with her? To take your place?" He pauses before asking, "To be *you*?"

"What? No!" I stop my pacing to face him again. As identical twins, trading places was something we'd done often as kids but never as adults. "I mean, yes, you stay with her. As yourself. I'll use the kids as an excuse to get out of it, not that they're an excuse. It's the truth. They need me at home."

Rafe nods. "At least you're not thinking like an idiot any-more. But I want to know why you really can't do it."

He knows me too well for me to prevaricate. When I hesitate, he states flatly, "You still have feelings for her."

I don't bother to deflect. "Hell, yeah. But I don't know which feelings. A part of me is still pissed at her. And the other part of me..."

When I trail off, he finishes for me. "Wants to fuck her."

My hands tighten into fists at Rafe's crude words. Words that wouldn't normally bother me at any other time except that he's talking about Stevie. I force myself to stay silent. She's no longer my girlfriend and doesn't deserve my defense of her.

After a moment, Rafe nods. "Okay. I'll do it. On one condi-tion. I literally take your place."

I immediately shake my head. "No." I don't want to delve too deeply—hell, not at all—into the reasons for my adamant denial.

"Then I guess you're going to have resist either of those temptations." The asshole sits back down and puts his feet up, locking his hands behind his head.

I narrow my eyes at him. "Why the fuck do you want to pretend to be me?"

"Not for the reason you think, so don't worry."

"Then what?"

He grins. "I need a little excitement in my life. It's been nothing but work for months. It's been years since we've played this trick. Come on. Don't you want to see if we still got it?"

"It's not going to work," I say with confidence. "She'll know you're not me. Look at your hair and your scruff. And your tattoos are different from mine."

"It's been ten years. She doesn't know what we've gotten inked since. Besides, I don't plan on taking my clothes off, bro."

"It never worked with her," I insist. "She always knew when we were messing with a teacher or someone."

"Don't you want to know if she can still do that?" Rafe narrows his eyes, thinking. "She hasn't seen me yet."

"What are you talking about? You were there at Luc's when Stevie came."

"I swear she didn't even look in my direction. I've never felt so invisible to a woman before." He tries to appear wounded but his laugh ruins it. "Look, it's been at least a couple of years since she's seen me in person. And the only way my clothes are coming off in front of her is if she tears them off me." He quickly adds when I take a step toward him, his eyes wide with fake innocence, "If she thinks I'm you, of course. I'll set her straight if it gets to that point, don't worry."

He grins before continuing with his plan. "It's cold out. I'll wear a hat to hide the hair."

It's a dumb and immature idea. I'm being ridiculous for even considering it. Easier just to tell her to either go back to Luc's or let her put her life in danger if she wants to be reckless.

Remembering her stubbornness, I'm afraid she'll go with reckless, so I can't give her that ultimatum. Her family would never forgive me if anything happened to her. Despite everything, *I'd* never forgive myself if she got hurt.

At the same time, I wasn't kidding when I told Rafe I have the urge to both fuck her and hurt her the way she hurt me. After not seeing her for years, I can't handle the intimacy of spending nights with her.

"Fine," I finally agree, against my better judgement.

7

$\mathcal{S}$tevie

G ABE FINALLY COMES BACK out, wearing a beanie. It's a few degrees colder here than in the city, but hats were never his thing. But then, a person's likes and dislikes can change over the years.

I cross my arms and look straight ahead when he gets in the car. "I was about to go in and see if you forgot I was out here," I grumble.

"Had to go over some things with my brother."

"And did you need to shave too?" The beanie wasn't the only thing I noticed in my quick glance when he came out of the trailer.

Out of the corner of my eye, I see him running a hand over his jaw that no longer has any trace of his late-day scruff before he grins my way.

"Also got a call while I was in there. Going to see someone after I get you settled."

It takes a second for his inference to sink in. When it does, I inhale sharply at the implication he's going to meet a woman.

Unable to look at him for fear of what he'll see on my face, I stare out the window and ask, my voice tight, "If it's okay to leave me at home alone while you go on a date, then I think I'll be okay at home alone during the day."

"Change of plans," he says, driving further into the compound instead of toward the exit. "You'll be staying here tonight."

"What?" My head snaps around to look at him. Away from the floodlights of the trailer, there are too many shadows in the car for me to see him clearly. "No."

"Yes," he counters. "Because it's not safe for you to be home alone while I'm out. I'll be getting back very late."

In self-preservation, my brain refuses to process what that means.

"And I'm safe here? Who else stays at the compound? I assume you're not going to stash me somewhere by myself?"

"I st—I sometimes stay here, but Rafe always does when he's not in the field. And the new hires we're training are here too. One of them is a woman, so I'll put you with her in the barracks."

The building we pull up to looks very similar to what I imagine military barracks look like, albeit smaller. It's a squat, U-shaped, one-story stucco building. When Gabe puts the car in park, I get out before he comes around to my door. He continues toward me anyway and stops a little too close. I take a step back but don't get very far with the car at my back. He takes my arm, preventing me from sidling away.

I hold my breath and brace myself when his hand brushes over my cheek. My heart doesn't speed up, not like it did when I sat next to him at dinner. The shivers I expect from his touch don't go through me the way they did when his leg brushed against mine. And my body doesn't flush with heat and desire as it did when I looked up at him as he towered above me at the dinner table, my face—my mouth—inches from his jean-clad cock.

What the hell is happening? Where did all the pent-up emotion and heart-thumping desire go? Disappointment and a sense of loss envelop me at the unexpected awkwardness. It's reminiscent of the end of a first date with a stranger. Except Gabe isn't a stranger and there had been no date leading up to this moment.

Is it because of the actual date he's going on tonight? Are my organs blocking once familiar sensations to protect me the way my brain is doing to keep me from falling apart from that soul-crushing knowledge?

Then what about him? His eyes are not burning with desire as they were just a couple of hours ago. The floodlights from the building allow me to see him clearly. He's watching me expectantly, observing me like a bug, waiting for its reaction to a poke. Except I don't feel the poke.

"Aren't you curious about this place?" he finally asks.

Confused, I reply, "Sure, I guess."

With a hand on my back, he guides me past the car and turns me around to face away from him. He holds me so close, I'm just short of leaning against his chest. He points to a building that's bigger and taller than the barracks. "That's the indoor training facility."

His outstretched hand moves several degrees to the left before resting both hands on my shoulders.

"Right over there, we're going to build guest quarters for clients who want to come here to learn self-defense and survival skills." His warm breath brushes over my cheek. And yet I feel nothing but awkward and uncomfortable—the way I would if I was getting unwanted attention from a guy at a bar. As confused as I am by my body's reaction, or lack thereof, I like it. It beats the hell out of feeling the earlier mix of lust and hurt and resentment.

He nudges me to face a different direction and lowers his head closer to my ear. Still no shivers when his breath tickles my ear. "Down the hill are the tactical areas where we train for situations involving vehicles and protection in exposed spaces. We also do target practice there, so steer clear of that area."

He moves his hands up and down my arms, trying to caress them despite my puff jacket. I try to step away when he turns me around to face him, but he holds on, keeping me in place. Why is he doing this to me when he's going to be with another woman as soon as he leaves me here?

"What do you think?" he asks, keeping his voice soft, almost intimate.

What do I think? I think he's playing games with me, but why? A sudden thought pierces the confusion. Was he playing at dinner, toying with me to deliberately hurt me? It's the only explanation. Tears well in my eyes, and I blink them away before they fall.

He lets go of me just as I jerk away from him, almost making me stumble. "Shit, Stevie. I'm sorry. I—"

"I'm cold. Can I get my bags so I can go inside?"

"Of course."

In the blink of an eye, he morphs into a polite stranger as he carries my suitcase inside. Several voices call out, "Hey, boss," when we enter an open space that has couches, a TV, a round kitchen table that's doubling as a card table at the moment, and a kitchen where someone is making a late dinner for themselves. Gabe introduces me to a few of the trainees and employees who are staying at the compound. He asks "Shep"—Kathy Shephard, whose room I'll be sharing—to show me around. From what I can see from the common area, the accommodations are going to be the no fuss, no frills type. That's fine. I've occasionally stayed in hostels similar to this during my travels.

Gabe wishes me good night before he leaves me there, like I'm nothing more than a hotel guest.

8

Gabe

"**W**HAT ARE YOU STILL doing here?" Rafe asks me as he barges back into the trailer. "I thought you were going to go home?"

I look up from the never-ending paperwork. "I FaceTime'd the kids. I was going to miss their bedtime anyway. Thought I'd get a head start on tomorrow's work so I can spend time with them in the morning instead."

And I wanted to see how Rafe's little experiment went.

"Uh-huh." He gives me a knowing look as he removes his beanie and runs a hand through his shoulder-length hair.

While it's true the kids are in bed, Rafe knows exactly why I stayed. I raise an eyebrow, silently asking him to tell me what I want to know.

"She's over you, bro." He sighs at whatever he sees on my face. I don't know what that is because I'm not sure how I feel.

"And how did you come to that conclusion?" I ask, leaning back in the chair, staring at the pen as I twirl it between my fingers.

"First, she didn't even blink an eye when she saw me and called me Gabe."

"That means nothing. Your hair was tucked into your hat and you shaved."

"Yeah, about that."

My fingers stop moving the pen as I wait for him to continue.

"She noticed that, so I kind of implied I got a booty call, and that's why I couldn't take her home."

I close my eyes. How did this get so fucking complicated?

"You need to tell her she's going to have to stay here until the new team starts." He sits at the other desk and picks up the folder he was looking at when I'd interrupted earlier.

"That isn't necessary. I can—"

"No, you can't," he says definitively. "You can't stay up at night keeping watch after working all day and then work again the next day on no sleep. And where's the security if you're sleeping—or in her bed, *not* sleeping?"

I don't say anything for a while, thinking over his words. Despite everything Rafe just told me, a part of me wants time with her. Until he said I no longer have to, I didn't realize how much I wanted to.

"You said 'first' earlier."

He looks up from the file, his head cocked. "What?"

"When I asked how you know she's over me. You never said what the second thing was."

A slow grin forms, his expression full of mischief. "Oh, right. Well, I tried coming on to her, but she—"

The chair hits the wall as I stand in one quick move. The pen clatters to the floor. Rafe throws the folder on the desk and puts his hands up to stop me from coming at him or raging at him. I'm not sure yet which if he doesn't start talking soon. Probably both.

"But she backed away," he explains. "She wasn't feeling it, and trust me, I know when a woman is feeling it." He grins but I am not amused.

I scowl at him. "And what would you have done if she'd leaned in instead?"

He shrugs and grins. "Seen how far I could have gotten before she realized it wasn't you."

I glare at him when he laughs. "Do you have a death wish?"

"Don't worry. I would have let her in on our little game before she got too carried away by my charms. But why are you getting worked up? I told you she wasn't feeling it."

"How do you know she wasn't feeling it because she knew it was you?" She had looked at me with desire in Luc's kitchen. I'm sure of it.

"Grasping at straws?" he taunts. "Look, I know for a fact that if you were blindfolded in a room full of women, you'd know which one was Stevie. From the moment you told me you were going to marry her, you never looked at another girl."

It's true. Even while I waited almost a year until she was ready to have sex.

"Now that you know, you can stop feeling so conflicted and move on. You need to face the reality that she's over you."

I cringe at his sympathetic expression.

"Gabe, I don't want to see you hurt again."

"I have no intention of getting hurt. And I don't know what you think you saw, but I know the chemistry is still there. I wouldn't mind a trip down memory lane in her bed. That's all."

I'm not sure which one of us I'm trying to convince.

9

Stevie

AFTER A RESTLESS NIGHT in yet another bed that's not my own, I'm left to my own devices for the day. Everyone else has left to either work their shifts or to train. Apparently, there are enough safety precautions set up on and around the property for me to be left alone.

I've gone stir crazy all day with nothing to do. I already called Mom and Andi and kept them on the phone longer than necessary. Bored, I walk to the trailer Gabe went into last night. I take my camera in case there's anything interesting to capture, though there's not much around. The flat and mostly clear part of the property has the trailer, the barracks, and the indoor training facility, which was locked when I went to check it out earlier.

I can't see beyond the trees that slope down to the driving course and shooting range. Kathy, my temporary roommate, passed along strict instructions from "the boss" to not venture near there or leave the premises.

"What are you doing, wandering around?"

I turn and feel a jolt upon seeing Rafe striding toward me. I can't believe how alike he and Gabe still look, except for the slight scruff. Gabe liked to be clean-shaven. I'm not sure I would have known it's Rafe if he didn't mention Gabe. In high school, I'd always been able to tell the difference, just by their presence. Georgie said she was only able to start telling them apart when Gabe and I started dating.

"The way he looks at you—*for* you as soon he walks into the room...I know right away who it is and isn't." She'd sighed with the drama of a fourteen-year-old and added, "It's so romantic. It's exactly how I picture my Prince Charming will look at me some day."

Could it be that's how I'd always known too? Can I not tell them apart anymore because Gabe no longer looks at me in that special way? Not that he has any reason to, of course. He's apparently seeing at least one woman, a fact that contributed to my restless sleep.

So why the hell is my heart thudding now with *Rafe* standing in front of me. Feeling sick at my reaction, I let my camera hang around my neck so I can cross my arms in front of me. I need the physical barrier, since my protective emotional barrier from last night has deserted me.

"I didn't know I was going to be left alone all day. I was bored."

He quirks an eyebrow at me, so much like Gabe does, but Rafe adds a taunting smirk. "Just say the word if you want to go back to Luc's, sweetheart."

The endearment jars me, coming from Rafe instead of Gabe. And the word doesn't sound so endearing when uttered in a sarcastic tone that conveys how little he cares about my disappointment. I don't blame Rafe for being mad at me on his brother's behalf. The two had always been close. But I'm not going to give either of them the satisfaction of leaving.

"No, I'll wait."

"Then you'll stay here where it's more protected instead of at the house. Which means you won't be going home tonight."

I huff at his unsympathetic tone. "You're enjoying this, aren't you, Rafe?"

"I'm not—" He frowns, then runs a hand over his unshaven jaw, his brows clearing. "No one is enjoying this."

"Wait." His previous words sink in. "I'm staying here again tonight?"

"Until we have a team in place. Gabe can't be on guard all night after working all day. He needs to sleep."

I still don't think I need protection. Luc is being overly cautious because he doesn't want Charlie to worry. But Rafe is right. I can't expect Gabe to stay awake and then work on no sleep the next day because I am too impatient to go home. That would be dangerous.

"Besides," Rafe continues, "he needs to be at home with his kids."

I narrow my eyes at his antagonistic tone, tempted to let loose with a few choice words for him, but I bite my tongue. If I was standing in front of one my sister's ex-boyfriends, one who had broken her heart, I wouldn't exactly be warm and welcoming either.

"Fine," I retort. "But can you at least take me home so I can get my laptop and hard drives? I need something to do."

Letting out a long-suffering sigh, Rafe reluctantly nods. "Fine. Let's go." He walks to a black SUV parked in front of the trailer—the one Gabe drove last night. I look around, almost expecting to see him appear, then I realize it's likely a company car. They are probably all identical.

When we get in and he starts backing out, I say, "By the way, nice to see you again too, Rafe. How have you been? I think I last saw you at the memorial the summer before last?" My knees had almost given way when I'd seen him across the lawn, thinking Gabe had come to pay his respects to my father and RJ, who had been one of his closest friends.

Rafe doesn't respond. I hold on to my patience despite his silent, surly attitude. His current hostility likely has as much to do with the extra work of taking me home as my history with his brother. I am *persona non grata* with the D'Angelos. They are an even tighter-knit family than my own, especially Gabe and Rafe, being twins.

Not that being twins meant much to Charlie and Georgie, since their personalities are complete opposites. They love each other but they aren't as close as twins stereotypically are.

In fact, Georgie and I had been closer growing up, having similar interests when we were little. Where the two of us had been more "girly," Charlie had been a tomboy and had become instant best friends with the like-minded Joey when they'd met.

Rafe ignores my question and drives through the gate, spewing gravel as he speeds down the long driveway. "Buckle up," he demands, making me realize I haven't done so yet.

I give him a dirty look, which he doesn't see because he's driving like a speed demon. "If you want me dead, you can just leave me at home. Maybe you'll get lucky and Victor will come looking there tonight."

He throws me an annoyed look. "Why would I want you dead?"

"Oh, I don't know. Maybe it's the waves of aggression coming from you and the way you're driving."

Instantly, his body transforms as it relaxes. He eases off the accelerator and his mouth quirks in apology. "Sorry. It's been a rough day. We're down two guys. One got hurt during a training exercise and I had to let another one go, for sending the guy he hurt to the hospital and failing the exercise."

His sudden openness distracts me from my irritation. "Really? But isn't taking someone down the point of a bodyguard?"

"We're looking for brains as much as muscle, if not more. This one got a little too carried away by his physical strength. We'd never want that in a situation where a client's safety comes first."

"What do you mean?"

"If he's too busy doing more than he has to in order to restrain the bad guy, and forgets to keep an eye on the client, that wouldn't be very smart."

"Because someone else could get to the client."

"Exactly." He glances at me with approval. "Get some muscle on you and maybe you can work for us. Become one of our Angels." He laughs at his joke. "Get it?"

I roll my eyes at him. "Yeah. Lame. And thanks, but no thanks." I couldn't put anyone I love through the anxiety and fear I have about dangerous jobs. I don't know how Teresa handled having one son in the military and another getting beat up in a MMA cage. And now both of them are bodyguards whose job it is to put themselves between their client and any potential danger. But then, having married a firefighter, she's obviously not affected by it the way I am.

I turn to him in my seat. "But if this was a training exercise, wouldn't the guy you fired have learned something and not do it again?"

"He wasn't fired because of his mistake. He was fired because he refused to own up to it. Got aggressive after the fact, insisting he did everything right. Can't keep him if he didn't learn anything."

"This kind of behavior doesn't show up in the background checks you must do?"

"Yes, it should." He slams the palm of one hand on the steering wheel in frustration. "And now I have to look into that to find out why it didn't. Did we hire someone too inexperienced to have come across a situation where this would have eventually occurred? Or am I going to have to fire our HR admin too? I don't have time to do her job on top of everything else."

"Well, good thing you caught it during training."

"Yeah, good thing." He blows out a harsh breath. "But that means we have to start the hiring and training process again for someone new, which takes time I don't have."

Time that I'm costing him by having to watch me separately.

"I'm sorry," I say softly, my turn to be apologetic.

His expression softens as he sighs again, more quietly this time. "Shit happens. But it does mean getting a team at the house might be delayed."

Unwilling to add to his stress, I don't express my disappointment. We're quiet as he turns into the long driveway of my family's property and up to the house. "Stay there. Get your keys ready. I'll come around to you and you stay glued to me."

Rafe transforms again, this time into full bodyguard mode. As much as he dislikes me, protecting me is his job. Just as he did while driving, his eyes scan our surroundings before getting out. He comes around to my side of the SUV and opens the door, taking my hand to help me out.

I almost drop my keys when I feel a familiar electric charge at his touch. *What the hell?*

I've only ever felt that with Gabe. But I thought it had magically disappeared last night, knowing he has moved on with another woman.

So what the hell is going on now? I've never felt anything but brotherly affection for Rafe, so why am I feeling for him what I've only ever felt for Gabe?

A horrifying thought occurs.

Has my attraction somehow transferred to his brother now that Gabe is no longer available?

Rafe drops my hand and ushers me up the steps to the front door. "Unlock the door," he commands.

Once we're in the entryway, he re-locks the door while I enter the code to the house alarm to disarm it.

"No dawdling. Get your stuff in three minutes and we leave."

"Do you really think Victor is hanging around here waiting for Charlie or one of us?" I ask, not looking at him.

"Probably not. On the other hand, we have no idea where he is. There are a lot places to hide on a tree-filled property as large as this one. Which is why we need a whole team in place to keep you and your family secure. Stay close."

Yeah, no. I'll keep my distance, thank you.

He climbs the stairs first, making sure it's safe to proceed. I wait until he's halfway up before following. I don't want to be face level with his ass, as perfect as it is.

"Which room?" Rafe visited often in our childhood, but the house had been smaller back then. A bedroom for my parents, one for us girls, and the other for RJ and Brent. Brent did a complete remodel after he signed with the NFL, adding bedrooms and bathrooms upstairs and expanding everything downstairs, including a first-floor suite for our mother and a gym with an indoor pool.

"End of the hall," I tell him.

Rafe enters my bedroom, the first man to do so since the remodel. The thought makes me feel a little queasy. He gestures for me to wait just inside the doorway while he checks out the closets and en-suite bathroom.

Satisfied that it's safe, he closes the bedroom door and stands guard. "Three minutes," he reminds me.

I get busy, going to my desk and pulling out a couple of hard drives as well as a binder of memory cards. Grabbing a leather satchel from my closet, I carefully put everything into it. From a smaller closet lined with shelves, I collect my laptop bag and check that the charging wire is still in there where I left it. Turning to him with a bag over each shoulder—but not quite meeting his gaze, I say, "Done."

Rafe doesn't move until I'm a couple of feet away from him. I gasp and take a step back when he reaches for me. He gives me a puzzled look, but without a word, he takes the bags from me and gestures for me to follow him back downstairs. It's not until we're back in the SUV that he speaks again.

"I'm starving. I missed lunch. Let's stop at a drive-thru on the way back. Fast food okay?"

I've lost my appetite despite hardly eating anything since lunch yesterday. I'd barely eaten my dinner last night, and all I managed this morning was a granola bar and tea. Kathy said I could help myself to anything stocked in the kitchen unless it had someone's name on it, but nothing looked appealing.

"Whatever you want to eat."

Rafe makes a choking sound. I look at him to make sure he's okay, but he's concentrating on driving in the quickly falling dusk. Maybe he was just clearing his throat?

An uncomfortable silence fills the car in the growing darkness, until Rafe finally comments, "So I hear you're home for good this time. Finished traveling the world?"

"No. I'm done living out of a suitcase and sleeping in strange beds. Which is why I'm impatient to finally sleep in my own."

"Slept in a lot of strange beds, have you?"

His voice is no longer conversational. It sounds like he's implying something unflattering.

What the hell is his problem? What does he care how many beds I slept in and with whom? Not that there were that many "whoms," but Gabe was married and had two children by the time I left home. I don't need to defend myself to his brother.

Instead of reacting with outrage, I reply with equal double-meaning, projecting a cheerful nonchalance I'm not feeling. "Every time I went to a new place."

Turning to Rafe to catch his reaction, I'm satisfied to see his jaw flex and his hands tighten on the wheel.

10

Gabe

"HI, RAFE," CHARLIE SAYS to me when I enter Luc's family room to give everyone an update on Victor, such as it is. There's nothing to report except what we've done in conjunction with law enforcement to try to locate him. So far, we've followed a lot of leads, but none of us have had any luck.

"It's Gabe," I correct her, leaning over to kiss Charlie's cheek.

She wrinkles her nose and touches my jaw, reminding me of the growing stubble. I skipped the last couple of shaves so Stevie would think it was my brother she was seeing around the compound. I had no intention of pretending to be him when I took her to the house yesterday, but when she called me by his name, I foolishly didn't correct her. It was an impulsive omission, but I liked how the pretense felt like armor against the confusion of being near her. His name on her lips and the scruff on my face reminded me to keep my distance from her, emotionally and physically.

"You're getting ready for a twins photo shoot or something?" she asks.

"Nah," Brent says. "They're probably getting ready to trade places. You guys still do that?" he asks, slapping me on the back and shaking my hand.

I laugh without answering, changing the subject instead. "Has Stevie always been so bossy?" I ask.

Though I direct my question at Brent and Charlie, it's Joey who answers.

"How do you not remember that about Stevie?" she asks, her face alight with humor. "Didn't you date her?"

"Yeah, for over three years," Charlie answers for me.

"Three?" Brent asks, frowning. "I didn't think it was that long."

"Oops." Charlie winks at me. "Should we tell him about the year the two of you spent sneaking around until she turned sixteen?"

"I think you just did. Thanks," I say dryly.

"How do you know about this and I don't?" Brent asks Joey. "You weren't even living with us yet."

I had already moved to San Diego by the time Joey came to live with the Hutchinsons, after her mother's death. I'd never gotten to know her, but Charlie used to talk about the long-distance best friend she'd met while on vacation.

"Charlie told me about it," Joey answers.

"I'm the last one to find out about Luc and Charlie," he grumbles, sending an annoyed look at his teammate, who shrugs apologetically. "And now, about you and Stevie—ten years later." He shakes his head in exasperation. "Are there any more secrets this family is keeping from me?"

"If there are, we'll make sure you're the...*last*...to know." Charlie scrunches her nose at her brother, then asks me, "What has Stevie done to aggravate you?"

"She insists Thanksgiving has to be at home and everyone has to be there."

She called me last night shortly after I'd dropped her back off at the compound. She apologized for the inconvenience, that "Rafe" told her we were down two men, but I have to do whatever is necessary to move the security team to the Hutchinsons' for Thanksgiving.

"Well, of course it does, Gabe. It's Thanksgiving. It's where we always have it." Charlie looks at Brent for support, who nods in agreement.

I should have known. The Hutchinsons were a tight-knit bunch, big on tradition like the D'Angelos. I suppose it was her tone when Stevie called that rubbed me the wrong way. Or that I was still thinking of what she'd told "Rafe" about all the strange beds she'd slept in.

"I'm sorry I didn't mention it myself," Charlie continues. "I figured your team would just follow us when we went there."

"It doesn't work that way, Charlie. I need to scope things out, check out vulnerabilities, see where to put the team..." I sigh when she looks at me in apology and I relent. "Fine." I have the men available, since no one will be at Luc's house to guard, but it's extra time and effort to do the prep work. I have only a few days to make it happen in addition to the coordination required for the clients who will be traveling for the Thanksgiving weekend. With Rafe and I pitching in, we'll have enough staff to split the shifts over the three days, which will include Brent and Luc's football game on Sunday. And of course, Charlie insists the family has to be at the stadium to cheer on Luc and Brent in person.

I've already arranged for a suite with Niko Anastasios, majority owner of the Firebirds. At least I can contain everyone in one area.

"Great!" Charlie beams. "Now let's talk about going to Florida for Christmas."

I narrow my eyes at her. "Please tell me you're fucking with me."

She smiles sweetly and bats her eyes at me. It reminds me of when Stevie used to do that to get her way, though the two have little more than a passing resemblance to each other. Charlie favors their gray-eyed, blond father while Stevie takes after their blue-eyed, darker-haired mother. But the smile and the mannerism are the same.

"DeeDee is upset over not spending Thanksgiving with our aunt and uncle. I'd bring them here, but they spend it with my uncle's family. Charlie and I promised her we'd invite them for a vacation over the Christmas holidays," Luc explained. "Sorry, man. I'm sure this mess with Victor will be over by then, but we should have plans in place, just in case. We'll be staying at Niko's island in the Keys, so at least it'll be harder for anyone else to get to it."

I sigh. This should have been over by now already. I don't know what I could have done differently other than putting a tail on Charlie—except I had no idea she was secretly dating Luc. I remind myself we all do the best we can in the moment, and hindsight is useless, since we can't change the past.

But I can have a plan in place for Thanksgiving and Christmas and a football game.

Fuck. I don't mind the work, but I do mind spending so much time away from the kids, especially during the holidays. Yet I can't blame Stevie or Charlie or anyone else. If Rafe and I weren't working on their security, we'd be working on someone else's as we continue to keep pace with client demand.

I nod again. "Fine. I'm afraid to ask, but anything else before I head out?"

"Yes," Charlie says, an unholy gleam in her eye. "While we're there, we want to see the game in Miami."

"Jesus, Charlie. You're fucking killing me. What did I ever do to you?"

"You kids carry on," Brent says, standing and holding a hand out to Joey. "Ready for bed, baby?"

Charlie's attention turns to her brother. "What's your hurry? Is it time for your weekly proposal?"

Joey ducks her head and blushes. Brent glares at Charlie, which does nothing to prevent her from continuing to needle her brother.

"Joey, when are you going to put the poor guy out of his misery? He looks like a lovesick puppy..." She looks Brent up and down, despite his narrow-eyed warning to shut up. "Well, maybe more like a Saint Bernard."

I hold back a laugh when he throws his sister a narrow-eyed glare. He does appear a little lovesick when he looks at Joey. It's clear by the way she returns his gaze that she is crazy in love with him as well. Whatever her reason is for turning down Brent's marriage proposals, it's not for lack of love.

It sure as fuck wasn't how Stevie looked at me when she'd turned down my proposal. No, all I'd seen were pity and condescension, like she was doing me a favor by turning me down.

I shake off the memory and stand. "I'm going to head out." I shake hands with Luc and Brent and kiss Joey's and Charlie's cheeks.

"I'll be in touch," I say with a parting salute. I've never felt like a fifth wheel as much as I did in those last few minutes in Luc's family room. It makes me think of what it would be like to be a part of that group with Stevie at my side.

Our relationship had ended, but the feelings hadn't gone away as quickly, at least not for me. And with her return, they have become more complicated. I have three years of memories and emotions that haven't died a natural death. When I walked out of my house after she'd turned me down, I'd buried my feelings deep and cut off all thoughts of her if they ever tried to push through.

Seeing her again and being near her has brought everything to the surface, like a volcano that has been lying dormant all these years and is now overflowing with lava. Unfortunately, my big feelings aren't hardening like lava when it cools. Instead, they're burning hotter than ever.

I scoff at the fucking poetic ramblings in my head. Am I wallowing? *Fuck, I'm pathetic.*

I focus on the city traffic, but my mind wanders back to thoughts of her as soon as I hit the Merritt Parkway. We have unfinished business between us even though her rejection of my proposal had been pretty damned final. Not one to sit around when there's a problem to be solved, I decide to confront it head-on.

Instead of heading straight home, I take the exit for the compound. There's one emotion I can take care of. And there would be nothing poetic about it.

11

Stevie

I ROLL MY HEAD, trying to ease the crick in my neck. I spent the day organizing my recent photographs, categorizing them and setting a few recent ones aside to enlarge for framing. Pulling up the last few photographs I shot—the black and white shots of the empty fields and gray skies, I'm pleased to see my skills have improved over the years despite no formal training.

At first, I took pictures on my phone to send to my family and as mementos of the places I've visited. Once I switched over to the bigger camera, I found myself capturing more of the people and places that had stories to tell rather than the typical tourist attractions.

What I'll do with the tens of thousands of photos on the hard drives, I have no idea. Maybe I'll enter a few in photography contests, which is what Mom suggests whenever she gushes over any of my photos. And I'll continue to use some of them as gifts.

I also spent part of the day going through the local help wanted sites online, hoping to be inspired to find my passion. Or at least a somewhat interesting job. Unfortunately, nothing sparked my interest, and I'm unqualified for anything that pays above minimum wage.

Frustrated and impatient to find a direction for the rest of my life, I grab my jacket and go for a walk. The temperatures have warmed up some from the freezing lows of the past few nights.

Kathy finished her training and went home for a couple of days before she started her first assignment. I had watched in disappointment as she left, hoping she'd be assigned to our house today so I could go home. I should have gone back to Luc's, since I'm still not in my own bed, but I prefer it here than being around two couples madly in love and a pregnant Charlie. I talked to Mom and she doesn't appear to be in any hurry to return. After living quietly at home with a couple of us at a time for the last eight years, she loves being at Luc's with three of her children and the soon-to-be new additions to the family.

I haven't seen Rafe, except from a safe distance since he took me home to get my laptop. Confused and repulsed by my reaction around him, I went with the slightly less awkward option of calling Gabe earlier, whom I haven't seen or heard from since he dropped me off here. I practically begged him to do what he can so we can have our traditional family Thanksgiving dinner at home.

Until I missed the holiday the first year I was away, I hadn't realized it was my favorite. I used to think only of the hours, from early morning until late afternoon—and the day before—spent in the kitchen. I was thankful I didn't have to do that until I spent it at a restaurant with strangers. I made it a point to be home for the major holidays after that, no matter how far away I was.

"Isn't it a little late for you to be out here?"

I jump at the voice and spin to see Rafe coming out of the darkness. I still can't get used to the fact that I only know it's him because of his scruff. It used to be from the way Gabe looked at me and the way he made me feel. I turn away in guilt and confusion when that rush of feeling flows through me for his twin.

"I've been inside all day and had to come out for some fresh air." I keep walking, hoping he gets the hint and leaves me alone.

Instead, he walks beside me. At least he keeps a bit of distance between us. I add a few more inches.

"Well, you'll be happy to hear that we'll have a team in place for you soon. You'll be in your own bed in a couple of days."

I'm so happy and relieved to hear the news that I close the distance between us without thinking and hug him in gratitude. I instantly realize my mistake. The electric current I felt yesterday is nothing compared to what's surging through my body now. Forget current. I'm hit with bolts of lightning and fireworks are going off inside me.

How can this happen with Rafe? Is it just physical? After all, if I think Gabe is gorgeous and sexy, so is Rafe, because they look exactly alike. Yet it was Gabe I'd been in love with for years—and thought I still was until the other night. Did my feelings transfer to Rafe because Gabe is no longer available? Or, now that the emotional connection with Gabe is severed, did it open the door for my heart—and body—to seek a replacement? And what better replacement than an exact replica? Gabe was my first, my only, until long after we'd broken up. Am I just looking for Gabe in Rafe?

The questions bombard me as I stand frozen in Rafe's arms, my face buried at his throat, bare at the collar of his unbuttoned jacket. His skin smells just like Gabe's.

A shocking thought strikes me. Had they changed places on me when I was dating Gabe—and I never knew the difference?

The thought horrifies me, even as my brain denies Gabe would have ever done that to me. Still, I try to back away, but Rafe's arms tighten around me. He ducks his head, his nose skimming over my jaw. Like Gabe sometimes did as a prelude to kissing me. Before I know it, his lips are on mine. I stop thinking altogether.

I respond to the mouth on mine, the taste so familiar. He slides his tongue between my lips, making my toes curl as they always did when our tongues met.

I kiss him back desperately, trying to make up for the years I've gone without. God, I've missed this. Missed him...his kisses, his arms around me, how he always made me feel so safe and loved.

"Fuck, I've missed you," he murmurs, echoing my thoughts. He kisses me like he's been starving for the past ten years.

"Gabe," I whisper when we break away to fill our lungs with oxygen before diving back in again. I bring my hands to his face to cup his jaw. My fingers instinctively flex at the unfamiliarity.

It feels wrong.

I hold Gabe back when he tries to bring his mouth back to mine. Why does it feel so wrong when it felt so right just seconds ago?

We stare at each other as my fingers brush over his cheeks. His unshaven cheeks.

Time slows. No, it stops. Everything around me is silent. The only image I see is Gabe's unshaven face, even as the nerves in my hands tell me what I'm touching is not bare skin.

My eyes widen as it finally sinks in and everything comes rushing back into focus. My gasp sounds like a roar in my ears. I jerk back, stumbling out of Gabe's arms—

No, not Gabe's. Rafe's.

Rafe's.

Right?

I back away when he reaches for me. I shake my head, rubbing my lips with the back of my hand, trying to erase what just happened. The thought that I can feel as strongly kissing him as I used to with Gabe is appalling and disturbing.

I turn and run.

12

Gabe

H OLY FUCK! WHAT JUST happened?

I stare after Stevie and know I'm in trouble—in more ways than one.

The look on her face—shock, horror, shame—gutted me. I don't know what will be worse—that she thinks she was kissing Rafe, or that she knows it was me and realizes I've been tricking her the last couple of days.

Okay, that's a no-brainer. For me, at least. Letting her think she kissed Rafe would be better, because she is going to be fucking pissed if it's the other. She'll never forgive me.

But she called me Gabe. So she probably already realizes the truth.

Fuck!

I need to go talk to her before she has too much time to think about this and come to the wrong conclusions—although they wouldn't be wrong, since I had every intention of making a move on her tonight. She just happened to make it first.

Still, I need to fix this. But how? What do I say when my own emotions are in freefall?

Having her in my arms after ten years and kissing her again felt like heaven. Everything in my world suddenly felt right. In reality, there's still so much wrong. My bitter anger and resentment have not suddenly evaporated. They are embedded in a part of my heart that's been walled off for a decade.

Looking back, I can admit that I fucked up ten years ago. Just because we loved each other did not mean we were ready for marriage. Flying off the handle and running away proved that I certainly wasn't.

Not wanting to worry about her husband every time he went to work was a reasonable requirement on her part. I wish I'd been reasonable about it back then and found a way for us to work through it, though I'm not sure how when we wanted polar opposite things.

Have her feelings changed since then? While I'm still in a profession where there's still some risk, I'm not a cop who faces danger every day. And it's nowhere near as dangerous as being a SEAL.

If my circumstances hadn't changed with the divorce, I would likely still be in the military. Since I had to leave for the sake of my children, I'm grateful to have found a way to earn a living utilizing the skills I learned. I love what I do and I'm damn good at it.

It's also my business, which Rafe and I are still trying to build up. Though more of my job has become administrative, I'm hoping to change that soon by hiring people to take over those responsibilities for me. I consider sitting at a desk a necessary evil while I grow the business, but I don't want to make it a full-time role.

Would Stevie make me choose between her and my job again? *Maybe not.*

My heart expands with hope at the thought. After all, it's been fifteen years since the deaths of her father and brother. She's ten years older and has had the chance to live a little, see the world, and grow up. She was only eighteen at the time and had already been burdened with too much.

My heart softens, remembering all she'd borne, all the responsibilities she'd assumed without complaining, watching her friends and her siblings live their lives.

Not that she couldn't have, but she was never one to put herself first. It's one of the things I loved most about her—how caring she was. In turn, I took care of her, helping her however I could, taking her out so she could have fun, spending what little money I had on things she'd never buy for herself. Most importantly, I was her rock, her strength, for when she was tired and overwhelmed.

Though she felt the heavy weight of her responsibilities, she hardly ever complained, except at the unfairness of fate. She did what needed doing, and what her family needed was for her to step up at home while Brent pursued his financial goals via football.

She used to talk about going to college to become a teacher, making a difference in young children's lives while having a work schedule that was conducive to the large family we'd planned to have. Did she still have those dreams? Was it possible we could make them come true together as we'd talked about so often?

Yes.

Yes, I want another chance with her. That kiss proved the physical attraction was undeniably still there, despite what Rafe said. And I'd be having a talk with him about that, the fucking liar. I grin when I realize he believed the attraction was gone because she didn't react to *him*. Subconsciously, she'd known it wasn't me.

The only way to know if she is willing to try again despite my job is to talk to her. Fighting enemies isn't all I learned as a SEAL. Communication had been just as important. Too bad I didn't remember that before I fucked up. Again.

It's never too late, right?

Figuring there is no time like the present, I mentally gird myself and walk in the direction she'd run. I find her sitting on the steps of the office trailer, forehead on her knees, her arms wrapped around her legs.

Her head pops up at the sound of gravel under my feet. My heart hitches at the tears streaming down her cheeks and the tortured look in her eyes. I rush to her but stop when she scrambles back to stand, shrinking away from me. It kills me to see her reaction.

"Stevie," I say gently, desperately. "I'm so sorry."

She looks at me in confusion. Shaking her head, she asks, "Gabe?"

"Yeah, babe. It's me. Gabe." I take a tentative step closer, relieved when she doesn't back away.

"What?" She stares at me, looking directly into my eyes and sees the truth. "What?" she asks again, shaking her head, her voice still confused but rising in anger. "What the fuck?"

In the next instant, she launches herself at me and starts pushing and pummeling. I allow it for a few seconds before grasping her arms. I deserve it, but I don't want her to hurt herself.

"Stop," I command, keeping my tone gentle. "Stop, sweetheart."

"Fuck you." She pulls away from me with a jerk. I let go of her before she tears her arms off trying to get away. She crosses them across her chest. "What kind of sick mind-fuck games are the two of you playing?"

"No games. Well," I clarify when she scoffs, "not exactly."

She narrows her eyes at me, ready to launch a verbal attack. I hold up my hands, asking for patience while I explain. "I had no intention of switching places with Rafe. I swear. I only wanted him to take over staying with you because I was…"

I haven't talked about my feelings in so long, I think I've forgotten how. I take a breath and blow it out fast before admitting, "A lot of stuff came up for me while we were driving back from Luc's. I didn't trust myself to be alone with you. Rafe wouldn't take over watching unless he could pretend to be me. But it was only when he took you to the barracks the first night. That was Rafe. He left the next morning and you haven't seen him since that night. It's been me the whole time."

"Pretending to be him."

"Yes." As soon as the word comes out of my mouth, I can feel my foot take its place. Fucking hell.

"Tell me how the hell that isn't trading places?"

It had made sense in my head when I allowed her to think I was Rafe, not take his place. Obviously, she's right, yet I try to justify it, needing her to understand. "Rafe stayed away, so he wasn't pretending to be me."

"But you've been pretending to be him. And he did switch places with you at least once—with your knowledge."

I rub the tense muscles at my nape. How the hell am I going to get out of this so we can move forward?

Blowing out a breath, I say honestly, "Yes, he did. And yes, I have been. I'm sorr—"

"How do I know you haven't traded places before, back when we were dating?"

"Jesus, Stevie, we'd never do that."

When she raises her brows at me, knowing the tricks we'd played on other people, I correct myself. "I would never do that to you, you know that. And Rafe would never do that to me. You were the girl I was going to marry, and he knew it. I loved you and I would have knocked out anyone, even my brother, if they got near you like that. I almost punched him the other night when he said he tried to come on to you."

"I'll be sure to let him follow through next time I see him," she retorts with heat.

Saying nothing more, she stares hard at me. I want to respond with a "hell no, you won't," but I hold my breath, afraid of doing or saying the wrong thing that will turn this into a bigger clusterfuck.

"Why, Gabe?" she finally asks. "Why did you do it?"

I sigh. "I suppose it's because avoidance was my only armor against you. Against what I feel when I'm around you."

She's silent again, staring at me, eyes still narrowed, but perhaps in thought instead of anger. I hope.

"What do you feel?"

I'm unused to sharing my feelings but I want to share with her. "Everything. Every big emotion, Stevie. Anger. Hurt. Bitterness. Resentment. Those were the first ones when I saw you at Luc's. After the shock."

I don't even know what I said after setting eyes on her for the first time in over ten years. "But then it was like a feeling of loss, like we let something slip away. And the chemistry. Fuck, the way you stared at my mouth when I tasted your ribollita...I wanted to fuck you, even if I hated you while doing it. Sitting next to you at dinner was torture, and I wanted to make sure you were suffering too."

The flicker of her lashes and momentary look away told me she had been. Progress, finally.

"It was you the rest of the time? Since my first morning here?" she asks, giving me hope that she understands and will forgive me.

"Every time. Couldn't you tell? When I touched your skin for the first time, helping you out of the car at your house, you felt it too. I know you did." My short laugh is tinged with a touch of triumph. "Fuck Rafe for telling me you didn't feel anything for me anymore. I know it was because somehow you knew he wasn't me."

"Oh, thank God, that was you," she says, her stiff body relaxing with temporary relief. Then she hardens her gaze again. "Do you know how shitty I felt thinking I was attracted to your brother?" She punches me in the abs. A corner of my mind registers the lack of strength behind it and wonder if she is pulling her punch, literally, or if I really do need to get some muscle on her for her own self-defense.

I take her fist and hold on to it when she tries to snatch it back. "I'm sorry, but I was sure you'd figure out it was me if you felt something. I had no idea you would think you were feeling that way toward Rafe. You called my name when we were kissing."

Her mouth tightens at the reminder. Shit. My big mouth just got my other foot stuck in it.

"Yes, but I thought it was Rafe when the kiss started." She tilts her head. "Let's make sure I really haven't seen Rafe since the other night. When is he back?"

Based on the cunning look in her pretty eyes, I'm not going to like whatever scheme she's cooking up. Warily, I answer, "Tomorrow morning. Why?" I ask, suspicious.

She shrugs and skips down the trailer steps. I stare after her as she walks backward and says casually, "I need to test out a theory. Good night!" she calls out, her voice almost cheerful as she jogs away into the night.

What the fuck does that mean?

13

Gabe

I'M STILL FUMING OVER Stevie's words when I see Rafe early the next morning. There is no way in hell she is going to test any kind of theory on him. I hope to hell she was just yanking my chain to get back at me for my stupidity. Afraid I was going to make the situation worse, I let her go last night. I was already feeling like an asshole for making her cry. Otherwise, I would have gone after her and shown her that any theory of hers would prove she belonged with me.

"Thanks a lot, you fucker." I kick the chair Rafe is leaning back in, almost making him crash onto the floor. As a former martial arts champion, he's quick enough with his hands and feet to save himself.

"What the fuck?" He glares at me. "Wake up on the wrong side of the bed?"

"I woke up alone. Because of you," I accuse. "If it hadn't been for your asinine idea the other night, I wouldn't have—" I stop, feeling like an idiot. My brother had nothing to do with it. Well, almost nothing. I created this mess. Rafe doesn't know what I've done and I don't need him holding this over my head for the rest of our lives. I wouldn't put it past him to find it hilarious to cooperate with Stevie on her little experiment to test out whatever theory she's come up with.

"What?" he asks, righting his chair and taking up his previous position. "What wouldn't you have done?"

"Nothing," I growl through gritted teeth. "Just stay away from Stevie."

He raises his eyebrows, then smirks. "Ah. Blue balls. Got it."

I glare at him and stalk out of the trailer. I need to go work out and burn off some of this frustration—sexual and otherwise—before I finish training the recruits on the driving course. Performing evasive maneuvers at a high speed without a clear head would be stupid. I've already filled my quota of stupid for a while.

While I warm up on the treadmill, I realize warning Rafe is unnecessary. He'd never been interested in Stevie or her sisters, despite our mothers' half-joking hope that the D'Angelo twins would marry the Hutchinson twins.

Instead, it was Stevie who'd suddenly caught my eye the first day of swim practice her freshman year, despite years of hanging out with her at family gatherings. She'd filled out between summer and swim season and our eyes had met across the pool. I was sure we'd have been electrocuted if we'd been in the water, the spark between us had been that strong.

I'd broken up with my girlfriend that night and told Rafe I found the girl I was going to marry. When I told him it was Stevie, his first reaction was, "Isn't she a little too much like a sister or close cousin?" followed by, "You better not tell Brent."

I asked her out the next day. Rafe had accepted it and helped keep it a secret from our families for almost a year, treating Stevie no differently than he always had. No, I don't have anything to worry about.

And yet, I can't help the flare of jealousy when I see them together at the training facility later in the day. She and Rafe are standing side by side, almost touching, as they watch Shep practice with Fraser, one of our experienced employees. Rafe shouts out a suggestion, then leans his head closer to Stevie's to explain something to her. They appear almost intimate, making my primal instincts clamor, even though I know better.

She laughs and my heart hitches at hearing it. I've missed hearing that sound. Fucking hell, I've missed *her*.

I lengthen my stride when Rafe pulls a still laughing Stevie to an empty space on the mat to demonstrate something. Seeing her in another man's arms, even my brother's, brings out unfamiliar feelings of insecurity and jealousy, even knowing it's innocent.

Or is it? Stevie looks up at Rafe almost shyly and bites the inside of her lip. What the fuck?

She'd never been shy. No, that's not true. She became shy with me when I first asked her out. She'd looked up at me just like she is looking at Rafe now.

A second before I'm about to snatch her out of his arms, I catch her glance at me out of the corner of her eye. Almost as if making sure I'm watching. I grin. Realizing what she's up to, I divest myself of my jacket, weapons, shoes, and socks before stepping onto the mat.

"Rafe, why don't you help out Fraser. I'll work with Stevie."

The asshole shakes his head. "That's okay. I'll stay right here," he says, barely able to control himself from laughing. "You can take over for Fraser if you want."

I narrow my eyes at him, letting him know he'll pay for that later. And for the flirting he does for the next ten minutes with his hands all over her. Granted, my own hands are on Shep, but I'm not teasing her and grinning like a loon while I do so.

When Fraser calls an end to the session, I have a few words with them about their new assignments starting in the morning. After he and Shep grab their things and head to the barracks for dinner, I turn to find Rafe standing with his arm around Stevie's shoulders.

I see red when I notice she has her arm around his waist. Fed up with their little game, I growl at Rafe, "How about a sparring session, little brother?"

He smirks and shakes his head, still holding Stevie close. "No, thanks. I'm going to grab a shower and then take this beautiful girl out for dinner."

I'm ready to pounce on him and take him down to the mat like we used to as kids. I resist the urge when Stevie removes her hand from him and takes a half step away. I manage a forced smile and say, "Great. I'll join you."

"Sure, if you really want to be a third wheel. See you in a bit, beautiful." He plants a kiss on Stevie's cheek and winks at her, then heads out of the gym, whistling a cheery tune.

Stevie stares after him like a lovesick fool. "You can cut the act now," I snap. "He can't see you."

Her features immediately transform to give me a dirty look. "I wouldn't embarrass myself by staring at his fine ass if he could see me."

I look at my brother's ass as he disappears out the door and wonder if it's any different from mine. Jesus fuck! What the hell am I doing? She's driving me fucking insane.

Scowling at her, I decide to get a little payback. My brother will get his later. Taking two long strides toward her, I grab her wrist and spin her around so her back is against my chest, my arms around hers.

"What are you doing?" she screeches in outrage. "Ever heard of consent?"

I scoff. "As if your assailant is going to ask permission first." I try to ignore how her own fine ass is wriggling against my hardening dick as she tries to break free of my hold. At least I'm not the only one reacting. Her nipples are tight points as her full breasts rub against my bare forearms.

"Let's see what you learned so far. Or were you too busy fawning over Rafe to pay attention to anyth—" I break off with an oomph as her elbow rams into my ribs. I manage to hold on to her, making her writhe and push harder against me in frustration until she suddenly gasps and freezes.

"What are you doing?" Her voice is breathy, her breathing fast. I doubt her struggle is the entire reason. My erection is trapped between us, and her body is softening and surrendering into mine instead of away. I swear I felt a little wiggle of her ass against my straining cock.

I smile in satisfaction because this is not how she reacted in Rafe's arms. I tilt my head to see her face and find her eyes half-closed and her mouth half open.

"If you're out of breath from that little struggle, you'd be in big trouble if I were a stranger about to assault you." I keep my voice low and against her ear. I'm rewarded with a hitch in her breath even as she tilts her head away, exposing her slender neck. The temptation to bite and lick the spot that used to drive her wild is almost too much.

"I would have been more aware if a stranger got too close to me," she protests. "I traveled alone without incident, after all." She pauses to glance up at me, her gaze lowering to my mouth then skittering away. "It seems being home is far more dangerous."

I smile, because despite her words, she's making no move to break free. She's holding on to my arms instead of trying to pull them away. My hands are on her biceps, which I squeeze gently. "You're so much softer than I remember."

She shoots me a glare. "Are you calling me fat?"

I chuckle. "Never in a million years." I slide my fingers under the short sleeves of her T-shirt and squeeze again. "Don't get me wrong, babe. I love how you feel. And you look fucking amazing. You've filled out some, in all the best ways."

She'd been long and slim during her swimming years, maybe a little too thin during the swim season. As often happens when the intensity of training stops, metabolism slows down and the body gains weight. The addition of a few pounds suits her perfectly, making her curves more rounded. My hands itch to wander over those curves...To palm her ass...To cup her breasts and feel exactly how much fuller and heavier they are.

I forget myself, lost in my fantasy, and nuzzle her neck.

She jerks—in surprise or something more?—then huffs out a breath. My grip is loose enough for her to easily escape—if she wanted to.

I change the topic before she decides she wants to. "So how did your little experiment with Rafe go?" Unable to resist, I lower my mouth to whisper against her neck, "Did you prove your theory?"

Her already fast pulse goes crazy, but she doesn't pull away. I press my mouth to the sensitive spot in the curve of her neck and lick her. She shivers, her breathing quick and erratic. Yes. It still drives her wild.

"Did he make you feel that?" I bite her gently this time, then lave the spot before pressing a kiss on it. A soft moan escapes, despite her teeth biting into her bottom lip.

"Can he make you shiver and moan? Can he make you lose your breath?"

I kiss my way up her jaw, made easier because she's involuntarily lifted her face to me. She releases her lips and parts her mouth. I take it as an invitation. I press my mouth to the corner of hers, taking her lower lip between mine to lick and suck before biting it softly. She moans and turns her head before following the movement with her entire body. I gather her close and take her mouth in an open-mouthed kiss, my tongue searching for hers.

Fuck, I've been dreaming of this since last night.

Her hands encircle my neck for leverage so she can go on her toes and rub her spandex-covered pussy against my cock. I help her by putting an arm around her hips and pulling her closer to my aching erection that is weeping for relief.

I want her. Right now. I need her. It's been too fucking long.

A tiny sane part of my mind reminds me we are in the gym. While the mat is soft enough for what I have in mind, it's not exactly private. Anyone can walk in.

I hesitate to let her go, afraid she'll come to her senses and back away again. Bending my knees slightly, I slide both hands to her ass. I moan at the fullness that fills my palms and dig my fingers into her soft flesh to pull her tighter against me. I grind against her pelvis, knowing I've hit the right spot when she gasps and digs her nails into my nape.

She's ready to climb me, one thigh coming to rest against my hip. Instead of lifting her so she can wrap her legs around me, I keep a subtle, circling rhythm against her damp heat and murmur against her lips, "Let's take this to your room."

"Yes," she breathes.

I shout a mental "Fuck, yes!" only to stumble back a half step in surprise when she unwraps herself from me and gives me a push.

"No!"

I almost whimper. So fucking close.

"Okay, we can stay here." I don't care. I just need to be inside her. ASAP.

"No," she pants, her palm up and out in a stop sign.

"Why not?" For fuck's sake. I'm whining.

"I'm not sleeping with you, Gabe."

Who the fuck said anything about sleep?

Rafe wasn't wrong about blue balls. Unfortunately, being afflicted by them means there's no room for tact and sensitivity. "Why the hell not?" I'm almost shouting, and I make an attempt to lower my voice when she flinches. *Fuck.* "There's obviously still something between us."

"Yes, there is. Your girlfricnd."

Huh? I can't even remember the last time I had a one-night stand, never mind a date. Every spare moment I'm not working is reserved for my kids. When am I supposed to have time for a girlfriend?

"What? I don't have a girlfriend."

She raises her eyebrows. "Really? The reason you couldn't stay at my house the night you brought me here? Remember?"

My fucking brother. I'm going to have to think back to our younger days to find a way to get back at him for all the trouble he's causing me.

"You shaved for her at nine o'clock at night! You're clean-shaven again. For her, for all I know."

I finally shaved last night, once she realized it was me, not Rafe. It was a relief since I'm not fond of facial hair. And she thinks I do it when meeting someone for sex. Her expression is accusatory but she can't hide the hurt in her voice. I'm going to add something extra to Rafe's payback for that.

"Babe, that was Rafe, remember? I haven't had a girlfriend since you."

Her eyes widen and her mouth pops open for a second before she laughs. Laughs! I hate to admit I'm an idiot who half-expected her to throw herself at me in relief. Having the woman you want to fuck laugh in your face might be the cure for blue balls.

"Gabe, you had a wife. Did you pick a random woman off the street and marry her?"

Close enough. She was someone I hooked up with occasionally who happened to get pregnant, despite taking precautions.

I don't want to get into all that with Stevie, but she's waiting for an answer. "We weren't dating. I married her because of Leo. And I don't have a girlfriend now. I haven't even dated anyone since I've been home." When she continues to look at me in disbelief, I add with complete candor, "Sure, I've hooked up here and there, but I never stayed over. Not once." Her expression is slowly transforming, softening. So I give her a little more truth. "There hasn't been anyone in over six months. I swear it."

"Oh," she breathes. Her eyes run over me like she doesn't understand how I'm still standing. I don't either. I'm dying for her, the way I always was when we were dating. We couldn't keep our hands off each other, frustration mounting because it was often days before we could be alone again.

Assuming we're on the same page when she continues staring silently, I take a step toward her. But damn if she doesn't take a quick one back, putting that fucking stop sign up again.

"It still doesn't mean I'm going to sleep with you." She walks off the mat and slips into her shoes.

Once again, who the hell said anything about sleep?

She bends over to tie her sneakers.

Fuck me. Her ass in the spandex has me swallowing hard. "It's just physical attraction," she continues, standing and reaching for her jacket from the peg on the wall.

How did we go from ready to fuck on the mat to her getting ready to leave? I run a surreptitious palm over my dick that was anticipating relief. I hadn't noticed the lack of sex in my life until Stevie came back into it. Annoyed at being reminded of the lack without the remedy, I ask bluntly, "What the hell else do you need?"

"I don't just hop into bed with anyone I find the least bit attractive."

When her eyes shift away guiltily, I feel a fierce stab of jealousy. I already admitted I haven't been a saint since my divorce, so I have no right to stand in judgment of Stevie, no matter how much it pains me to think of her with other men. I'd been her first and only, and I had reveled in that fact when we'd been dating. As hypocritical as it makes me, since there had been a couple before her and many more after, I experience the loss of that claim deeply.

"Besides, it's not a good idea to start something when we have unfinished...history."

It had felt pretty damn finished at the time, which is why I had needed to get away from her. The thought of being in the same town, seeing her at family functions, having to pretend to be friends with her the way we were before...The thought had suffocated me. I'd had to get as far away as possible to breathe again.

But while I'd learn to breathe air that I didn't share with her, I hadn't been fully alive without her. Standing before Stevie now, it becomes so clear. All the turmoil I've been feeling since seeing her again is from the pain of coming to life again.

And she's right. The way we—I—ended things was meant to be a clean break. Instead, it had left jagged edges in both of us. I—we—need to fix them. Take out the sharp pieces that can still hurt us and smooth out the edges, so if—*when*—we make our way back to each other again, both of our healed parts can fit together like one solid piece, with love as our glue.

While I've been standing there, waxing poetic thoughts I'll never admit to even under torture, Stevie has almost reached the exit.

"You're right," I call out. "Let's dump Rafe and go out to dinner to talk about it. Then we can start over."

She faces me and shakes her head. "I'm not going out with you. And we're not starting over. Nothing's changed." Her gaze goes to the gun and two knives lying on top of my jacket.

I go to her, even as my frustration rises at her lack of cooperation with my plan. I keep my tone calm as I open my mouth to say something reasonable, only to stick my size thirteen foot in it. "You don't want to fix things and you don't want to fuck."

Shit. That's not what I meant to say. I jump ahead of her when she turns to leave and block the door so she can't escape before I fix this. Panic replaces frustration. "I'm sorry. I'm sorry, Stevie. I didn't mean that. I only meant to ask what you want. If you don't want to start over or go out with me, what do *you* want to do?"

She sets her chin at a stubborn angle and states, "I want to go home."

Despite the dread that sets in at the thought she won't change her mind, that my job is still an issue for her, I back off. For now. Projecting a lightheartedness I don't feel, I say with a smile and small bow, "Your wish is my command. You can go home tomorrow. We'll have a team bringing your mother and sister to the house in the morning. In the meantime," I continue, opening the door for her, "enjoy your dinner with Rafe."

She walks out the door but turns back to me. "You're not coming?"

Is she disappointed or am I hearing what I want to hear? Either way, that she asked is enough to improve my mood. Feeling hopeful again, I check to make sure the door is locked. "No," I respond, turning to grin at her. "You just proved my theory." Raising my hand in a casual salute, I leave her staring at me in confusion. My steps light, I quicken my pace so I can make it home in time for dinner and bedtime with my family.

14

Stevie

I BREATHE DEEPLY AND stretch my entire body, fingers and toes pointing in opposite directions. I'm so happy and relieved to be waking up in my own bed. And I'll be doing it every morning for a long time to come.

Home. I'm home to stay.

Why did I stay away so long? Why had I been so eager to leave?

Oh, right. Feeling stuck. Spending the years since my dad's and RJ's deaths taking care of my mother and baby sister while everyone else had moved forward with their lives. Especially Gabe. He'd been the first one to leave. And when I heard he was coming home, I decided it was time for me to go, unable to face him and the children that were meant to be ours.

Instead, he had two babies with another woman. As if on cue, my hand goes to my heart and I rub the physical pain that always comes with the thought. When I heard about the birth of his first child, I cried, then went to a bar, got drunk, and slept with the first man to hit on me. I had done the same a few months earlier when the news of his wedding had reached me. I'm not proud of it, but I needed something to escape the deep, searing pain.

Pain that did not lessen in intensity over the years.

But it was my decision to turn down his proposal, the only choice I thought I had at the time.

My thoughts continue to wander through the past to the what-if scenarios. What if I'd accepted Gabe's marriage proposal? How different would the last ten years have been? Where would we have ended up today? I certainly wouldn't have seen as much of the world as I have. If I'd stayed, I'd have been lucky to see much of anything beyond driving distance on his police officer's salary. Without a college degree, any job I worked wouldn't have paid much more than minimum wage.

I lie in bed, resting my head on my bent arm as I stare at a large poster of one of the first artistic photos I took. It's a picture of one of the prettiest views I'd seen up to that point, from inside a lighthouse in Puerto Rico. The arched window with its green shutters opening up to sun-bleached sandy ground, a white picket fence, and a vast blue sky with the darker blue ocean visible beyond the cliff's edge. I had the photo enlarged almost to scale and placed on the wall across from my bed. Every time I look at it, I feel like I'm back there, staring through the opening at the bright world outside while I stand in the cool, dim interior.

I always thought of it as a relaxing, meditative image to wake up to. Today, it's more of a reflection of my life. There's this big beautiful world out there and I'm standing in the dark—which is how it felt when I first stepped into the lighthouse from the blazing sun. But my vision adjusted then and it will eventually do so here, metaphorically. I need to be patient.

My thoughts move forward in time to my conversation with Gabe yesterday. Is starting over with him part of the adjustment? Can I risk my heart to him again? Ten years ago, he dismissed my fears like they didn't matter and left me without a word.

Maybe it was for the best that he left instead of trying to work things out. The years have given us both time to grow, to mature, to see more of the world and learn what's important in life. And perhaps be better prepared this time around?

What am I thinking? Am I actually considering Gabe's proposal to start over, to try again? No, it's too early to start thinking about that. There's too much to fix between us. First and foremost is his job. Is it something I can live with even though it's not as dangerous as a policeman's? Yet he does a carry a gun because the people who hire him need protection from some type of danger.

I sigh, knowing from past experience I could spend the rest of the day going in circles with my thoughts. Determined to look ahead to my future from now on, I throw the covers back and get out of bed.

Thanksgiving is in a few days. My mood brightens at the thought. As I shower and dress, I make a mental list of the menu and everything I'll need for it.

Hmm. Maybe I can become a chef and open a restaurant. I let that idea float around in my head while I make breakfast for me, Mom, Bobbie—and some extra for the two men watching the house today.

"What do you think, Mom?" I ask her when she walks into the kitchen a few minutes later. She's carrying her cane but not using it. Her limp, leftover from the stroke, will get more pronounced as the day goes. She'll reach for her cane then.

"Can you see me being a chef?"

She raises her brows and gives me a wry smile. "Perhaps you'd like to cook all the meals for the next little while and see if you like it as much as you think you do." She presses a kiss to my cheek. "It's so good to have you home, sweetheart. I hope you really are staying for a while this time."

I keep my emotions in check so I don't squeeze too hard when I wrap my arms around her. "I'm not going anywhere," I whisper, my throat tight. "Don't worry. I'm home for good. I promise."

"We'll see. Being stuck here, you might start getting itchy feet again."

I let go of her reluctantly, the hissing and popping of the grease reminding me to check on the bacon. "These last few weeks, I actually missed being stuck here. And all the little things that happen while I'm gone. And I missed you." I grab the tongs to take the bacon out of the pan and place the strips on a napkin-lined platter. "But I do need to figure out what to do with the rest of my life."

"You don't want to go to college?" Regret curves her mouth downward. "I'm sorry you didn't get to go with your friends."

I shrug, pouring the whisked eggs into the pan. "It wasn't in the cards. I got to travel the world instead."

"Well, it's not too late, honey," she reassures me as she makes her tea. "Weren't you planning on becoming a teacher?"

"God, I can't remember. It was so long ago." I chuckle and tell her, "I was told I could get a job as a bodyguard if I get into shape." My smile slips away when I remember it was Gabe, pretending to be Rafe, who made the offer as a joke.

"If you ever decide you want to go to college, don't worry about paying for it. Brent has given me more than I'll ever—"

"Nope. Uh-uh." I turn the stove off and spoon some of the scrambled eggs into a casserole dish to keep warm in the oven. "I'm so grateful for the funds to travel, but Brent has done more than enough."

He set up an account for each of us when he signed his big contract with the NFL and added to it when he signed his next contract. Charlie attended college with hers and Georgie left to chase her dreams of stardom. Mine sat unused, collecting interest. When Charlie graduated college and moved back home, Mom convinced me it was my turn to do whatever I want. I didn't know what that was, so I took a tropical vacation and then kept traveling. I used up a big chunk the first year, staying in luxurious accommodations and indulging in things I didn't need, making up for all the lean years. I was more frugal after that, so I still have a little money left until I get a job.

"If I decide to go to college, I'll take out a loan. Besides," I say before she can protest, "I don't even know if that's what I want."

But the thought of sitting in classes next to eighteen-year-olds holds no appeal. It wouldn't be the same as if I'd gone at that age. I already missed out on the dorm life, the carefree days with nothing to worry about but grades and boys, the sisterhood of a sorority...

"What about your photography? Couldn't you do something with that? You've taken beautiful photos."

I open a cabinet and pull out three plates. "Maybe." Mom will wave away the doubts I have about doing anything as a professional photographer, so I keep them to myself. I make up a plate for Mom and set it on the table at her usual seat. "Let's eat while it's hot. I tried to wake Bobbie before I came down, but it looks like she's going to have leftovers."

"No, I'm not," Bobbie announces, bouncing into the kitchen.

I hand her an empty plate so she can take what she wants before I make up a plate for myself. "Any particular dishes you're craving, Bobbie? I'm making a list for our meals and for Thanksgiving."

I'm hoping I can go to the store to pick out everything myself with one of the bodyguards. We had the staples delivered yesterday to get us through a couple of days.

"Your sister is thinking of becoming a chef," Mom tells Bobbie, who wrinkles her nose.

"Ew. Does that mean we're going to be eating weird-looking things? The only good thing about those fancy dishes is the portions are tiny."

"Not that kind of chef. I was thinking more of a family restaurant. Italian maybe. Or a diner."

"Cool. The diner in town has new owners. They fancied it up and changed the menu. Took out the booths and jacked up the prices."

The news saddens me. Mom and Dad would take the five of us there almost every Sunday for brunch. Picturing the homey atmosphere of the place as I remember it, I realize that's the image I had when the idea of becoming a chef popped into my head. I wanted to recapture that feeling of enjoying the meal with family.

Being the one to make the food—for multiple families—did not sound as appealing.

"Bobbie and I went for brunch when it reopened," Mom says. "There were hardly any families with young kids there. We would have been kicked out if it was that kind of place when we used to take you rowdy bunch." She smiles nostalgically at the memory.

"We've been trying new places since, on the lookout for our new favorite," Bobbie says.

I'm glad she has her own memories with Mom of the place that had been special to the rest of us.

Thoughts of my future and its direction consume me as I offer breakfast to the guards and do chores around the house. Mom is right. I should see if I really missed cooking as much as I think I do. And if it's opening a place of my own I want instead, I need to figure out a financial plan that doesn't involve taking money from my brother. Then there's the steep learning curve of opening and running a restaurant.

Just thinking about it makes me feel exhausted and unfulfilled. I sigh as the short-lived dream fades away. Back to square one.

Though I've been on the move constantly for the last three-and-a-half years, being back home makes me feel like time has stood still. I'm twenty-eight years old and being a lifeguard is the only real job I've had. I suppose I can get back in shape—not enough to be a *body*guard, but to be recertified as a *life*guard.

As I picture it, the notion of sitting at a pool for hours every day—and indoors during the cold months—has no appeal. Thinking of the pool Brent included in the remodel, I change into a suit and go for a swim as my thoughts continue to swirl.

Cooking and lifeguarding are the only things I have experience in besides being a caretaker, but I have no license or certification to back that up. A reference from my mother won't mean much to future employers.

Frustrated with getting nowhere in figuring out a direction for the rest of my life, I flip onto my back and switch to a backstroke.

I'm out of breath after just a couple of laps. Walking instead of taking cabs and occasionally hiking during my travels did not keep me as fit as I thought.

I hold the last backstroke and reach for the wall with my hand so I don't hit my head on it. I tip my head back to see how much more I have to go and see a little human standing over me at the edge of the pool. Startled, I flip over, going under for a second as I try to find my footing, only to realize I'm at the deeper end. I get myself upright, inhaling a splash of water on my way up. I attempt to cough it out of my lungs and take in air, unable to speak.

"Hi."

I look up for the source of the child's voice. I whip off my swim goggles and find wide, curious eyes staring at me. A little girl is kneeling, leaning over to peer at me with big blue eyes, a little too close to the edge.

"Scoot back so I can get out," I tell her, trying to keep my voice calm so I don't panic her into falling over.

"Arianna! What are you doing in here?"

At the bellowing voice, the girl stands and whirls around, only to stumble and lose her balance. Her arms windmill for a second, but it doesn't keep her from falling backward into the pool with a splash.

15

Gabe

I'M ALREADY RUNNING EVEN before the splash that Ari makes has a chance to land back in the pool. Not knowing her location or if I'm at the deep end, I skid to a stop at the edge instead of diving in. My heart starts beating again at the sight of my little girl clinging to Stevie like a monkey.

"I got you, sweetie. You're okay," she murmurs. Her hand is cradling Ari's head and my heart stops again.

"Did she hit her head?" I ask.

Stevie looks up at me, her soothing expression hardening. "No," she responds, her voice tight with anger. "Luckily, she fell straight back into the water."

She'd windmilled backward when I startled her with my panic at finding her at the edge of the pool. She was next to me by the mud room one minute and gone the next.

When Ari burrows her face further into Stevie's neck, her voice lightens. "Just like a starfish." She jostles her gently. "You okay, sweetie? Does anything hurt?"

Ari shakes her head without lifting her head.

"Good. Then let's get out of the water so we can dry off. What do you say?"

She shakes her head again.

"No? Why not?"

"Daddy's mad at me," she mumbles around the thumb in her mouth. At four-and-a-half years old, she's mostly outgrown the habit, but falls back to it when she's overly tired or upset.

Stevie's eyes snap up to mine and narrow. "Daddy's not mad."

"He is. He yelled real loud."

"He only did that because he was scared you were going to fall in and get hurt. Weren't you, *Daddy*?"

She's right. I was scared. I should have known better than to frighten her into sudden movement, but I panicked. It's not something I've ever done as a SEAL or as a bodyguard. But seeing Arianna at the edge scared the bejesus out of me. My fear hadn't been her falling into water. I was right here to go after her. It was picturing in that split second what would have happened if she'd already fallen in and I hadn't been there.

I get down on one knee. "Hey, baby. Stevie is right. I'm not mad."

Ari finally lifts her head to look at me. "You're not? Pwomise?"

"I promise, sweetheart."

"You were scared?" Her eyes widen at the improbable thought of her big, strong daddy being scared. If she only knew how often I lay awake worried about her and Leo's well-being.

"Yeah, I was."

"How about we have your daddy take you out so I can get out too? I think my fingers are turning into raisins." Stevie chuckles and waves her fingers in front of Ari, who giggles. "Hold up your arms so he can lift you out, okay?"

Stevie looks up at me while instructing Ari. I give her a look of gratitude and grab my daughter under her arms to lift her up and out. I wrap her in a hug to reassure her I'm not mad. I watch as Stevie gets out of the water, my gaze taking in her cleavage, jutting nipples, and the tight fit of her dark red one-piece bathing suit as she uses her arms to pull herself out of the water. Rivulets of water stream down her long, bare legs.

When she passes us, my gaze follows her almost bare ass, the fabric bunched at her crevice. *Fuck me.* Despite the circumstances, I'm not able to look away until she wraps a towel around herself, hiding the mouth-watering view.

She comes to us with another towel and hands it to me. I smile in thanks at her but she turns away. "I'll go find some clothes for her. There's a bathroom through there if you want to rinse her off or warm her up with a shower." She points to a door on the other side of the pool, then leaves.

"Let's get you out of these clothes, baby." I carry Ari to the bathroom and help her out of her wet shoes and clothes and into a warm shower. I figure she has time, since Stevie has to shower and change too. Might as well wash her hair too. One less thing for me to do tonight.

Once we're done, I dry her off and wrap her like a burrito in a dry towel I find on a shelf. She shrieks with laughter when I pick her up in a fireman's carry over my shoulder and take her back out to the pool. I sit on a pool chair and hold her in my lap, cupping her chin to make sure she looks at me.

"Ari, you know you're not allowed to go near pools by yourself. Why did you come in here alone?"

"But, Daddy, I wasn't alone." She glances at the glass entry door. "I saw someone swimming."

Well, fuck. The kid has me there.

"I only wanted to watch. I wasn't gonna go in the pool. I know I'm not supposed to," she says, her little face full of earnest assurance.

"Alright. Good. But you were standing too close to the edge. This is why I give you rules, right? Like staying near me while I did some work instead of wandering off like you just did. It's for your safety. I don't want you to get hurt. I love you, sweetheart."

"I love you too, Daddy."

My heart expands when she lays her head on my chest, her arms still encased in the towel. I place a kiss on the top of her head, wondering when I'll be able to stop worrying this much about her.

The sound of someone clearing their throat makes me look up. Stevie, dressed in black sweatpants and a long-sleeve jersey, moves from the door with clothes in her hand. She puts them on the chair next to us. Straightening, she appears self-conscious as she runs a hand over her wet hair that's pulled up into a bun on the top of her head. I want to tell her she has no reason to feel insecure, if that's what the gesture meant. It's been a while, but I often saw her looking exactly like this after a swim practice. To me, she was prettier with wet hair and no make-up than any other girl with styled hair and a done-up face.

"These are my godson's," she explains. "They'll be a bit big, but they should do until her clothes dry. I'll put them in the dryer now."

"I'll get them." I stand and set Ari on the chair in my place. "Ari, this is...my friend, Stevie," I say, having a surreal moment as I look at the woman I thought was going to be my wife and introducing her to my daughter, a child that should have been ours. "Stevie, this is my daughter, Arianna. This is not how I expected you two would meet." I hadn't planned on them meeting at all until Stevie and I had figured things out.

She smiles, but it doesn't reach her eyes. I leave them to get Ari's wet clothes. Does she not like children? We used to talk about having a big family, so what changed? As I pick up the wet pile from the bathroom and wrap them in Ari's used towel, a troubling thought occurs. Is it *my* children she doesn't like?

I come out of the bathroom and stop in my tracks. Stevie is kneeling in front of Ari, helping her into clothes that are at least two sizes too big while Ari talks to her a mile a minute. My heart lurches at the sight, especially when Ari holds Stevie's face still for one of her special nose-kisses. Both of their noses scrunch adorably.

My heart stutters. I have a sense of déjà vu, the feeling I had when I looked across the high school pool and knew she was the one for me.

Stevie is still the one for me. *Always was. Always will be.*

I felt it in my gut when I saw her again at Luc's, though I'd fought it, still angry at her for rejecting what we could have had.

She says something to Ari, who giggles, then gently towel-dries my daughter's curly black hair. She stops when she sees me and stands, all traces of a smile gone.

Her gaze meets mine when I hold the clothes out. I don't let go when she tries to take them.

"Thank you," I say softly.

She shrugs. "I had no choice but to dress her when she threw off her towel."

"I meant for being here and keeping her calm in the pool."

"You're welcome. But you should really get her into swimming lessons." She tugs the clothes out of my hand. "I need to get these into the dryer."

She walks out without another word.

I want to follow her, but I need to fold the bottoms of the overalls Ari is borrowing before she trips over them. By the time we reach the kitchen, Stevie is coming out of the laundry room.

She gives me an annoyed look, but sighs when her gaze falls on my daughter. I'm relieved to see her expression soften. Thank fuck. I don't know what I would have done if she didn't like kids, and mine in particular.

"Is it okay to give her a snack?" she asks me.

"That would be great. She normally has lunch when she comes home from preschool, so she's probably hungry. Ma will give her lunch when I get her home, but a snack would...be great," I repeat, smiling. She doesn't return the smile.

"Any allergies?"

"Nope, not that I know of." When she raises an eyebrow at me, I clarify, "I mean, none so far that we've found. Hopefully, it stays that way." Why am I fumbling like a nervous nerd with a pretty girl I want to impress?

"Why don't you turn the TV on for her?"

The kids have a "no TV while eating" rule, but I don't say anything. Keeping Ari occupied will give me a chance to talk to Stevie.

While I settle her in front of a show for preschoolers in the adjacent, open area family room, Stevie washes an apple, then cores and cuts it into eight slices. On a small plate, she arranges the apple slices and a spoonful of peanut butter. She retrieves a juice box from the pantry and stabs the attached straw into the opening.

"Here you go, sweetie." Stevie places the plate and drink on the coffee table for Ari.

"Why do you look like you have a lot of practice doing this?" I ask her when she returns to the island in the kitchen.

"Because I have, between Bobbie and my godson, Alex."

"Godson? Whose child?"

"My friend Andi. Someone I met after you...we..."

"After you turned me down and we broke up. And—" I hold my hand up to stop her from interrupting. "And I ran away like a child instead of trying to work things out."

She shrugs as she pulls open the fridge and stares into its contents. "No point in talking about it, Gabe. We didn't want the same things. There was nothing to work out."

How can she say that, as if what we had, the love we shared, meant nothing? But I can't get into it with Ari sitting a few feet away. I also don't want to say anything until she's in the right frame of mind to listen and I've figured out what to say.

She closes the fridge without taking anything out, filling the tea kettle instead. She pulls out a mug and holds one up for me, brows raised. I shake my head. I'd rather have coffee, but I don't ask for any.

"What I'm wondering is why your daughter was at the pool. Alone. And at the house to begin with. Is it Take Your Daughter To Work Day?" she asks sarcastically.

"Hilarious," I deadpan. "I was on my way here to check a camera that's been acting up. My parents were at a doctor's appointment that was running late, so I picked her up at preschool and brought her with me. I thought she was standing right there with me while I worked on the camera."

"Lucky I was there," Stevie continues, "though she insists she wouldn't have come to the pool if I hadn't been there. She doesn't know how to swim?"

"She's four," I say, on the defensive.

"Never too young to start."

When am I supposed to take them for swim lessons? As it is, I almost never pick them up from school and often miss having dinner with them. I can't add one more thing to Ma's plate.

But fuck, Stevie's right. It reminds me that I've pushed off hiring someone to ease the burden on my mother, though she insists she doesn't mind. She's almost sixty and has health issues—minor but still requiring self-care and medical follow-up. And she takes care of my recently retired father, who has his own health issues after forty years with the fire department. I've relied on my mother for three years, but I can't keep expecting that of her, as much as she says she doesn't mind.

As Stevie stares at the kettle, waiting for it to whistle, I narrow my eyes at her profile.

"You're right. You're hired."

She spins to face me, her eyes wide. "What? I'm not—"

"You were a competitive swimmer and a lifeguard. I'll pay for you to pick her up and bring her here for the lesson. Name your price. When can you start?"

She laughs in disbelief. "Gabe, I'm not giving her swim lessons. I'm busy!"

"With what? You were swimming just now."

"I was actually trying to figure out my life. I'm not giving her lessons."

"Daddy?"

We both look over to see a teary-eyed Ari standing with her thumb in her mouth. I rush over to her and crouch in front of her, wiping at a tear with my thumb. "What's the matter, baby?"

"Stevie don't want to teach me to swim? She don't like me?"

I glance at Stevie whose expression is filled with guilt and apology that morphs into resignation. She comes over and kneels next to me. My mouth curves into a smile, her action confirming what I'd already determined at the pool.

"Of course I like you, honey. I just need to check my schedule."

Taking mercy on Stevie, I give her space for the next few days. I'll see her tonight when Rafe and I take a shift at the Hutchinson house. I took most of the day off to spend the holiday with my family. Some relatives lingered after the early Thanksgiving dinner, but I take Leo and Ari for a walk. I don't get enough alone time with them and a day off is even more rare.

I hold Ari's hand as she skips beside me while Leo takes a pebble along with us, kicking it ahead as we go.

"How's it going, buddy?" I ask him, wondering why he's so quiet.

"Good."

I was hoping one-word answers were still a few years away.

"Aren't you going to ask me how work is?"

Without looking back, he asks, "How's work?"

"Good," I reply in the same morose tone he used.

I raise an eyebrow at him when he looks over his shoulder and grins, showing off a gap from a front tooth that fell out last week. I woke up in a bit of a panic in the morning when I forgot to have the tooth fairy visit during the night until I remembered he told me the night before he knew who the tooth fairy really was.

I smile and hold out my hand. "Walk with us."

He looks around to make sure no one else is around before taking my hand. My hand engulfs his and I give it a little squeeze.

"Something bothering you, T-Rex?"

He kicks the pebble a few feet down the road and says nothing.

"Everything okay at school?" I try to remember what second grade was like and can't come up with anything that troubled me. But then, I had Rafe at school with me and two parents who were home more often than I am now. Dad guilt is real.

He hitches a shoulder. "It's okay."

Whatever is bothering him, looks like I'm going to have to pull it out of him.

Ari pipes up, "Nonna gave him a timeout 'cuz he push me yesterday."

Or I can just ask the little pixie holding my other hand.

"Shut your big mouth!" Leo yells, glaring at his sister.

"Hey," I admonish Leo, giving him a stern look. "We do not talk like that. It's disrespectful."

"That's how he talk to me yesterday too, Daddy. He was mean and dissispetful."

"Leo, want to tell me why you pushed your sister?"

"She was being a brat!" His eyes flare with angry frustration. He kicks the pebble hard so it flies through the air and disappears into the grass. "She kept trying to climb on my back for a pony ride when I was playing with my Legos."

"Okay, I'll talk to her about that. But you know you're not supposed to push her. She's smaller than you."

I stop and crouch down to his level. "Look at me, son." Once he does, I ask gently, "Tell me what's going on."

My heart cracks when his eyes well with tears. I can't stand to see either of them cry.

"Geoffrey called me an orphan because I don't have a mom."

Fucking Geoffrey, whoever he is. I bet he's a lot smaller than me and yet I want to break the edict I gave Leo and scare the shit out of him.

Leo no longer asks about his mother, but when he did, I only said she wasn't able to visit them because of her job. I figured the white lie of a job was the easier—the right—thing to do.

"You have a mother. She's just—" I glance at Arianna. Her eyes are also wet, but the tears are for her brother, not a woman she has no memory of. Despite her occasional brattiness toward her brother, usually because he's ignoring her, she hates seeing him upset. I bet she spent Leo's timeout sitting next to him, talking and singing, until he forgave her.

Turning back to Leo, I reply with tact. "Your mother isn't here, but you have me, so you are not an orphan."

"I wish I had a mommy," Ari says, her voice small with impending tears. "Mommies bwing all my fwiends to school and come get them after. And when Nonna took me to the park, everyone had a mommy there 'cept me."

I close my eyes, suddenly exhausted and sick at heart for all of us. Leo and Ari don't deserve the hand they were dealt. I'm filled with guilt, but at the same time, if I hadn't married Camilla, I would hardly have seen Leo and Arianna wouldn't have been born.

When Camilla became pregnant, she told me she would return to Brazil after the baby was born. She admitted to overstaying her visa, so she would not be able to return for years. It meant I would hardly see my child. After confirming the baby was mine, I offered to marry her so she could stay in the States. It took me some time after the divorce to stop questioning that decision.

"Dad, it's okay," Leo whispers. Shit. He's comforting *me*, making my throat tight. I enfold the two of them into my arms before they can see my own damp eyes.

When I'm able to speak without my voice breaking, I sit back on my heels and glance between the two of them. "You have me, and Uncle Rafe, and the best Nonna and Nonno in the world. And all the cousins that were at our house today...Do you know how lucky that makes you?"

They both nod, Leo a bit more reluctant to agree than Ari. "And today's Thanksgiving, so let's be thankful for them, okay? What do you say?"

Another nod.

"And do you know what I'm most thankful for, more than anything in the world?"

Leo tilts his head but stays silent, his blue eyes unblinking.

"What, Daddy?" Ari asks, eyes wide with curiosity.

"You two." I smack loud kisses on both their faces, making Ari giggle. Even Leo cracks a smile as he tries to escape.

"Come on, let's head back." I stand and hold out a hand to each of them. "Because I'm also thankful Nonna makes the best tiramisu."

"And the best rainbow cookies!" Leo says, his eyes brightening again. "Nonna said she made extra for us and hid them away in case everyone finished them today."

"Now, doesn't that make you even more thankful?" I ask as we head back home, holding a small hand in each of mine. Ari resumes her skipping and Leo tells me about the latest *Beyblade X* episode.

Despite everything, I'm very thankful for having these two in my life.

"Thanks for today, Ma. And for everything you do for me and the kids."

I lean down to kiss my mother on her cheek as she puts away leftovers while my father sits in his favorite armchair in the family room with the newspaper.

Pop is a good father and grandfather, if somewhat set in his traditional ways. He was the breadwinner while Ma took care of the house and children. Since Camilla had never shown interest in pursuing a career, it's the way it had been with us also.

"You're thanking me for taking care of you and my grand-children?" she huffs, genuinely offended.

"Yes, because I want you to know I don't take any of it for granted."

"I know, son." She pats my arm.

We're silent as I pour myself coffee and take a few sips. "Hey, Ma. Have you noticed anything going on with the kids? Especially Leo?"

When she frowns at me, I clarify, "I mean emotionally. Have they seemed sad or upset?"

Her frown of confusion changes to that of concern. "Leo becomes quiet sometimes. Lost in his head."

"He still thinks about his mother."

"She's no mother!"

The venom in her tone is not surprising. She'd been excited when she'd learned her Brazilian daughter-in-law was actually of Italian descent. It quickly changed when Camilla made no effort to have a relationship with her, and it went downhill from there. Before she can go on a rant about my ex-wife, I continue.

"Maybe I should take him to see a child psychologist again."

Ma ponders the idea before answering, "I suppose it wouldn't hurt. Make sure you talk to Leo first and explain to him there's nothing wrong with him. The psychologist is someone he can talk to about things he can't talk to you about."

I tsk. "But I want him to talk to me. About anything."

"Of course you do, but he won't if he thinks it will upset you."

Ready to argue that point further, I blow out a frustrated breath instead. She's right, of course, no matter how much I assure Leo he can tell me anything.

"I'll call the one Leo saw when he first came here," she offers. "She seemed to help him at the time."

I thought so too, but maybe I should have continued the sessions even after Leo appeared to have adjusted. When we first left San Diego, he'd either act out in anger or retreat within himself. I thought it was because of too much change at once—moving across the country, a new home, his mother not calling or visiting after promising...My anger begins to boil as it always does when I think of how easily Camilla gave up her children.

"It's okay, I'll do it. I want to talk to her too. But thanks, Ma."

"There you go with the thank you again."

"Okay, no more tonight. I have to head over to the Hutchinsons' anyway. I'll be home in the morning."

"Wait," she says, wiping her hands on a kitchen towel. "I wanted to ask you. What's this about swimming lessons? Ari hasn't stopped talking about it since you brought her home from school the other day."

"Oh." I'm not sure how Ma will feel about the kids and Stevie in the same room, never mind bonding over swimming. Leo needs lessons too, though I have yet to tell Stevie. Ma loved Stevie like a daughter even before we started dating. But after the breakup, she blamed her for my decision to enlist and move across the country.

"Something you want to tell me?" she asks, already knowing what I'm going to say.

"I stopped by the Hutchinsons' and Ari saw the pool. Figure it's a good time to start her on lessons so she's safe around water," I prevaricate.

"Hm. Do you want me to sign her up at the Y?"

"Uh, no, that won't be necessary." I drain the last of my coffee and put the mug in the dishwasher. When I turn back, she's looking at me, brows raised, arms crossed, mouth tight. Fuck.

"I've asked Stevie to give them lessons. She'll pick them up and drop them off so it's not one more thing on your plate."

"My plate is big enough to hold everything just fine, Gabe. Don't use me as an excuse to do something foolish. She broke your heart once already and changed the course of your life."

I sigh. Apparently ten years isn't enough time for my mother to forgive or forget. "Ma, you can't blame everything on Stevie. She was eighteen years old and I shouldn't have pushed her to marry me."

"You were also young."

"My point exactly. I was two years older, but we were both too young to take the next step."

"She came looking for you," she says out of the blue, wiping the countertop that is already squeaky clean and not looking at me.

"What? When? What did she say?"

"A couple of weeks after you left. I gave her your address at bootcamp."

"You didn't tell me." Had she changed her mind about marrying me? The hope that flares brightly burns out just as fast when I remind myself she never reached out to me.

"Contact was very limited while you were in bootcamp," Ma explains. "I didn't see the point when you were going off to BUD/s training soon after. I didn't want you distracted and getting injured."

I let her know it's okay with a kiss to her cheek before leaving to protect Stevie and her family.

We all left things unsaid back then.

16

Stevie

I CHECK ON THE turkey, satisfied to see it browning nicely.
Wiping my hands on my apron, I sweep my gaze around the
kitchen, trying to think of anything I might have forgotten.
There isn't, of course. I made a massive list with every menu
item and when it needed to be prepped, cooked, or put in the
oven, as well as tasks for everyone. Brent and Luc have already
added the extra leaves to the kitchen table so that Bobbie and
Daphne can set the table with instructions I provided them.

Thanksgiving feels extra special to me this year and I want to
make it that way for everyone else too. Except for Georgie, who
missed last Thanksgiving as well, we're all here, including Andi
and her son—my godson—Alex. With the addition of Luc and
Daphne, the kitchen table is extended to its fullest length, with
enough room to squeeze in a couple of more chairs if needed.

Our house never had a formal dining room, and Mom insisted on not adding one during the remodel. She said it was a
wasted room, preferring to have a bigger kitchen that opened
into the family room. It's where we spend most of our time as
a family when we're all able to get together.

I went a little overboard this year. Okay, more overboard than usual. There is enough food to feed an army. Luckily, there is a small army outside that is guarding everyone inside, so the food won't go to waste.

In addition to several pies and the twenty-pound turkey, we have at least one dish of everything there can possibly be at a Thanksgiving dinner. Joey, Charlie, and Andi each brought an appetizer and a dessert. Mom and Bobbie helped me prep everything yesterday and everyone pitched in today, one way or another.

We are fortunate that Brent and Luc aren't on one of the unlucky teams who are scheduled to play on Thanksgiving this year, so they are able to enjoy the holiday with the family. They'd arrived after finishing their volunteer work at a food pantry in Manhattan. Luc had also gone with Brent to drop off pies at the area firehouses and a generous check at the local food bank. Of course, they were accompanied by one of Gabe's men as well as Reggie, Luc's best friend and personal bodyguard, who left once Luc was safely in the house.

"Come on, Stevie. You've been in the kitchen all day. Come sit down with us." Charlie grabs my arm and starts dragging me to the family room.

"All right, all right!" I laugh. "Let me take this apron off."

"It suits you," Charlie said, smirking. "Now you just need to take your shoes off and put a bun in the oven."

I ignore the lurch in my heart at the words. Charlie doesn't know why her joke about being barefoot and pregnant would hurt me. No one does because I didn't tell anyone my secret. Not even Andi. The right time never seemed to come up again once the time to say something had passed. I wonder sometimes if my mother has guessed.

Pasting a mock scowl on my face to hide the pain, I swat Charlie with the apron. Charlie laughs and darts away, one hand on her expanding belly. I follow her into the family room where the TV is tuned to a football game, of course, though no one is really paying attention to it except Brent and Luc, who throw an occasional glance in its direction. The two are sitting on the floor, along with the younger girls and Alex, deeply involved in a game of Monopoly set up on the large square coffee table.

Charlie pulls me down to sit on the sofa opposite the one Andi and Joey are on. Mom sits in her usual rocking recliner chair, appearing content to be surrounded by her loved ones. Luc leans against the sofa next to Charlie's legs. He absentmindedly rubs her calf with one hand while continuing to play the board game. I have to look away from the intimacy of the gesture. It brings back memories of Gabe doing something similar when our two families gathered for evenings like this—once we revealed we were dating.

A burst of shouts and groans from the coffee table brings my attention to the board game.

"You're a shark, Alex!"

"How did you get that many properties already?"

"You must have picked up a couple of cards when no one was looking."

"I didn't. I don't cheat!" Alex protests. "Mommy told me you don't actually win if you do it by cheating."

Andi gives Alex a proud smile before she notices all eyes on her. She lowers her light green eyes, appearing uncomfortable at the unintentional reminder of how close to home the moral lesson hits. The adults in the room are aware she's changed her identity to distance herself from her father's criminal reputation. He died shortly after being caught, but she's still afraid of being recognized as his daughter. Some of his victims had directed their anger at her, and all of her friends had turned their back on her.

"You won because you got your brains from your mom," I tell Alex. Andi is one of the smartest, hardest-working people I know. She went from having a baby at nineteen, with no family or money, to owning her own boutique in Greenwich. Loads of talent and a need to succeed for her son's sake also had a good deal to do with getting her this far so quickly.

"Your mom is right," Charlie says. "And cheating will only get you so far."

"Yeah," Brent agrees. "Most likely alone with no friends."

"Don't worry, kid," Luc says, ruffling Alex's hair. "I don't think you cheated. Not when you have a smart mama like yours." Luc winks at Andi, who gives him a star-struck smile in return. We've all gotten used to Brent being a celebrity, but Luc is on a whole other level. No wonder Bobbie was squealing with excitement when she called me. Had it only been two weeks ago?

"Stevie, did you see the newest pictures of the baby?" Charlie asks as the others put Monopoly away and debate which game to play next.

No. I'd avoided looking at them when she'd brought them out, claiming to be busy at the stove and promising to look at them later.

Knowing there's no way out of it now, I force a smile and hold out my hand to Charlie. "Let's see the little nugget."

She looks around, frowning. "They're in my purse."

A reprieve. "It's okay. I'll see them later. It's dinner time anyway."

"I'll get your purse." Daphne jumps up. "I want to see the pictures again."

I hold back a groan. What's wrong with me? I should be happy for Charlie. I *am* happy for her. I just can't help feeling sad for myself, knowing I will most likely never have this experience. I had my chance with Gabe and lost it ten years ago.

17

Gabe

I WALK INTO THE Hutchinson family room and have to pause to separate out all the faces—except one. My gaze finds Stevie right away. She's staring down at a photo.

"Hello, Gabe, honey," Sandra says.

Since I'm still looking at Stevie, I see her jerk slightly before her gaze meets mine. It darts away guiltily, but not before I see the sheen of tears in her eyes. What the hell? I take a step toward her, but Sandra's voice stops me as she continues.

"You're just in time for dinner."

I drag my gaze away from Stevie and smile at her mother. This is not the place or time to continue my campaign to win Stevie back.

"Thanks, Sandra, but I already ate. Ma would never let me leave the house without eating first." I sneak a quick look at Stevie, glad to see her smiling again and talking quietly to Charlie. Maybe I was mistaken about the tears and it was a trick of the light. But that guilty look...? Something to think about later.

I grin at Sandra and pat my stomach. "I'm more stuffed than the turkey was. Rafe and I are here to relieve a couple of the guys."

"Well, come in for dessert later, then. And send your team in to eat. We have plenty for everyone."

I nod. "I'll let them know." I signal to Brent and Luc, who grab their jackets and follow me outside.

When we step off the front porch and away from the house, I tell them, "Victor was spotted in Atlantic City a few hours ago."

"Great. He's finally in custody now and we can be done with this," Brent says.

I shake my head. "Unfortunately not. My guys followed the lead, but he was nowhere to be found and the security tapes don't show him leaving. It seems he's using disguises and changing them frequently as he moves around. He's disappeared again with no hint of which way he went."

"Damn it!" Luc growls.

"I'm sorry, man. I get your frustration, but we'll get him, I promise."

"I don't understand how he's able to stay hidden for so long." Luc frowns. "Disguises, transportation, basic needs..."

"I'm guessing he has cash hidden away in a few different locations. If he's been in debt for a while, he was probably ready to hide if needed. He hasn't been near a bank, at least not under his name. It's possible he's using aliases. Law enforcement is looking into that."

Luc exhales in frustration, running a hand over his short curls. "Charlie's going stir crazy in the house. I'm not going to be able to keep her tucked away in there much longer."

"I'm surprised she's stayed this long," Brent said.

"Wrapping up her projects was keeping her occupied, but her idiot boss has her doing busywork. She finally gave her notice. As glad as I am about it, it's going to be harder to keep her at home when she has more free time." Luc grimaces. "I'm using Daphne and the baby to guilt her into staying indoors as it is. Dee fell a little behind on her homeschooling since she's come to stay with me, so Charlie is keeping an eye on that and helping her."

"She's helping your sister with homework? You better keep an eye on what Charlie's teaching her or Daphne might end up going back a grade."

"I heard that, you big jerk."

Brent grins at Charlie. He must have seen her come out on the porch and baited her with his teasing. Some things never change in this family. He pulls his sister to his side in a half hug and kisses the top of her head. "Just make sure you teach her more than sports stats."

She shrugs his arm away and lightly punches his bicep before moving to Luc, who instantly puts his arm around her and kisses her temple. She rubs a hand over the mound of her belly and asks me, "Any updates?"

After giving her a quick summary, I tell her with a pained smile, "Sorry, Charlie. We have to keep playing it safe a little longer."

She sighs loudly. "You're killing me, Gabe. I'm going to die of boredom soon."

"At least that's temporary." Luc pulls her closer and wraps his arms around her. "Better than dying from a bullet. I don't know what I'd do if anything happened to you." He cups her face and tilts his head to kiss her.

When the kiss deepens and goes on for longer than it should in front of an audience, Brent shakes his head in disgust and heads back inside. As if he wouldn't be doing the same every chance he got if Joey wasn't so shy.

I clear my throat when the two still don't come up for air.

"Okay, then. I'll see you two later."

Leaving them to it, I walk down the driveway to Rafe. He's talking to two of our men who have been with us from the beginning. Ortiz was an MMA fighter Rafe trained with, and Morris is a SEAL from my unit who'd retired and drifted until I hired him.

"You two were invited into the house for dinner, if you'd like."

Both shake their heads. "Got a buddy north of here, near Hartford," Morris says. "Told him we'd come see him."

"They'll check him out to see if he's a good recruit for us," Rafe adds.

I nod. "Good. See you in the morning then."

When the two men leave, Rafe turns to me. "We have enough coverage out here if you want to go back inside, Romeo."

"What are you talking about?"

He grins. "I'm talking about the jealous fit you had the other day at the compound."

I glare at him. "That reminds me. I still owe you for that, you son of a bitch."

"Hey, that makes you one too. And I'm going to tell Ma you—"

I grab him and put him in a chokehold, keeping my arm loose around his neck. It's a move I'd never have gotten away with if he wasn't busy laughing his head off.

"Hey, why are you mad at me? For helping her prove to you what an idiot you were pretending to be me when you *kissed* her? She marched up to me, mad as a hornet, and demanded I kiss her."

"So you did?" I growl at him and squeeze my arm a little before pushing him away.

He holds up his hands in surrender. "Of course I didn't do it. I told you she didn't feel a thing when I took your place for a few minutes that first night. I guess she knew deep down it wasn't you. I never believed in that shit, but that's some serious pheromones you two have for each other."

Pop always said he knew Ma was the one for him the second he set eyes on her. I didn't believe him until the day I recognized Stevie as my soulmate.

"Fuck off."

Rafe becomes serious. "What's the deal between you two now?"

"Hell if I know. She's hot and cold." Mostly cold until she's in my arms. I kick at a pebble in frustration.

"Lost your touch?" he teases.

"No, she still melts in my arms."

I've never talked to Rafe about my sex life with Stevie the way I did about the girls that came before and after her. She'd always been off-limits, because I was sure she was going to be my wife. It hadn't felt right to talk about her like that.

"But I'm not giving up this time. I'm no longer a hot-headed twenty-year-old and I've learned patience." Between SEAL training and raising a couple of kids, I had no choice but to master the trait. "I let my anger push her away before. I'm not going to do that again. Because, Rafe," I say, staring at the house, its lighted windows glowing in the falling dusk, "she's still the one."

He claps a hand on my shoulder. "I remember when you told me that back then. Really hope it works out for you this time, brother."

"Me too." I don't know what I'll do if I can't convince her to give us another chance. There's still something between us, but she's resisting it.

"You going to introduce her to the kids?"

"Ari met her accidentally. I asked Stevie to give the kids swim lessons."

"Are you sure that's a good idea?"

No, but it's the only one I have right now to give her a chance to bond with them. "As far as they're concerned, Stevie is just a friend, like Charlie. They've mostly adjusted after everything that's happened, and I want to keep it that way. If Stevie decides she wants nothing to do with me, they'll miss her for a little while like they would any other teacher. Or as a family friend."

"And what about you?"

"I don't know. Let's hope she's not stubborn enough to let it come to that, to let go of what I know we still have."

Rafe laughs. "I suggest you not call her stubborn to her face. It won't help your cause any."

I smile. "Another thing I learned is that honey works better than—"

"Okay. I don't want to hear about your sex games," Rafe protests, covering his ears playfully. "Let's go do a perimeter check and touch base with the others."

I hadn't been thinking of sex, but I am now. Dabs of honey on her lips, her nipples...her clit...so I can lick every drop from her.

No. Forget the honey. She doesn't need the added sweetness. Her mouth tasted as good as I remembered. I'm sure the rest of her does too. Everywhere. And there is no sweeter honey than hers.

18

Stevie

"I'M GOING OUTSIDE FOR a walk," I say to no one in particular. "I shouldn't have eaten that second helping of pie."

In a sugar coma after polishing off yesterday's leftovers, everyone is sprawled around the family room for a movie marathon,

.

"I'll go with you," Gabe says, standing up and stretching his arms high. He'd come for his shift a couple of hours ago. Due to the sudden dip in temperatures, he and the rest of the team were rotating locations so no one was outside for too long.

His shirt molds to his muscles when he re-tucks the ends into his pants. He catches me staring, so I scowl at him. "You just came in from the cold. Besides, I don't need a babysitter by my side. Your men are already on watch."

It was bad enough he'd taken the empty space next to me on the sofa with his pumpkin pie. I made myself sit until he finished the dessert, then used the excuse of taking his plate to the sink to move away.

I thought a walk would help me avoid sitting next to him again, the only seat available.

"They have their posts and can't leave to follow you."

"Whatever," I mumble under my breath, heading to the mud-room. Gabe follows me and watches as I don my puffer jacket and pull on my boots. He's right behind me when I step out. My breath catches at the bone-chilling cold and billows out in a cloud of white steam. Too busy being annoyed at Gabe, I forgot to grab a hat and gloves. I shove my hands in my pockets, which does nothing to help because they're lined with thin, cold nylon.

I walk at a fast clip down the gently sloping backyard, solar lights on the edges of the paver stone path guiding me. Fairy lights outline the shape of the gazebo waiting at the end. The bench that Dad had built still sits at the edge of the pond, but it's too cold to sit there and draw comfort from it. I head for the enclosure instead.

A sideways look shows Gabe is a step behind, his gaze watchful as he scans the area. His coat is unzipped for easy access to his holster, but he's wearing gloves.

"What are you annoyed about now, babe?" he asks, opening the door of the gazebo and signaling me to wait. He turns on the lights, makes sure it's all clear, then turns them off again and gestures me inside.

"Stop calling me babe." It's a generic term of endearment, but it was one he used when we were dating. It still gives me a tingle when he calls me that. Our friends would tease us, calling us Gabe and Babe. In private, he'd laugh and call me Gabe's babe.

I don't want to think of the laughs we had or feel the tingles. Having him just a foot away is already more than I can handle, especially in the dark near the place where we used to hang out for hours, talking and making out.

"And why did you turn the lights off?" I ask, not that we need them. The exterior fairy lights provide enough illumination to see, but the dim glow makes the gazebo feel romantic.

"So I can see outside without any reflections on the glass," he answers, pulling me to one of the side walls that has no glass. There are oversized windows looking out over the pond and wide sliding doors facing the house. In the summer, the glass on both is replaced with screens to keep out the mosquitoes and any other critters looking for a home while allowing the air to flow through, with the help of the overhead ceiling fan. But the glass in the winter provides some relief from the wind chill.

I sit on the cushioned bench along the wall and turn sideways to look out over the pond. The full moon reflects off the water, providing a magical glow to the surroundings.

I lean my head against the wall and breathe in the peacefulness of the night...Only to have Gabe disrupt my peace by sitting next to me and turning to face me. He's close enough I can feel his body heat near my bent leg. I'm tempted to inch closer to absorb more of his heat. Instead, I rub my hands together to warm them up.

"Cold?"

He takes off his gloves, and instead of giving them to me, takes my hands into his warm ones. I'm not sure if it's his touch or the sudden warmth, but I'm racked with a full body shiver. He slides closer, pulling my legs over his thighs and enfolding me against him. When he wraps his jacket around me, I only resist for a millisecond, too grateful for the warmth. I don't know what I was thinking, coming out in this weather for a walk.

I tell myself I'm moving closer only because it's too damn cold and place my freed hands on his chest, holding onto his shirt to prevent them from sliding down into his lap. Allowing my body to relax, I lean my head on his shoulder. I breathe in his familiar scent that's mixed with the chill of the outdoors. The soothing sense of peace returns.

"Remember the last time we were down here?" he murmurs.

"I'd rather not," I whisper, unwilling to let the past intrude.

But the question brings it all back. It had been shortly after Mom's stroke. I'd come out to the old bench at the edge of the pond after helping Mom into her bed. It had been her first night home after a short stay in a physical rehabilitation facility. I'd had to help my mother, a grown woman, use the bathroom before giving her a sponge bath. My siblings had done their share of work, but the experience of seeing my mother as weak and helpless as my baby sister had been terrifying.

Gabe found me at the old bench, exhausted, scared, and bawling my eyes out. He'd held me, comforted me, and promised me everything would be okay. He swore he'd take care of me forever and told me how much he loved me. His declarations and my need for comfort soon led to some heavy petting. We didn't have the privacy of an enclosed gazebo back then, so we'd moved under the shelter of the weeping willow tree.

"That was a tough time for you. But I was referring to what we did, hidden under the overhanging branches over there. We had to move from the bench because it creaked so loudly when you moved to straddle—"

I jump up from his lap, not wanting to revisit that memory either. "It was a long time ago."

When Gabe slowly stands, he's too close. I take a step back and he follows, stalking me, the reflection of the string lights glittering like stars in his midnight blue eyes. I hold my palms up as a signal for him to stop. He leans into them so they're pressed against his chest. His heart beats strongly under my fingers, only his shirt separating them from his hot skin.

"It may have been a long time ago," he rasps, "but this hasn't changed between us."

He puts his hands over mine to keep them on his chest. No worries there as my hands like being right where they are.

I shake my head. "Everything's changed."

"Nothing that matters."

"How can you say that? You got married, had children—"

"What does that have to do with us, right now, right here?" he asks, his voice harsh. Before I can think of a response, he kisses me. No, his mouth devours mine. When he lets go of my wrists to cup my face, my hands remain, fisting into his shirt. And then, all rational thought escapes. Only sensations remain...the feel of his mouth, his tongue, his teeth as they clash against mine in a kiss unlike any we've shared before. It's hard, frustrated...desperate.

Yet under it all, it's familiar. It's Gabe. My Gabe. *Mine.*

I return the kiss with equal fervor, my body on fire for him as I open wide and meet every thrust of his tongue with mine. My arms go around his back and I bring my body flush against his hard chest. His even harder erection presses against my stomach, making my core clench as I imagine the feel of his thick length inside me. My hands pull at his shirt to get to the warm skin of his back. I move my hands to his waist to pull more of the fabric out, only to encounter something unfamiliar.

His hand grabs my wrist at the same time I realize it's his gun holster. I come crashing down, pushing him away and stumbling back, only to come up against the hot tub. I'm panting, my legs quivering. My brain has short-circuited and I can't form a complete thought, never mind words. Desire, fear, regret, and anxiety roil through my system in confusing chaos.

"Easy there," he murmurs, his voice rough with passion but calm and soothing despite his raspy breathing. I detect a slight trembling of his fingers as he inserts the earpiece that I dislodged back into his ear.

"Hey, it's okay. The safety is on."

He thinks I'm worried about the gun. Okay, I am, but not in the way he means. It's everything it represents. And proof that nothing has changed for us except our age.

"No need to be scared." He rubs his thumb over my wrist.

"I'm not," I lie.

"You're shaking." His eyes lighten from concern to hope and humor. "Unless it's because of that kiss. What the fuck was that and can we get back to it when I'm done with my shift?"

There's no point in feeding his hope. Admitting to how much I want him, need him, would only add fuel to the fire, so I admit, "Okay, it is the gun."

His mouth tightens, all humor gone. "I have to carry it for your protection. It's part of the job."

"Right. Your job is to protect people from someone out there willing to harm them. To stand between them, putting yourself in the line of fire."

"Fuck!" He spins away, fingers rubbing his temple like I've given him a headache.

Hoping I've finally gotten through to him, I say, "Like I said, nothing's changed. The only difference from you wanting to be a cop who serves the general public to what you do now is you get paid more to protect fewer—wealthier—people."

"Which now includes your family," he shoots back, his eyes blazing with bitter anger. "It's my job to protect them. Would you rather Charlie was in danger without us here?"

I gasp. "Of course not! But I don't want you in danger either."

I realize my mistake with that foolish slip of the tongue when his voice and expression soften. "Because you still care for me."

Refusing to acknowledge the full truth of his words, I sidestep them. "I've known you almost my whole life. Of course I care about you. I don't want anyone to get hurt."

"No, it's more than that."

"Even if that's true, it's not enough."

"Stevie, it's everything."

We're both talking about the L word without actually voicing it.

"Look at my mother," I argue. "She lost the love of her life and endured so much alone. I couldn't bear it if—"

I stop before admitting what losing him would do to me. He doesn't need any more ammunition in the battle I'm fighting with myself. Every time I'm in his arms, I'm tempted to give in and take what he's offering, no matter the risk to my heart.

Straightening my spine, I look into his eyes with defiance. "You may not agree or understand, but it's a valid fear."

He sighs. "I don't disagree and I do understand. But are you going to live the rest of your life in fear?"

"Better than to live it in grief."

"Oh, baby." He comes back to me and enfolds me in his arms before I can move away, placing a gentle kiss on my temple that nearly undoes me.

I close my eyes and soak in his tenderness. I wish I could shut out the world and stay here forever. His warm embrace gives me the sense of security I've yearned for since my father's death. He makes it seem like everything will be okay, just as he'd promised on that bench by the pond. But it's not possible, because love and happiness aren't guaranteed to last forever.

If he didn't mean so much to me, it would be easy to give in to the chemistry and have a physical only relationship with him. But I know continued intimacy with him would mean an ever-deepening emotional attachment. We'd be making more memories, new ones that I'd have to try to forget, that would hurt so deeply to remember, if he was gone from my life again.

I can't afford that heartbreak again.

When I ease away from his arms, his eyes search mine. I lower my lids, not sure what he's looking for and afraid he'll see what I don't want him to.

"Good night, Gabe."

He lets me go without a word, leaving me to wonder where we go from here.

19

Stevie

"**S**TEVIE, THESE PHOTOS ARE beautiful!" Charlie exclaims. "I want one. Or three."

I smile at my sister's enthusiasm over the photographs from my recent trip to Yellowstone National Park. I'm screen mirroring them from my laptop to the big screen TV so I can see which ones are good enough to enlarge and print.

She and Joey are staying in Connecticut until the game tomorrow to come up with preliminary plans for Charlie's baby and wedding showers, as well as the actual wedding.

Gabe tried to convince her to stay home and watch the game, since Victor had been sighted in Atlantic City. For all they know, he might be making his way north. But she stood firm, insisting on going to the stadium for the home game.

"I refuse to postpone living my life indefinitely," she announced at breakfast this morning, her mouth set in stubborn lines. "I don't want that for any of you. So let's use the suite and have some fun."

Not even the combined charm of Luc and Rafe made her budge. Gabe finally agreed, saying they'd use it as practice for the game in Miami after Christmas. Only Andi won't be going, having left yesterday to open her store for Black Friday shopping. And Brent and Luc, who are staying in the city tonight after practice, will go with the team. The rest of us will go with the security team tomorrow.

"Well, if you've been a good girl, Santa might bring you a couple of prints," I tell Charlie as I continue swiping through the photos.

"Really? Can I tell Santa which ones I want?"

"No." I laugh at her pout. "Don't worry. Santa knows what you like." The photos she squealed about as they appeared on the TV screen were a big clue.

"You know, you could make money selling these prints," Joey says.

"Oh, please," I scoff. "These aren't unique. Millions of tourists visit these parks and take photos."

Charlie shakes her head. "Not this good, not unless they have a good camera and, more importantly, a great eye. I work in the visual media industry, which makes me an expert."

"Yeah, okay, Rachel Morrison."

With a blank look, she says, "I don't know who that is," then flips her hair and continues, "But if you're talking about producers, you can call me Margot Robbie." She flips her hair again and poses, her chin tilted at an angle.

I roll my eyes at her. "You don't even work in film, you ninny. And Rachel Morrison is the only American female cinematographer nominated for an Oscar."

"Hey, see? You're the one who referred to me as someone who works in film." She brushes away the words with a wave of her hand. "But never mind that. How do you know about cinematographers? Are you thinking about working in film?"

"God, no. I just like her work."

"Do you have a favorite still photographer?" Joey asks.

"I don't know the work of enough photographers to have a favorite—besides Annie Leibovitz and Ansel Adams."

"The ones you have here are definitely good enough to put up on stock photo sites," Charlie says. "You get paid a licensing fee when people use them. One of our videographers does it on the side."

"Or what about creating calendars or postcards and things like that from them?" Joey suggests.

"You really think these are good enough for that kind of stuff?" I never took pictures thinking I'd do anything except look at them and maybe gift a few. I simply looked through the lens, made setting adjustments once I learned how, and shot what felt right.

"Absolutely. I can help you figure all that out since I'm not working anymore," Charlie offers.

"Your photos are amazing," Joey confirms. "You should be proud of them."

"You can take photography classes if they would help you feel like a professional," Mom chimes in from the kitchen where she'd been paying bills at the kitchen table. She moves into the family room to take a seat in her favorite recliner and picks up her knitting.

"Will you send me some of your photos for me to look at if I tell you what I'm looking for?" Joey asks. "I need to add some color and life to Brent's place—"

"Your place now, too, Joey," Charlie corrects.

"*Our* place," Joey continues with a happy smile, "needs a break from the neutral monochrome. I'll be your first customer for exclusive rights to a couple of your photos."

"Okay, all this flattery might go to my head. Enough about me."

"What about you, Charlie? What will you do until the baby is born?" Mom asks. She looks up from the baby blanket she's knitting.

Charlie shrugs, looking a little despondent. "I don't know. It's going to be weird not having a job for the first time since I was fifteen. And it's going to suck staying close to home for now. I want to go shopping to get the nursery ready. Until then, I guess I'll figure out what I need for grad school applications and plan the wedding."

"Do you know which programs you're going to apply to?" Joey asks.

"I'm still researching which ones offer a master's in trauma psychology. I've reached out to your former professor for advice. I have a serious crush on her after she helped Luc remember his trauma."

"Dr. V is the best," Joey agrees.

Before I can ask about how this professor helped Luc, Mom asks, "Have you and Luc set a date yet?" Her face lights up at the prospect.

"No," Charlie sighs. "I'm trying to decide if it's better to look like I'm having a shotgun wedding or to have a child out of wedlock. Do you think my beach ball will care?"

I laugh. "First, I think she might care more that you called her names based on how big your stomach is." A couple of weeks ago, it was "my basketball."

"Second," I continue, "did you just time travel from the 1950s? Who cares?"

Charlie pouts. "What if my beach ball does?"

"Honey," Mom interjects, "I'm sure she won't."

"Okay, but I don't want to have a giant belly in my wedding photos for all of eternity. The earliest we can get married is in February, after the Super Bowl, since it's more than likely the Firebirds will be playing in it. I'll be eight months pregnant! Who knows how huge I'll be by then?"

"We'll call *you* whale," I tease, laughing, "but what are you going to call the baby?"

She throws a pillow at me.

I catch it and suggest, "You can take your pictures from the back and no one will know. Look over your shoulder at the camera, maybe a little bit of a silhouette?"

"Ohh, that sounds pretty. Alright, you're hired...at least for the photos you're not in. You can direct the rest." She turns to Joey.

"What do you say, bestie? Brent asked me to convince you to have a double wedding with me and Luc. How about Valentine's Day?"

Joey laughs and shakes her head. "I don't think so."

"Have you at least said yes to him and put him out of his misery?" I ask her. For some reason, she keeps turning down his proposals. And yet, Brent hasn't run off and done something impulsive, like kicking Joey out or enlisting in the military. They live together and their PDA, mild in comparison to Charlie and Luc's, is sickly sweet. It's obvious how much they love each other. Whatever the issue is, Brent is not giving up on her.

Why did Gabe give up so quickly when I said no the first—the only—time he proposed?

"Not yet," Joey replies. "We've only been together for a couple of months—"

"If you don't include the months before that when you were pretending to be just his physical therapist," Charlie interjects.

"That's still not enough time for him to be sure."

"He'll wait until you're ready, honey," Mom assures her. "So take your time."

"Mom, she's waiting for Brent to be sure he's ready," Charlie clarifies.

"Oh, sweetheart." Mom stops the clicking of the needles. "That boy has never been more sure of anything in his life."

I snicker to myself at hearing my six-foot-seven, two-hundred-something pound brother still being called a boy.

"What makes you think he's not?" Mom asks, concerned. "Has he had any more nightmares?"

"No, those have stopped completely." Joey's face is flushed with all of our attention on her, even with her slightly tanned skin tone. The blushing gene of her Irish mother is stronger than the melanin she inherited from her South Asian father.

"I'd say that's a sign he's sure," Charlie says. "As are the multiple proposals. How many times has it been so far?"

Joey's shoulder hitches as she bites her lip bashfully. Either she doesn't want to admit how many or she's lost count. Despite her reluctance to rush to the altar, her eyes glow with love.

I can't understand how Joey and Charlie are the best of friends. My sister is bold and confident whereas Joey is quiet and diffident. Yet their connection was instant at ten years of age. It became stronger through letters, emails, and phone calls and the occasional visit. Their friendship reminds me of how Georgie and I used to be, long before she took off for the bright lights of a big city. The years after Dad's and RJ's deaths changed us all.

"Charlie," Joey admonishes, "we were talking about your wedding. Once you decide what you'd like to do, we can figure out your baby and bridal showers."

"Luc says the sooner the better, but I think I'm leaning toward waiting until after the baby is born to get married. Maybe June? That will still give us time for a honeymoon before the season starts again. And I think having our daughter with us would be kind of special." Charlie beams, running a hand over her belly. "There! I've got the perfect reason to give her as to why we waited."

"Not to mention you'd then get two separate showers," Joey teases.

"There is that," she laughs.

"And it's right around the time of the memorial," I say. "We can combine it. We'd make a killing on the fundraising with all of Brent's and Luc's millionaire friends," I joke.

Charlie frowns, shaking her head. "We want to keep the wedding small. But we'll have two charities guests can choose from if they'd like to donate in lieu of gifts. One to honor his mother and one that's for Dad and RJ."

"If it's a June wedding, we can have the baby shower in late February," Joey suggests. "Since there's a good chance we'll get to the Super Bowl this year, like you said, it'll give everyone a little break to recover from the craziness of that and still give us time to get everything ready for the wedding."

"And maybe time for Stevie and Gabe to get back together? How about you, Stevie? Double wedding?"

I widen my eyes at Charlie. "What are you talking about? Gabe and I aren't—"

"Oh, please." She waves a dismissive hand. "Even a blind person can tell there's still something between the two of you."

Yes, the thing that broke us apart in the first place...and what I did after.

I startle when she takes my hand in between hers. "It was shitty of him to leave like that when you refused his proposal. But, Stevie, you were right to do that. You were only eighteen."

I never told them it was because he was going to the police academy, afraid they'd agree with him and take his side. We all went through the same trauma but were impacted in different ways. For me, it was the fear of him dying on the job like my father had. Like RJ had before he even had a chance to become a full-fledged firefighter as an adult.

"I agree, honey," Mom says. "You did the right thing. You were both too young."

"Yeah," Charlie adds. "I can't believe he ran off and enlisted instead of waiting to propose again when you were ready. Like Brent is waiting for Joey."

Not liking that Gabe is being blamed for all of it, yet not ready to confess my reason for refusing, I admit, "He wants to try again."

Charlie claps in excitement, practically bouncing in her seat, making the beach ball belly bounce with her. "That's wonderful! You have a second chance to do it right this time, older, more mature, and able to go the distance."

My brows furrow. "What do you mean?"

"You two wouldn't have handled arguments well. He proved that by leaving instead of working things out."

I stay silent, giving myself time to process her words.

"Charlie's right," Mom says. "If the relationship hadn't worked out over time—I'm not saying it wouldn't have, but if it ended bitterly—you likely wouldn't be able to work your way back to each other if you left behind too much pain and resentment between you."

I don't know. There seems to be enough of that already. I was pretty bitter when it happened.

Mom continues, "I'm sure it didn't feel that way at the time and maybe still doesn't, but whatever happened might be for the best. You have a second chance now—if you want it."

Do I want it? How will it be different if I can't come to terms with the danger of his job? Not willing to delve further into this conversation, I deflect with, "Hm. We'll see."

Charlie nudges me with her shoulder. "Hurry up and get back together so we can have that double wedding."

"What's your obsession with double weddings? Sounds like you're unsure or nervous or something."

"Ha!" She tosses her hair and sticks her nose in the air. "Unlike the two of you, I know a good thing—a good man—when I see one."

I grab a throw pillow and stand, looking at Joey, eyebrow raised. She smiles, nods, and takes a pillow as well. We throw them at Charlie simultaneously. She yelps in indignation, then dissolves into laughter as she tries to throw them back at us.

Bobbie and Daphne run into the room to find out what all the commotion is, and a pillow fight ensues, accompanied by joyful laughter.

Despite my confusion over Gabe, I am deeply happy to be home.

20

Stevie

I TURN AND FLOP onto my side so hard, I bounce on my mattress. I've been flipping and flopping for the last hour since we returned from the Firebirds game. It's partly due to being revved up from the stadium atmosphere and the win, but mostly it's because my thoughts keep returning to the conversation from yesterday. Would Gabe and I have made it if he'd stayed—whether or not I accepted his proposal? The what-if scenarios have been playing in an endless loop, causing my restlessness as I try to sleep.

If he had joined the police force, would I have become anxious and clingy, requiring constant reassurance? It would have suffocated him and led to bitter arguments. Just like the last one that resulted in our breakup.

But if he'd taken a safer job, his resentment would no doubt have eaten away at the love that allowed him to make the sacrifice. It would have created an emotional distance—perhaps even a physical one that pushed him into the arms of another woman.

Either way, Mom was right. Trying to make our relationship work would have created a chasm that widened between us until we ended up falling into it, our love—and perhaps a marriage—in pieces.

And if we had a child? My hand goes to my heart automatically to soothe the ache. That is one what-if scenario my mind refuses to imagine.

There might have been another option, but we were too young and immature to find it on our own. We might have had a chance with the help of others, but his abrupt departure took away any possibility of finding a better way forward.

Could we do it now? We're older, more experienced, perhaps more mature. But are we wiser?

I flip to my other side and curse when the movement causes me to get wrapped up in the bedsheets. Cursing again, I disentangle myself, the covers rustling so much I almost don't hear the clink against the window.

I freeze and look toward the curtains, almost expecting the shadow of someone trying to break in. Could Victor have somehow made it past the security patrolling our property and climbed to the window? And avoided the cameras that Kathy is keeping an eye on from downstairs? Even as I realize there's no way anyone would make it to the house without discovery, the clink comes again.

It sounds like a pebble being thrown against the window, not someone trying to break in. Curious, I tiptoe to the side of the window and peek out from the edge of the blackout curtain. Thanks to the floodlights that are left on all night as part of the security measures, I recognize the figure standing in the yard, his dark head tipped back, ready to toss another pebble.

I unlatch the window and push it open. "What are you doing?" I hiss, shivering at the chilly air that rushes in.

He walks closer and grins.

"Hey. Want to go for a walk?" he whisper-shouts.

How many times had he asked me that while standing outside my bedroom window? Back then, it was on the first floor, and I shared the small room with Charlie and Georgie. We kept our relationship a secret from Brent at the beginning, afraid he'd disapprove of his friend dating his younger sister. Sometimes, the only alone time we had was at night, when we'd drive around aimlessly in Gabe's truck.

He's clearly trying to remind me of those nights by playing out the familiar scene. I wish I could say yes, could go back to our carefree days and be alone with him in the dark. But I can't, knowing we'll end up playing out another familiar scene—with our hands all over each other.

"No, I don't," I snap and start to close the window.

"Wait! I want to talk to you."

"Then use the front door." I stop myself from slamming down the window, closing it firmly instead and re-latching it. I consider ignoring him and going back to bed, but I wouldn't put it past him to come to my room. Gabe and a bed nearby is a combination I'm not sure I can resist. I flick on my small bedside lamp and slip into my warm robe to meet him downstairs.

Vanity is my undoing, because as I take the time to check my hair in the dresser mirror before heading down, I hear a creak outside my door followed by a quiet knock. I open it to let myself out, but Gabe is already crowding me back into the room with his hard body.

"What do you want, Gabe?"

"I just want to talk, hang out." He widens his eyes innocently. "As friends."

My own eyes narrow, not trusting his intention. "Friends?"

"Isn't that what you wanted when we broke up before?" he asks, removing his earpiece and holstered gun and reaching out to place them on the bureau. "I was an idiot—a hurt, humiliated idiot—who lashed out and ran away like a child because I couldn't handle a friendship back then. I'm willing to try now, if you are."

I was equally immature when I said that, thinking I'd be able to step back and watch him not only risk his life, but move on with other girls. Unsure of his motives or of my ability to handle a friendship with him feeling as I do, I shake my head.

"No, we can't be friends. And it's a little late for a talk."

"Okay then, no friendship and no talking."

The heat in his eyes should have warned me, but before I know it, I'm in his arms and his mouth is on mine. He takes advantage of my parted lips when I gasp in surprise and he sweeps his tongue inside. My toes curl and I'm lost.

My knee would have shot into any other man's balls by now, but this is Gabe. *My Gabe.* And I'm already drowning in sensation.

The tiny part of my brain that is still working knows this is a bad idea, but I can't summon the strength to care at the moment. No one could ignite my passion the way Gabe did with just a look, a touch. No one ever has since. His soul-stirring kiss washes away the memory of every meaningless soul-sucking encounter with strangers. Encounters that often failed to satisfy a temporary physical need and always left me feeling emptier than before.

Gabe's hands rove over my body, unbelting my robe and sliding under my pajama top. He leaves behind a trail of fire everywhere he touches. I'm burning up, melting, my panties getting damper by the second.

I mewl into his mouth, digging my nails into his back, trying to meld into his body, needing more. He hitches me up by my thighs, so I can wrap my legs around him. With his hands on my ass holding me up, I rub my sex against him. I moan in relief. His hard erection and the stiff fabric of his pants seam over his zipper provide some relief, but it's not enough. I'm panting, unable to keep up with the tongue-tangling kiss. I bury my face in his neck and focus on seeking relief, moving my flannel-clad pelvis over him.

So close but still not enough. I need more of him—all of him—to fill me up, body and soul.

The sensation of falling into bed distracts me from my mission to reach the peak as fast as possible. A flicker of awareness tries to break through, a vague thought that I should stop this, should think of the possible consequences.

In the next second, it's too late. I lose myself in sensation once again when he yanks up my top and latches onto my breast. His teeth scrape over the tip before sucking hard. I arch my back off the bed, whimpering at the current that zips through my body, straight to my clit, leaving behind a pulsing anticipation.

I wrap my arms and legs around him, clawing into his back, desperate for more, desperate for relief from this burning hunger.

"Please, Gabe," I beg with a not so gentle tug of his hair.

"That's right, baby. Tell me what you want." His low words vibrate against my chest, his mouth traveling to my other breast.

"I want you inside me," I cry out, pulling his head impossibly closer to my breast, encouraging him to suck harder.

Instead of complying, he removes his hand, his mouth, and lifts himself away.

21

Gabe

"N ooo," Stevie protests as I gently pull her arms away, breaking her hold to stand so I can strip.

"I'm not going anywhere, babe." As I toe my shoes off and unbutton my shirt, I think of how often I have dreamed of this moment, while awake and in my sleep. Sometimes it was when I was missing her, wishing I hadn't been so impulsive in leaving. Other times, it was with anger, hate-fucking my hand even as I screamed my love for her in silence. Or more recently, getting her as hot and bothered as I've been and leaving her high and dry. Or wet, in her case, I amend, eyeing the darker pink of drenched fabric between her parted legs.

Since the day at the compound, I've been picturing her like this, her pussy dripping and throbbing with unfulfilled lust, wanting me as much I want her but unable to have me. My cock screams at me in warning to not punish us when the prize that was denied on the mat the other day is ours for the taking. I give it a single stroke in reassurance. I have no intention of cutting off my nose—or my cock—to spite her.

But since the day at the pool when I decided I'm not giving up on her, my imagination has been providing a satisfactory ending for all concerned, as I stroked myself to climax.

I intend to stroke myself to climax tonight too, inside her sweet honeyed depths. But first, I need to taste that honey.

Removing my clothes, I gesture to her and say, "Take yours off too, baby. I want to see you. All of you." Her shirt is still on, bunched above her perfect tits, the nipples tight and a deeper shade of pink from the vigorous attention I'd given them.

Bringing her bent knees together, she lifts her hips and drags the thin flannel pants down her thighs. My cock jumps in excitement when she lifts her legs to tug the panties past her feet, giving me a glimpse of the gates of heaven. She pulls her shirt off next, and I simply drink in the image—the reality—of her, from her silky caramel brown hair to her pretty feet with toenails painted a seasonal pumpkin-orange.

On my perusal back up her body, I linger on her long, toned legs, one slightly bent to hide herself. That's okay. I'll be getting a close-up look there soon enough. I move my gaze to her slightly rounded belly where her hand rests as if to hide it. I'll be sure to give some extra attention there, letting her know I love every inch of her sexy body.

My gaze keeps going up, from the hourglass curve of her waist to her firm breasts that are definitely fuller. But the tips are still the same succulent pink that make my mouth water. Her tongue slips out to lick her bottom lip, calling my attention to her face. Her beautiful face with cheekbones that have sharpened with maturity and clear blue eyes lighter than mine. Her sky blue to my ocean blue, she used to say.

She flicks her gaze to my cock, standing at full mast for her, then looks back at me—directly, boldly. But the flicker of lashes and bite of her lip give her away. Between those slight movements and the hand covering her belly, I need to make sure she understands she has no reason to ever feel nervous or self-conscious around me.

"You are even more beautiful than I remember," I tell her fierce-ly. "And I remember you as fucking perfect."

I finally go to her, lying on top of her again. Her thighs part to make room for me and I settle against her, keeping most of my weight on my elbows and knees. Her breath speeds up at the full-body contact. We moan simultaneously when I notch my erection against her, her pelvis already rocking against mine. I pulse in response but don't move. I want to revel being with her again, skin to skin. Finally.

Jesus, she feels so good. Warm. Soft. Feminine. Her skin is still as silky soft as I remember, smelling of lavender with a hint of vanilla. I bury my face in her neck and breathe her in. When her arms lift to encircle my shoulders, her hands at my nape, I sigh and relax. For the first time in over a decade, all is right in my world.

Soon enough, my cock is weeping and throbbing, yelling at me to move things along.

Not yet, buddy. Not yet. I'm going to savor every moment like it's the first time all over again.

I lift my head and cup her face so we can stare into each other's eyes. Despite the low light of the lamp, I can see every fleck in her eyes. I'd memorized them and seen them in my dreams. We spent countless collective hours doing exactly this during our time together, lost in the moment, amazed and grateful to have found each other so early in life, content to be with each other and doing nothing more than holding one other, conveying our every thought and emotion with our eyes.

"Hi," I whisper.

"Hi," she whispers back, holding my gaze. Her eyes are full of emotions more complicated than the love, trust, and happiness that used to shine from the girl she once was. But beneath it all is the passion of a grown woman.

My eyes stay on hers as I slide a palm to her breast. Her pupils dilate and her mouth opens on a gasp when my thumb brushes over the sensitive, hard tip. Afraid I'm dreaming again, I dip my head to taste her one more time before she disappears into wispy images.

I lick her tight nipple, swirling my tongue around it, then suck it into my mouth. She makes a little sound in her throat and lifts her chest. Her fingers dig into my nape before wandering over my shoulders and back. Her touch causes a violent shudder of anticipation to roll through me.

I move to her other breast, giving it the same love, going back and forth between the two mounds while my hand drifts to the center of her chest and down her torso. When I reach her abdomen, I pause to thoroughly caress the soft curve of it before continuing to her pelvis, her mons, and finally, her slick folds. I sink a finger into her entrance and use my thumb to circle her clit.

"Oh, god, yes, Gabe!" she calls in ecstatic relief.

I abandon her breasts and kiss my way down her body, searching for the spots that used to drive her crazy. I place kisses around her navel, delving into it with my tongue, making her cry out with the overload of sensation.

Continuing downward, I place kisses on her mound, then swerve to lick the soft skin at the junction of one thigh. Brushing my lips over the area my fingers are busy pleasuring, I lick the other side. All the while, her hips are moving, circling, begging for more.

With her musky scent filling my senses and my mouth watering for a taste of her, I end the teasing. She moans in protest when I remove my finger from her. I use my thumbs to reveal her pot of honey and, ravenous, I dive in, my lips and tongue swirling, sucking, lapping from her entrance to her to clit. Still so fucking sweet but with a hint of spice now.

She grabs my hair and holds me close, pushing against my mouth. That's my clue to focus all my attention on her clit. I suction my mouth over it and flick my tongue, hard and fast. Her hips go wild. She's about to come. I suck and I flick until her body tenses for a second before releasing into powerful spasms. I hold her as she bucks, keeping my mouth on her as I make it last for her, for me.

When she finally lowers her ass to the mattress, I nip and nuzzle my way up her body, ready to thrust into her for my own impending release. I encounter her hand instead of her slick entrance. What the fuck? She is literally cock-blocking me.

"Babe, I'm dying. I need you." It's my turn to beg, my words coming out raspy between heaving breaths.

"Condom."

Jesus. Of course. I almost whimper in gratitude that she wasn't about to stop the show. I sit back on my heels and lean over the bed for my pants. I'd come prepared and filled with optimism, but I honestly didn't think I'd get this far tonight.

I almost topple over when her hand wraps around my thick length, her thumb rubbing over the crown. Ripping the condoms out of my wallet, I rear back onto the bed. I throw one on the bed and tear the other packet open. I nudge her hand away when it gets in the way of rolling the latex on. She places her hands on my chest instead, running her palms over my pecs and zeroing in on my nipples.

Unable to take any more stimulation, I hold her wrists in one hand and position myself at her entrance. She breaks free of my light grip to put her hands on my ass and dig in, lifting her hips at the same time. In one hard thrust, I'm in to the hilt.

I barely hear her groan over my own. I don't know how sound-proof these walls are, but at least her mother is in her suite downstairs and Bobbie is down the hall.

As much as I want to take my time, I'm too close. I set up a deep, hard rhythm that she matches, thrust for thrust, her fingers digging into my buttocks.

My climax is fast approaching and I hope to God she's with me. I put my hands under her, holding her luscious ass as I lose my rhythm, and thrust hard and deep. Once. Twice. Three times. I throw my head back and let go with one last thrust, holding myself still as I explode just as she screams into my shoulder and contracts around my cock, enhancing my orgasm. I think I black out for a few seconds from the intensity of it. When I come back to awareness, we're still pulsing gently against each other. I press my mouth to hers and kiss her softly, gently. We don't speak. No words are needed after what we just experienced. It was fucking mind-blowing.

Long moments later, our tender kisses of the afterglow turn to open-mouthed, lusty ones of rising passion as our pelvises grind against each other. Wrapping my arms around her, I flip us over so she's on top. Pulling off the condom, I reach blindly for the one I'd thrown across the bed earlier. She finds it and sheathes me with it before guiding me back inside her. My cock, which hadn't gone fully soft yet, soon swells with a rush of blood.

Well, hell. Not since the early days of our lovemaking have I recovered this quickly. I help it along with slow, shallow thrusts. I'm hard as a rock within minutes, ready to go again.

22

Stevie

N OW THAT THE LUST has been slaked, for the moment at least, regret is knocking on my conscience, but I keep the door firmly closed against it. Being held in his arms feels too good. Besides, that horse has already left the barn. So if he's up for it—he already has been twice—I'll count the whole damn night as one big mistake and move on in the morning.

Because being in his arms feels like I'm right where I belong. Home.

Is this what I've been fruitlessly searching for as I traveled across the globe? Is this the peace I was yearning for as I drove aimlessly through the Northern Plains?

How can it be, when nothing has changed? Well, one thing has. But I'm not ready to confront that yet. If it's this painful for me to even think about over ten years later, how will Gabe react when—if—I tell him? And I'll have to tell him if we get back together.

It would be easy to blame him for everything, but time and perspective have shown me that I was to blame for the breakup itself. He may have tried to rush me into taking a step I wasn't ready for, but I was the one that did the breaking up when he proposed instead of saying, "I love you, but not yet."

I'm still angry he went behind my back about the police academy, but did I have the right to force him to give up something that had been important to him? I should have figured out a way to deal with my fears, but at eighteen years old and trying to survive one tragic setback after another, it was more than I'd been capable of at the time.

Perhaps if Mom hadn't been going through her own health issues, she might have seen my struggles and helped me through them. I hadn't been able to bring myself to tell her and add to her troubles, afraid to trigger another stroke.

I should have gone back to therapy, something I'd done when Mom had insisted after we lost Dad and RJ. But finances had been tight, and I didn't have time for one more thing. As it was, chores, a part-time job, and caring for Mom and Bobbie had been more than I could handle.

Maybe I can start therapy now, to see if it helps deal with my issues of fear and loss. I don't remember it doing much for me back then, except as a place to vent.

"Penny for your thoughts?" Gabe murmurs against my neck. He holds me close, my back to his chest.

Not a chance.

"You'd be paying too much for them."

"I'll be the judge of that." He shifts, nudging me to my back and throwing a leg over mine, as if to make sure I don't run away. He rests his head on his palm, tracing my jaw with his other hand.

I force a smile and evade his question by asking one of my own. "Do you realize this is the first time we made lo—had sex in my house? Even when I finally got my own room after Brent went to college, you refused to do it in the house."

He chuckles. "Your house back then was so small, Sandra would have known what we were up to. No way I was risking that embarrassment, or the trouble we'd both get into."

"It might have been worth the risk instead of using your truck most of the time."

"Yeah, that truck was fine in the summer, if a bit small. In the winter, I either froze my ass off or one of us ended up getting cramps or bruises trying to maneuver in the cab." Becoming serious, but still smiling slightly, he brushes the pad of his thumb over my cheek. "And it's making love, babe. It's always been making love with us," he says softly.

Unable to meet his eyes and see the tenderness in them, I stare up at the ceiling. "This doesn't mean anything."

He pushes up on his elbow. The fingers on my jaw are firm when he forces me to look at him. "The hell it doesn't."

Putting some distance between us and removing his hand from me, I pull myself up to lean against the headboard. I drag the covers up to cover myself. Not that I'm shy, but having an argument fully nude is...awkward.

"Gabe, this was bound to happen, given our history." I keep my voice calm and reasonable. "But it doesn't mean we're picking up where we left off."

"You're right. It doesn't. Where we left off sucked. But we can start over. A clean slate, as adults."

I shake my head. "Your job is still dangerous and you know how I feel about that."

Gabe huffs out a breath in frustration and leaves the bed. For a moment, as he stands with his back to me while he rights the legs of his inside-out pants, he looks like a stranger. The man standing in my room is a smidge taller and a lot broader. Where he'd been more lean and lanky before, he's filled out and put on more muscle, likely due to his SEAL training.

He's harder in both body and demeanor, with new tattoos and scars, his carefree, fun-loving demeanor—the way Rafe still is—mostly a thing of the past.

"Jesus, Stevie," he says, jerking on his pants. He faces me while zipping up. "You traveled the world by yourself, yet you're still afraid of this one thing?"

"Yes," I say, my chin sticking out in defiance. "Because I learned that people die every fucking day and there's not a thing I can do about it except not get emotionally involved."

"That's a shitty way to live. And impossible. You love your family."

"That's different." It's a pathetic comeback. Especially since I'd still grieve if something happened to Gabe, even if we were no longer involved. But I feel as if it would be so much worse if we built a life together, if I came to rely on him always being with me.

"It's not different, and you know it. We are family. Maybe not by blood but in every way that matters. Hell, I've known you since you were a baby."

"If you're implying we're related, what we just did would be pretty sick."

He stares at me, eyes narrowed in anger, hands on hips. "I don't know why you're looking for a fight, but you obviously are. Is it because you're scared of what we just did? Of how right it felt?"

Damn it, he'd always been good at reading me. Of course, I'm scared.

Because I still love him. Have never stopped loving him. And I can't risk losing him again.

I hitch a shoulder. "I'll admit the sex was hot, but it's been a while for me. I was scratching an itch." I look at him squarely in the eye and insist, "This was a one-time thing. It's not going to happen again."

I expect him to walk out in anger. Instead, his frown morphs into a gorgeous, sexy smile, leaving me in thrall. I don't move when he presses his palms on the bed to lean close to me. "I'm not buying it, sweetheart. You're going to have to do better than that." He presses a quick kiss on my mouth and straightens, picking up his shirt and putting it on. "But if it makes you feel better, we can be just friends. For now."

I watch as he puts his comms equipment back on and tucks away his various weapons. Despite the danger they represent, he looks hot as hell. Even without the aviator glasses he sometimes wears, he's sex personified. I'm surprised I was able to resist him as long as I did. Keeping distance between us is the only way to resist him, so his next words are a welcome relief.

"I have to go away for a couple of days to do advance planning for that trip to the Keys and the Miami game Charlie insists on going to over Christmas. In the meantime, how about those swim lessons? It's all Ari talks about. She's really excited about it."

Unwilling to let a child down, especially Gabe's child, I nod. "Sure."

"I'll have my mother call you to set it up."

He picks up his jacket and grins at me. I'm under his spell again as I stare at the mouthwateringly sexy vision before me, with his tousled hair and shirt unbuttoned at the collar. I don't blink when he walks away, presenting me with an equally stunning view of his broad back and perfect ass. I wish I had my camera handy as he gives me one last lingering look over his shoulder.

Only when he steps out of my room and closes the door quietly behind him do his words fully sink in.

I groan and slide down, pulling the covers over my head. I'd rather cut out my tongue than talk to his mother.

23

Stevie

I'M ABLE TO AVOID talking directly to Gabe's mother by telling Mom about the swim lessons.

"That's a wonderful idea, honey," she exclaims. "And it gives me an excuse to invite Teresa over. We don't get together enough like we used to."

I look away in guilt. One more regret I carry on my shoulders—their cooled friendship. Mom had still been recovering from her stroke when I broke up with Gabe. Teresa had been an immense help to the family during that time, but her resentment toward me, who she blamed for Gabe moving so far away, had driven a wedge between them. While the two maintained a cordial relationship and Teresa continued to do what she could for our family, it hadn't been the same.

"She's been busy since the grandchildren came to live with her," Mom says, noticing my reaction. "Tell me what time is good for you, and I'll invite her over. You'll do weekly lessons?"

I haven't really thought about it. I remember many of our childhood activities were weekly, but we didn't have time for more, nor am I a business with lots of students. I could do it every day since my future is still very much undecided. Not that I want to see Gabe's mother every day.

"Let's see how it goes with the first lesson," I answer.

Either Mom really missed her friend or Ari was driving Teresa crazy with her excitement, because two days later, I'm giving Gabe's daughter her first lesson.

And the first lesson is safety.

"Absolutely no running at the pool, okay?"

Ari nods enthusiastically, bouncing in her eagerness to jump into the water.

"Any pool," I emphasize. "It's very slippery when the floor becomes wet. You can fall and hurt your head. And if you fall into the pool when you hurt your head, you might forget how to swim."

She stops bouncing and her eyes widen. Shit. Did I scare her? I've never taught children to swim but I've lifeguarded through lots of classes and no running is probably the first rule taught. And I've seen plenty of kids slip on the wet tiles because they ignored it. Most resulted in bruised tailbones and embarrassment, but there had been the occasional concussion.

"Okay, I pwomise not to run."

"Good. Thank you." I'm relieved to see her smile again, afraid I'd traumatized her. "You already know to never come in here without an adult." Does that cover the never-swim-alone rule? Deciding it's better to keep this short before I lose her attention or give her anxiety, I finish with, "And always listen to my instructions, okay?" That should cover everything, right?

She's nodding and bouncing again.

"Okay, let's get started and have some fun!" I channel what I think is a cheerful, preschool teacher voice. When we stand, she takes my hand. The gesture startles me. I glance down and find her adorable face, so much like Gabe with the ocean blue eyes and black hair, gazing at me with trust and innocence.

She could have been *my* child. *Ours.*

The ache in my chest throbs in agony. The hand that usually knows its job in trying to ease the pain is caught by a small, chubby one. Staring at our joined hands, then at the pure, open heart shining through Ari's eyes, I feel the ache lessen. It doesn't go away entirely. My heart will never fully recover, but it does melt a little when she smiles at me.

We start with the basics—how to enter the pool safely using the ladder, holding on to the wall, blowing bubbles, and making big splashes while kicking her feet.

Ari is impatient and unafraid, so I advance her to putting her face in the water while blowing bubbles and then bobbing under the surface for a second or two while holding her breath.

Deciding to keep the learning part of the lesson short so she doesn't get bored at the wall, we move to the fun stuff. I give her a foam noodle and hold her hands to drag her from one side of the pool to the other while she kicks. She laughs in delight, shouting, "I'm swimming! I'm swimming!"

Checking the time, I tell her, "I think that's enough for today. What do you think?"

Of course she wails, "Nooo!" Her face falls and turns to pleading. "More! Pleeease?"

I'd be a monster to say no after asking for her opinion. "Okay, how about a couple of jumps?" There I go again, asking a four-year-old instead of telling her, when I know her grandmother will be waiting for her.

Ari squeals in excitement. I tug her by the noodle to the ladder and show her how to get out, making sure she holds on with both hands. I stay in the pool and instruct her where to stand and how to jump.

"Ready? Three. Two. One...Jump!"

Without hesitation, she jumps toward my outstretched arms. I catch her but allow my arms to sink with the weight of her, so her head is under water for one quick second before I pull her up. I don't want her to panic when she eventually jumps in on her own and it happens. I expect her to come up laughing with excitement, but she comes up coughing instead.

Shit. Did I remember to tell her to hold her breath before jumping?

I pat her firmly on her back as she coughs in my face. She clings to me and wraps her legs around my waist, showing fear for the first time. "You're okay, sweetie," I reassure her. "You're okay. You swallowed a little water, that's all."

"Are you trying to drown my granddaughter?" a voice calls out in a very *non*-joking tone.

Of course Teresa would see this one moment of the lesson. Ari finally stops coughing and wraps her arms around my neck in a hug. I gently squeeze her little body to me for a second, then unwrap her arms from me.

"Ari, sweetie. We're going to do the jump one more time, okay?" I can't leave her feeling afraid, or she'll never come back. Wait. Don't I want that? If I'm not careful, she'll trap me in those big blue eyes of hers, just like her father does when I don't keep my distance.

"No, I don't want to," she whimpers.

"Hey," I jostle her lightly. "That was a great big first jump. But it's only the first. You need to keep practicing to get better at it."

She shakes her head, trying to wrap herself around me again.

"She said she doesn't want to."

I sigh at Teresa's interference but ignore her.

"Okay, I won't make you today, but you'll come back tomorrow for another lesson?" When she hesitates, I remind her, "It was a lot of fun today, right?"

She nods slowly. "But I don't want to jump again."

I agree, deciding to cross that bridge later. "Okay. How about…" No, no asking. "Let's end today with a nice relaxing float." I can't let her last memory of this lesson be the scary jump.

"Just a few more minutes, Teresa." This telling thing instead of asking comes in pretty handy. I suppress my grin as she regards me with her usual thinly veiled hostility. In the next instant, my bubble bursts when she nods regally, granting me permission to a question I did not ask. Damn. I should have looked away. Rookie mistake.

I look away now and make sure to hold Ari firmly, since this is not a lesson in learning how to float. I've seen kids flail and panic when they start sinking. She keeps her eyes on me, her body tense as I cradle her in my arms. I walk back and forth for a few minutes, gently swinging her until she finally relaxes. I ease my hold, keeping my hands under to prevent her middle from sinking, but allowing her body to float naturally.

"How's the lesson going?"

Ari and I both startle at Gabe's voice.

"Daddy!" She tries to jump out of my arms in her excitement, but I hold on to her. I don't need her sinking and breathing more water into her lungs, especially with Teresa watching.

But she is nowhere to be seen. Gabe stands alone at the edge of the pool, towering over us. My mouth goes dry at the sight of him in dark slacks and a white shirt that's unbuttoned at the collar. The sleeves are rolled up, revealing a gadgety black watch and my kryptonite…sexy, strong forearms with a dusting of hair and popping veins.

I tear my gaze away, catching his knowing grin, and carry his wriggling daughter to the ladder. She tears up the steps and runs—runs!—into her father's arms. So much for promises.

"No running," I call out.

She turns to me, shame-faced, excitement dimmed. "I'm sowwy. I fowgot."

I smile to ease the sting of the reprimand. "Remember next time."

"Okay." She nods then turns to her father, who picks her up, neither one caring she's getting his clothes wet.

I forget everything too when I climb up the ladder to find Gabe's eyes blazing with blue fire as his gaze runs over my body. I'm wearing another one of my old one-piece bathing suits. I figured there's no better motivation to lose a few pounds than wearing something a size too small. The tight fit makes it appear a little more high-cut at the hips and low-cut at the cleavage as it stretches to cover my curvier body.

Arianna is talking a mile-a-minute about what she did at her first swim lesson, holding his cheeks to make him look at her.

Gabe tears his gaze away from me, releasing me from his trap. I grab towels for me and Ari, wrapping one around my waist before taking the other to her. I hold it out for Gabe, but Ari turns to launch herself at me. Good thing Gabe holds onto her, because I was not prepared for that leap. He sets her down and takes the towel from me to dry her off. Over her head, he says softly, "Hi, Mermaid."

Hardly anyone uses that nickname anymore. My father began calling me that when I first started swimming, excelling in the butterfly stroke at a young age. Mom and my brothers sometimes would, so Gabe and Rafe did as well when they were teasing me.

But coming from Gabe, who got a new mermaid tattoo to commemorate each year we were together...in that tender tone...It feels like a soft caress over my body. Or maybe it's the way he's looking at me.

"Why you called her muhmaid, Daddy?"

He glances at his daughter, his eyes crinkling at the corners as he smiles at her before looking back up at me. "Because she swims like one, especially when she does the butterfly."

Ari looks at us, confused. "Then how come you don't call her butterfly?"

Chuckling, he says, "Remember we read that book about the caterpillar turning into a butterfly? Well, Stevie turns into a mermaid."

I roll my eyes at him. She looks even more confused.

"Your daddy is joking, Ari," I explain. "My daddy used to call me that because I was really good at swimming. Like a mermaid."

Her eyes widen in understanding. "Like Awiel in *The Little Mermaid*!" She bounces excitedly. "I want to be like Awiel! I want to be a muhmaid!"

My gaze meets Gabe's in amusement until I realize what this little tableau looks like—a shared moment between parents over their child's antics. Except I'm not Arianna's mother, and Gabe is not my partner.

"Is the lesson over?" Teresa asks from the doorway, glancing between the two of us.

"Nonna!" Ari takes a running step, then stops to look over her shoulder at me. She gives me a sheepish grin at my raised eyebrows before speed walking the rest of the way to her grandmother.

"All done, my little angel?" Teresa beams at her granddaughter. "Let's get you showered and changed." She throws a warning glance my way before walking away with Ari. Does she think I'm going to have my way with her precious son once she leaves us alone?

"How was the lesson, babe?"

"I told you to stop calling me that."

"You prefer Mermaid?" He smiles, raising an eyebrow.

I narrow my eyes at him. He's still as cheerful as he was when he'd left me in bed, despite me telling him we weren't going to have sex again. While he was gone, he sent me friendly texts and a few pictures he took from Niko's island—the ocean, palm trees, and a sunset. The last one came with two texts. First, *wish you were here.* It was quickly followed by *to see this.*

I ignored them all, only texting him once to tell him Ari's lesson was scheduled.

"I prefer you stop playing whatever game this is."

His eyes cool, but he maintains his easy smile. "I'm just playing the game of life, sweetheart."

Groaning and shaking my head at his corniness, I leave the pool to shower and dress in my room, waiting until I'm out of sight to release the smile that's been waiting to burst out of me. I'd forgotten how playful and charming he could be. All the best memories we had of the years before had been tainted by that one short, last memory of his hurt rage, frozen in time.

24

Gabe

I scan the SUV's passenger side mirror to check for suspicious moving headlights driving too close or swerving between lanes trying to catch up to us, then glance over my shoulder to look out the rear window for the same.

As I turn back, I catch Stevie's gaze. She's sitting with her mother and sister, who fell asleep by the time we reached the Bronx after leaving the West Village. Everyone had gathered at Luc and Charlie's for Daphne's thirteenth birthday party.

Our interaction at the pool after Ari's lesson reminded me of how much fun we used to have, of how much fun *I* used to be. Rafe isn't the only one who can be charming.

I wasn't able to make it to Ari's next lesson, but I called Stevie that night to ask her about it. After I waited patiently through her two-word answers, she eventually loosened up enough that we stayed on the phone for a half hour, talking about various harmless topics.

Whenever I have a free moment during the day, I send her a text asking how her day is going or call her at night to ask if she remembered something we did back in the day. The desire to make love with her is still burning—I want to pick her up and drag her off to bed each time I look at her—but now that I've had her once—okay, twice—I don't want to do anything to scare her away. I'm trying to take it slow, building our relationship back to the way it used to be.

I may have asked for her friendship the other night, but I have every intention of getting her back—into my life and into my bed—for good. Because she's the fucking love of my life, my soulmate, something I've known since I was seventeen years old.

At the thought, I smile at her. She smiles back but tilts her head at me, puzzled. My gaze goes to her mouth, and she immediately bites the inside of her lip. Despite the darkness, when I meet her eyes again, I can tell she's thinking along the same lines as me.

Hold that thought, baby. I wink at her before facing forward again, leaving all thought of taking it slow on the highway behind us. Ten days is slow enough when even a day feels too long.

I mentally urge Morris to drive faster. The sight of the Hutchinson house fifteen minutes later has never been more welcome. Morris and I check out the inside before letting them in. Sandra goes to her suite after giving me a knowing smile. I feel the heat creep up my neck with momentary embarrassment at having her guess where my thoughts are.

If she only knew what my plans are. I secure the house and check in with the team via the radio. Once they assure me they're all set, I let them know I'm going offline and climb the stairs. I pass Bobbie's room, where I can hear the radio playing loudly, and knock softly on Stevie's door.

She opens it a crack. Shit. I can tell from her expression that the moment we'd shared in the car has passed. Reminding myself this is not a sprint, I give her a friendly smile. "Want to go for a walk?"

"Now?" She looks at me like I've lost my mind. "It's freezing outside."

"How about a movie downstairs?"

She frowns. "Aren't you on duty?"

"I'm officially off the clock."

"Gabe, I'm tired. It's been a long day."

"Let me in, Stevie. Just for a few minutes."

She narrows her eyes in suspicion. "Why?"

"To talk. As friends. Didn't you used to have late-night gab fests with your girlfriends?" I grin, keeping my tone and expression innocent and charming. "We're still friends, right? Even though you're done using me to scratch your itch?" I feign a wounded look, though there's truth to the words.

She hesitates a long moment before backing up and opening the door wider but staying behind it. Triumphant, I step inside and add, "Feel free to take advantage of me again anytime you get itchy, babe."

I take off my sport coat as I move further into the room, noting the steam coming from her bathroom.

Fuck, I wish I'd been in the shower with her. We never had the pleasure of experiencing shower sex when we were younger. The vision of her, naked and wet, sends a bolt of lust straight to my dick along with a rush of blood.

I peek over my shoulder to see her standing in front of the door, her back and her palms pressed against it. She's wearing a robe. And nothing else if she just came out of the shower? One can only hope.

"Get that smirk off your face. You're not getting lucky tonight."

"Ah, babe. I already feel lucky just standing here with you."

She narrows her eyes at me suspiciously, making my smile widen. I lay the coat over the wingback chair by the window.

"But I'm holding out hope to be even luckier some other night, if not tonight." For now, I can only hope spending time with her will remind her that what we have is too special to throw away because of her fear over something that might never happen.

I remove my gun holster and the other paraphernalia hooked on my belt and hidden under my pants and set everything on her dresser. I don't want her to focus on them and remember why she doesn't want to be with me.

"Keep dreaming," she scoffs, but doesn't move when I edge closer to her, rolling up my sleeves.

"All I do is dream of you, Stevie," I say softly. "Don't you know that by now?" No longer smiling, I stop an inch away from her, so that she has to tilt her head back to look at me. My gaze falls to the curve of her long neck and to the pulse at the base that's jumping erratically. Her breathing quickens through slightly parted lips. I bet everything I have that her nipples are tight points of desire, but I don't take a peek. I maintain the connection with our eyes and my words.

"I dream of your soft skin, your beautiful sky-blue eyes, your perfect lips."

Her tongue runs over one perfect lip.

"And your mouth. I especially dream of your mouth. Kissing me. Moving over my body. Around m—"

"Gabe," she moans softly. In the next instant, her robe drops away from her shoulders. My eyes widen and I blink, making sure I'm not imagining her standing naked before me.

The shock and awe continue as she closes the short distance between us, her breasts pushing against my pecs. A shiver goes through me at the touch and my cock rises from half-mast to full. She grabs my face and pulls my head down, going up on her toes so her mouth can reach mine in an open-mouth kiss, her tongue seeking mine.

With my last working brain cell, I cup her face and pull us apart. With my lips a breath from her parted ones, I smile and give back her words from the day at the compound, "Ever hear of consent?"

Her gaze snaps to mine, but before she can take offense at my teasing, I cover her mouth with mine and gather her close.

Fuck yeah. I do a mental fist pump that she's the one to make the first move. While I would have happily talked to her all night if that's what she wanted, I'm thrilled we'll be doing more. Much more.

With a hand under her thigh, I bring it up to hitch it against my hip. Her hands are busy between us, unbuttoning my shirt, unbelting my pants...I push her fingers away before she can do any damage in her haste to unzip my slacks. I leave them on, not wanting to move too fast, especially if she tells me to leave as soon as her itch is scratched. I want to take my time, to savor these moments—to savor her.

We both moan when I pull her close and my erection finds its place between her legs. My boxers keep my cock from finding its way to its final destination when I lift her other thigh and she wraps both legs around me. I almost take her against the door, but remember there's a teenager down the hall and her mother downstairs, as well as someone from my team.

I carry her to the bed instead and sit on the edge. She's holding on to me as she devours my mouth, leaving my hands free to hold her breasts and rub my thumbs over the tight tips before rolling and pinching them.

She abandons our kiss to throw her head back, her hair like a waterfall over her back.

"Gabe!" she cries, offering herself to me. I take my time, kissing my way down her throat, pausing to suck and bite and lick her freshly washed skin until I reach the sweet pink nipples. I give one of them a nip as well, causing her to push her pussy harder against my erection.

"That's it, baby. Use me."

I continue to worship her breasts with my mouth while slipping my hands over her ass. After I knead and fondle every inch, I slide my fingers lower to between her cheeks. With her legs spread wide over my thighs, she's completely exposed to me, allowing me to explore all of her. As my fingertip circles her back entrance, she tenses. We never had the chance to play here either. I use my teeth on her nipple, just hard enough to take her attention off what I'm doing between her legs. Tonguing the hard nub at her breast, my fingers glide through her slippery heat that's fully exposed and waiting for my cock. For now, she'll get as many fingers as she can take. I slip the first one inside easily, pull it out and add another, sinking into her liquid heat with little resistance.

"Tell me if you want more," I demand.

"Yes, more...more!" She's squeezing my fingers as she rides them while grinding her clit against my cock, which weeps in protest because it's not inside her.

She's overflowing with so much desire that I'm able to insert a third finger.

"Oh fuck, Gabe! That feels so good! But I want *you*. I *need* you inside me," she wails.

She'll get me, all of me, but I want to see her come apart first. Not sure if she'll get there when my fingers aren't at the right angle to give her maximum pleasure, I remove them. She whimpers in protest but keeps going, circling against my cock. She's so close but can't quite get there herself.

I adjust my hand, twisting it, so I can circle her clit with my thumb.

"Ohmigod, yes! Right there! Don't stop!" Her movements pick up speed, her panting breath coming faster and louder, her perfect breasts jiggling in front of my mouth.

"Look at me, baby."

When she opens her eyes and meets my gaze, I lean forward to trap a nipple and suck hard. Her mouth falls open in a silent scream. I keep my eyes on her as she tenses then flies over the edge with a long, low moan. Her eyes flutter closed, her back arching as she rides out her orgasm against my hand.

"Oh, God, Gabe," she says when she's able to speak. She leans forward and kisses me, taking my bottom lip and biting it lightly, making my cock jump. Making me afraid I'm about to embarrass myself by coming in my pants, which I sometimes did during our heavy make-out sessions long ago. She soothes my lip with her tongue and presses her lips to mine.

She moans when I gently slide my fingers out. I smile against her mouth. She lifts her head and stares at me with her pretty eyes soft with satisfaction.

God, I love seeing her like this, sated and relaxed after lovemaking.

"Why are you smiling?" she asks. "You didn't get anything out of this."

"On the contrary," I reply. "I got the satisfaction of watching you come apart in my arms. You don't know how much I love seeing you like that."

I bring my fingers to my mouth. She watches me, her eyes widening as I suck on them, one at a time. "Mm." I run my tongue over my lips. "Delicious. Taste," I say, pressing a finger between her parted lips. They close around my fingertip. Her tongue circles it once before she bites it gently and lets go.

She shakes her head slowly. In a low, seductive murmur, she says, "I prefer the taste of you."

I grin at her wickedly. "Okay," I tell her, leaning back on my hands as she sits on my thighs.

She tilts her head, brow furrowed. "Okay?"

I nod, jerking my chin at my unbuttoned pants. "Go for it. I don't mind if you taste me."

She laughs. "I'm sure you wouldn't." She slides off, spreads my thighs, and drops to her knees.

Holy fuck. I groan at the sexy sight. And groan again when she spreads the zippered edges of the pants and lowers the front of my boxers to free my cock. It lands heavy against my navel. Her mouth is inches from it and going to be on me for the first time in a decade. My body trembles in anticipation.

I have no idea how we got here tonight, but I'm not going to question it—at least not right now. Not when she's taken my cock in her hand, wrapping her fingers around it to hold it steady as she leans forward. She licks her lips as if she's about to taste something mouth-watering.

I put a hand lightly on the back of her head and, as my eyes roll up to the ceiling, I say a silent prayer of thanks when I feel the first touch of her tongue.

Hallelujah!

By the time she brings me to the edge, almost swallowing me whole, I'm hanging onto control by a thread.

"Stevie, baby, stop." I try to gently pry her away, but she shakes her head and hums, making my eyes cross. "I'm going to come," I warn with a groan.

Another hum and the thread snaps. I cup her face and hold her still as I jet into the back of her throat, pulsing against her suctioning mouth.

I come back to awareness when she finally releases me and sits back on her heels. She is looking up at me, wiping the corner of her mouth with her middle finger. She sucks it clean, making my cock jump with envy despite its recent gratification.

With a daring grin, she holds her finger up to me like I did to her. I accept the offering, watching her smile turn to one of satisfaction, though I am the one thoroughly satisfied at the moment.

The saying "like a cat that got the cream" comes to mind. I suppose we both did tonight.

25

Stevie

I HUM ALONG TO a Christmas song from my Spotify playlist as I slice chicken breasts for the piccata I'm making for dinner. Since neither of my parents were very religious, we didn't grow up going to church, but we always played the popular holiday songs around this time. The nostalgia of the past and the contentment that fills me in the present moment soon has me singing along to Springsteen's version of "Santa Claus Is Coming to Town."

"You're in a good mood, honey," Mom says, entering the kitchen.

I smile at her over my shoulder. Her limp is a bit more pronounced, which means she just completed her daily physical therapy exercises.

"It's almost Christmas," I say, though it's much more than that. Though I am happy to be home and with my family during the holidays, it's mostly because of Gabe.

I don't know at what point I decided to give in to my attraction to him after telling him we were not going to have sex again.

Oh wait. I do know. It's when he walked into my room a couple of weeks ago and started undressing. Sure, he probably hadn't intended on getting naked, but when he rolled up his shirt sleeves, all rational thought fled, leaving only animal instinct to guide me. *That* moment had been the point of no return.

But it doesn't explain why I allow him—no, *invite* him—into my bed on a regular basis. I don't plan on making this permanent, but at what point will I be able to end it? And end it I will. I have to. Maybe when this Victor thing is over, I can use that as the convenient excuse. No need for security, no need for him to come over to check on his team or take shifts...

Except I'm still giving his daughter swim lessons and my mother and his have become reconnected as besties again. Apparently, all is forgiven there. Maybe it will help Teresa's attitude toward me soften.

When I came home last month, I accepted that I'd be seeing him again with both of us living in a small town, but I hadn't expected our lives to become quite this intertwined. I hadn't expected Gabe to be sneaking into my bed almost every night either. Unless he is working a guard shift, or is traveling, as he currently is, he has dinner with his children and puts them to bed, goes to the compound to work, then comes to me.

Most nights, he's so late because of work that he doesn't need to wait until Mom and Bobbie are in bed. They're long asleep by the time he slips in beside me and takes me in his arms. Depending on the kind of day he's had, we'll either make long, slow love or fuck hard and fast. Occasionally, he's too tired to do more than kiss and hold me while we talk and drift into sleep. Of course, he makes up for that in the morning before he slips away again.

I love sex with him every time, but the morning sessions might be my favorite. He'll wake me up with nuzzles and soft kisses, touching me gently, entering me slowly, and thrusting softly. When neither of us can take it anymore, he'll end it with deep, driving strokes that quicken to piston-like speed until we both burst into flames. Or at least that's how it feels because it's so freaking hot. Every time.

I don't know how he's able to move after that, but he showers in my bathroom where he's convinced me to join him, sometimes at night, sometimes in the morning. He'll dress in clothes he's brought and leave me with a kiss. He either goes straight to work, or if he doesn't have to be somewhere until a certain time, he'll go home first to see Leo and Ari at breakfast.

As much as I want to go back to sleep when he leaves, I feel guilty for being lazy. He's working so hard to grow his business and to spend as much time as he can with Leo and Ari. And now me. So when he sneaks back out, I haul myself out of bed and start my day with a workout in the pool.

Between the sex and the swimming, my old swimsuits are getting less tight and my current clothes are already getting a bit loose around the waist. Gabe noticed and growled, "I hope you're not losing weight because of what I said about you being soft. I was talking about your strength, not your perfectly shaped body." I assured him I was only trying to get healthier and working on building muscle.

"Good, because I love your curves, babe," he said, then added, "I'll always love your body, no matter how it changes." Hearts floated around my head at his words and immediately popped when I wondered if he meant changes due to pregnancy.

Of course, nothing gets by my mother either.

"Looks like all the exercise you've been getting lately is paying off," Mom says, coming to stand next to me after she puts the teakettle on. "You're looking very fit."

I stare at her bland expression, which gives nothing away, but I swear I saw her lips twitch and heard an emphasis on the word "exercise."

She chuckles and turns away for her favorite mug, saying, "I'm glad you and Gabe have worked things out, honey. And since the two of you aren't teenagers anymore, you don't have to sneak around like you used to."

I open my mouth to deny there is—or was—any sneaking around, but it's pointless to lie straight out to my mother. Picking up another chicken breast to slice into thinner cutlets, I clarify instead. "We're not back together, Mom. This is...casual and, um, temporary."

"Are you sure that's all it is? If you're only looking to fulfill your needs—"

"Mom!"

"—there are plenty of other fish in the sea than an ex-boyfriend who hurt you badly when he left," she continues, a bite in her tone.

Mom doesn't usually dig into her kids' love lives. I'm not sure why she is now, unless she and Teresa have been talking about it. Gabe's mother wouldn't hesitate to butt into her sons' love lives. I was fortunate that I was her best friend's daughter—until I broke her son's heart and "chased him out of town." Rafe's girlfriends weren't so lucky, though he'd never had one serious enough for her to worry about.

Keeping my back to her, I hunch my shoulders and admit, "It was my fault he left."

"I highly doubt it was *all* your fault." Her voice is harder now. "So what's going on now? Who decided this is temporary?"

Ah. Now I understand. "Don't worry, Mom. This is my doing. I'm the one who doesn't want to make this permanent."

She raises her brows, silently waiting for me to explain.

I sigh. "We're getting along now *because* we haven't faced our issues. The thing that broke us apart is still a problem—for me. He is ready for more, but I'm not."

"What do you—"

Gabe's voice unexpectedly carries into the kitchen as he speaks to one of the guards. I shake my head at my mother. "Mom, not now. Please."

Mom purses her lips and nods a second before Gabe saunters into the kitchen. "Hello, ladies."

"Speak of the devil," Mom says.

He glances at my mother with a wary smile, but his gaze comes back to me to drink me in with his eyes. That look…the way he used to look at me…it's there again, every time he sees me. It's intoxicating.

I stare back at him, looking so sexy in his midnight blue business suit and his thick, dark hair slightly mussed. Whenever he wears a suit, I imagine him taking off his jacket, loosening his tie and undoing the first couple buttons of his shirt. And then rolling up those sleeves…

I tear my gaze away from him before I start drooling—or jump him in front of my mother.

When the spell breaks, he answers Mom as if there hadn't been a long, awkward pause. "My mother would argue that with you, Sandra. She thinks I'm an angel. Even named me after one."

"Ha!" Sandra scoffed. "As I remember it, she called you everything but an angel."

Maybe when she vented to Mom, because that's not how I remember it. Teresa called Gabe and Rafe her angels plenty of times.

"What are you doing here?" I ask. "I thought you were going to get in late tonight." He had to provide additional coverage for a celebrity client who booked a last-minute public outing in addition to the meetings she had scheduled in Los Angeles. Knowing how worried I was, he checked in often, letting me know he was fine with quick texts during the day and long phone calls at night.

"Wrapped things up early. And speaking of wrapping, I had an idea for a gift for Ma's birthday next month. I thought she might like one of your photos."

"What a wonderful idea!" Mom says. "I've framed some of Stevie's beautiful photographs and put them up around the house."

"Do you mind if I steal her for a few minutes so I can pick one out?" he asks Mom.

"Of course. And you'll stay for dinner?"

Looks like her annoyance with Gabe was short-lived now that I've told her he wants more and I don't.

"Sorry, not tonight. I'm going straight home to spend some time with the kids before going to the compound to catch up on work there."

I cover the chicken and wash my hands before leading him out of the kitchen. "My laptop and hard drives are in my room." I give my mother a look over my shoulder. "Where the *photos* are stored."

Mom may know about Gabe coming into my room at night, but I don't want her thinking I'm taking him up to my room for sex while she's in the kitchen.

"What was that about?" he murmurs.

"I'll tell you in my room," I whisper back, going up the stairs.

He follows so closely behind me, I can practically feel his gaze on my ass as we climb the stairs. My suspicions are confirmed when his hand lands on my ass in a light slap followed by a not so light squeeze. I slap his hand away, hissing, "Stop it."

He laughs. "She can't see or hear us, babe. You think I'd risk it otherwise? I still remember the look she used to give me when I picked you up for our dates. Did its job of shriveling my balls. For a few minutes anyway."

"Did you come here straight from the airport?" I ask, leaving the door open when we enter my room.

"I wanted to let you know I was back in town."

"You could have called or texted."

He shuts the door, then grabs my hand and swings me around. I stumble into his arms and he kisses me senseless.

"I could have," he sighs against my lips. "But then I wouldn't be able to do this." He cups my face in his big hands and keeps his eyes open as he kisses me again before continuing. "I needed this." Another kiss. "It's been a long two days." Kiss. "And even longer nights."

I'm lost by this point, dazed, while we kiss, long and deep. With my hands at his nape, my fingers buried in his thick hair, I hold on to him so I don't melt into a puddle at his feet. How have I survived ten years without him when just the two days he was gone have dragged on forever?

Still kissing him, I loosen his tie and undo his top two buttons before he stops me with a hand over mine.

"We can't, baby. Your mother..." he says, but keeps ravaging my mouth. The way he's kissing me brings me back to when I was fifteen and not ready to go all the way. We spent endless moments like this, fogging up his truck windows with all the kiss—

His words sink in through the layers of desire. My mother. I forgot about her, waiting for our return downstairs. Our kisses get shorter until they're quick pecks as we reluctantly tear our mouths apart from each other.

"God. I feel like a teenager again," he says, his voice rough and eyes burning bright with passion.

"She reminded me we're not teenagers anymore and we don't have to sneak around."

He leans back, brows raised. "When did she say that?"

"Just before you walked in." I push lightly with both hands against his chest, not to get away from him, but to take him in. Mussed hair, loose tie, unbuttoned shirt. So fucking sexy.

"Stay right there. Don't move." I hurry to my desk and grab my camera, still sitting where I left it after taking a few pictures of the frozen pond this morning. I turn it on and check the settings quickly before turning to him and snapping a few shots before he can protest.

But he's doing no such thing. Not shy or self-conscious at all, he spreads the edges of his jacket to place his hands on his hips and gives me a sexy grin.

So. Fucking. Hot. I zoom the lens out to capture him from head to toe.

A quick zoom back in for a few medium shots when he checks his watch. And close-ups when he turns his head in profile to look at the bed before looking at me again. Each push of the button takes a burst of photos, capturing every minute change in expression and motion.

God, he's gorgeous. A beautiful face with Italian features—olive skin, thick eyebrows, full lips, strong nose, a five o'clock shadow covering a chiseled jawline...

"You could be on dozens of romance book covers," I tease. "I'd make a killing off these photos. I'll give you a modeling fee. Maybe even part of the profits."

"Don't you dare," he growls, straightening and coming toward me.

I zoom back out and snap a few more pictures of his scowling face. I finally stop and put the camera down when he's too close and out of focus.

"Please," I scoff. "As if I want other women—or men—drooling over you and fantasizing about you."

"What do you intend to do with all the photos you have?"

"Yours are for my eyes only." I grimace and add, "And maybe your mother. She won't see what I see when she looks at these." Shrugging, I say, "But I have no idea what to do with the tens of thousands of other photos I have. Or with the rest of my life."

He takes my face in his hands and places a kiss on my forehead. "You'll figure it out, babe. You've only been home...what? Just over a month?"

"I guess. I've started putting some of them on stock photo websites to see if I can make a few bucks off them. But not the ones with people's faces, since I didn't get signed releases from anyone."

"That's a great idea. Except for the ones you just took," he warns. "I'm not signing anything."

I laugh. "Are you sure?" My eyes widen and I giggle when a thought hits me. "I'll ask Rafe."

He gives me a quick, hard kiss. "Shut up and show me what you've got."

"Babe, you've seen everything I got," I tease, giving him a sultry look from under my lashes.

He swats me on my behind, then pulls me close with both hands on my ass. "And I want to see it as often as possible. But first…" He turns me to face my laptop, "I was thinking Italian countryside, if you have any."

"Only hundreds of them," I mutter, looking through the labeled hard drives until I find the one I'm looking for. "Here it is." I plug it in and open a folder labeled "Italy."

Gabe sits in my desk chair and pulls me onto his lap. Scrolling through the sub-folders, I look for the one labeled "Tuscany countryside."

"Wait. Stop." Gabe reaches around my body to scroll back up. "What's this?"

He clicks open the "Earthquake" folder. They were pictures I took in the days after an earthquake when I was on my way to Florence from Rome.

"I was curious about the damage in this little village where the epicenter was." I also wanted to see if there was anything I could do to help, even if it was donating some money from my funds. "Fortunately, this was a small one, though some older buildings had collapsed. No fatalities, thank God, but there were some injuries. Not like the one in Nepal. That one was terrifying." Just thinking about it makes me shudder.

"You were there during that earthquake? Fuck, Stevie." His arm tightens around me.

"Not the epicenter, but it was still bad where I was. I hadn't called Mom to check in yet since I'd just arrived, so she didn't know I was there when it happened. I'm glad she was spared that worry, but at the time, I thought I was going to die there, alone, halfway across the world from home."

"Jesus, babe. I'm so fucking glad you didn't." He places his mouth to my shoulder and holds it there, both arms around me.

"Thousands weren't as lucky. In a country that was already poor, so many were left with nothing, not even the little they'd had to begin with. So many lives lost." I tear up thinking about it.

"You have photos from there?"

"I do." I lean down to reach the bottom drawer of the desk and take out the hard drive. I plug it into another port on the laptop. "I haven't been able to make myself go through these to organize them."

I find and click on the "Nepal Earthquake" folder. As Gabe scrolls through them, I tell him about hanging out with a group of international travelers at a hostel when it struck. The fear and the panic as buildings started to collapse, wondering if ours would be next. And then the horror of the aftermath, the devastation it left behind. In less than a minute, everything had changed, and for so many, it would never be the same again.

"When we crawled out from the tables we'd sheltered under, our little hostel was somehow still standing."

The photos show buildings lying in massive piles of rubble, people still covered in dirt because there had been no running water or electricity. The hardest ones to look at, even now, were of grief-stricken residents and terrified children huddling in front of their destroyed homes. It felt too wrong to take pictures of people crying over the bodies of their loved ones. I didn't need photos to remember those moments, since the heartbreaking images are embedded in my soul.

Our little group had slept in an open field for days afterward, too afraid of what might happen during the unpredictable and fairly strong aftershocks.

I stare blindly at the screen while Gabe scrolls slowly through the photos. "I wanted to get on the first plane out and run away as fast as I could. Then I saw people trying to dig others out with their bare hands, giving what little first aid they could to complete strangers..."

Leaning against Gabe, I take comfort from his touch, his hand rubbing along my arm. "It changed my perspective on my traveling."

"How so, sweetheart?"

"I felt so selfish for wanting to get out of there, especially when the relief groups came in with supplies and volunteers. I donated money to a couple of the groups, but it didn't seem enough. Donating money, which wasn't even mine, was easy. But volunteering my time and working for hours on end until my body ached felt so much more satisfying, like I was making a difference."

I blow out a breath and continue. "After I did what little I could there, I began to look for ways I could help wherever I went. And I took some pictures along the way."

"You did more than that. You captured stories. These are amazing photographs, Stevie. The portraits...I mean, you've captured their emotions perfectly."

I practically glow from his praise. Not wanting to worry my family, I've never shown them these photos, only the pretty ones.

"I'd love to see them all some time and you can tell me the details behind them. I bet you could submit articles or something to magazines. Hey, you could be a photojournalist."

I switch over to the folder of the Italian countryside. "No, I'm done with traveling for a long while, and writing is not my thing. You used to help me write my essays, remember? Besides, I couldn't stand by and capture the moments without doing something to help. Isn't there some rule about reporting what you see without becoming a part of it?"

He kisses my shoulder again. "You always were soft-hearted—" He breaks off when he sees the photo on the screen. Rolling green hills, a winding dirt path, and an old gray stone building in the distance. "That's it. It's perfect. Ma will love it."

"I have hundreds more. I'll put them into a folder and you can go through them when you get a chance."

"I think this one's perfect, but why you don't you pick out one more? Email them to me so I can have them enlarged. You know what my mother will like."

"I know she doesn't like me," I mutter under my breath.

He pulls my head closer and kisses my temple. He was always touchy-feely with me when we were dating. I've missed being held with care and affection by a man. My infrequent one-night stands were almost clinical, fulfilling a bodily need—and not very well at that.

"Don't take it too personally," he says, grinning. "Nobody is good enough for her boys."

"Not even your wife?" Immediately regretting my question, I wave my hand, even as he tenses. "I'm sorry, that was—" Jealousy prompted the question, jealousy that I have no right to feel, especially when the woman isn't in his life any longer.

All playfulness is gone when he answers. "Ex-wife. As far as Ma is concerned, Camilla's only redeeming quality was that she gave birth to Leo and Arianna."

Despite being jealous that another woman had the privilege of giving him children, I feel a twinge of compassion for him. "I'm sorry things ended that way. It must have been hard, especially with the kids—"

"Don't be sorry." His voice is hard, his eyes flat. "The kids and I are better off without her."

I freeze, not sure how to respond. "I'm..." Sorry? I'd be a hypocrite if I said I'm sorry he didn't miss her, wasn't pining for her. "What happened?"

"It's a long story for another day." He looks at his watch then picks me up and stands before lowering my feet to the floor. His tone is lighter when he says, "Your mother probably thinks we're having sex in every position by now."

I gasp, wondering how much time has passed. He kisses my parted lips, sneaking in a little tongue. My body strains to be closer to him while my mind tells me I need to get back downstairs.

"And I need to get home to see the kids." With one last kiss, he asks, "I'll see you later tonight?"

It makes me happy to see his eyes are bright again, his lips curved in a smile that I return. "Sure. And you can come a little earlier and work here if you want, now that Mom knows. You don't have to wait for her to go to bed."

He winces. "I'm a grown man and yet I feel like a teen, weirded out that your mother knows I'm having sex with you under the same roof."

I laugh. "Is that going to be a problem tonight—you know, performing?"

I shriek and leap away when he tries to swat my butt one last time on his way out of the room.

26

Stevie

"I'M DONE PACKING," BOBBIE announces, walking into the family room with Daphne at her side.

"I thought you were wrapping presents," Mom says. "If you procrastinate much longer, you'll be up half the night."

I don't understand how someone can wait until after dinner on Christmas Eve to start wrapping presents. Or to pack for a trip when you're leaving the next day. But that's Bobbie.

Just like at Thanksgiving, the house is full for Christmas, if a little quieter for now. Brent and Luc are somewhere studying film for their next game—homework, since they have the day off tomorrow. Andi is putting Alex to bed in the guest room that they'll share.

"The wrapping is done too," Bobbie says, sending a smile to Daphne.

"Did you make DeeDee do it?" Charlie narrows her eyes at our baby sister.

"I didn't make her," Bobbie denies, eyes wide with innocence.

"I didn't mind, Charlie," Daphne says. "I like wrapping presents, and I usually only get to wrap three." One each for Luc and their aunt and uncle, her adoptive parents. "Besides, I offered to do it when I saw the way Bobbie wraps." She wrinkles her nose and giggles.

I've only recently met Luc's little sister, but Charlie has told me some of what she and Luc went through with their mother's tragic death. Daphne was a toddler at the time and was in the car accident caused by their father, the man responsible for our current need for security. Her injuries had resulted in scars on one side of her face and neck that continue down the side of her body. She's sensitive about them, using her curly hair to hide her beautiful face.

"In that case," Charlie said, winking at Daphne, "I would have let you wrap mine too."

"You two girls and Brent are just like your father," Mom said, shaking her head. "The first time he gave me a wrapped present, it looked like used wrapping paper crumpled around a box. A box! I can understand if it's something odd-shaped but..." She shakes her head and smiles. "I tried to teach him, just like I did with all of you, but he never got any better at it."

Joey chuckles from her perch near the fireplace. "Brent put his present for me in a gift bag, then shoved a pile of tissue paper on top and called it a day."

"Sorry, Mom," Bobbie says, not appearing sorry at all. "Looks like only Stevie and Georgie got that gene."

Georgie had again called to say she couldn't come home for Christmas but had sent beautifully wrapped presents through the mail. Once this Victor thing is over, I have every intention of flying to Missouri and camping out at her doorstep if I have to in order to see her.

"Well, let's hope your packing is better," I say. "Did you at least use the packing list I texted you?" I'm a little out of practice at looking after her, but the instinct is still there.

"Yeah, thanks for that," Bobbie says. "I would have forgotten half of the stuff otherwise." She smiles with excitement. "I can't believe we're going on a private jet to a private island!"

She's practically squealing in excitement, the way she did when she told me Charlie was secretly dating Luc. We're leaving the morning after Christmas to spend a few days on a private island in the Florida Keys owned by Niko Anastasios. He is the majority owner of the Firebirds and Brent's friend and business partner. While there, we'll attend Luc and Brent's game in Miami, per Charlie's request.

"The jet was the only way Gabe would let us go," Charlie says. "He's still annoyed with me, since I insisted we're all still going to the game too."

I don't blame him. He told me last night about the logistical nightmare of getting us all from the Keys to Miami and back. "At least I can take my entire team from here with me, instead of leaving some of them behind to watch you and your mom," he said in resigned acceptance. He would have preferred we all watched the game at Niko's island home, which was already a fortress.

"I wish we could leave now and have Christmas in Florida," Bobbie continued. "It must be really cool to wake up to palm trees and warm sunshine instead of cold and snow."

"It's not that cool," says Daphne, who's lived in the South her whole life until recently. "It's like waking up on any other day. I've always wanted to wake up to a white Christmas. Like it is in all the carols and movies."

"Well, you're in luck, sweetie." Charlie holds out a hand to her soon-to-be sister-in-law. When Daphne takes it and sits next to her, she continues, "We're supposed to get snow tonight. It will make it look all fresh and pretty in the morning." She runs a hand over her protruding belly.

"Is the baby kicking?" Bobbie asks, taking a seat on the other side of Charlie. "Can I feel?"

She guides Bobbie's hand to the side of her belly. "This one is a night owl. It's like she knows when the sun is setting and she wakes up, making sure I stay awake with her for half the night." She looks over to see Daphne watching closely and gestures to her. "Go on, sweetie. Put your hand here and say hi to your niece."

I watch as the two girls feel the baby's movements, their eyes wide with wonder. I can't help but imagine how it would feel to experience the miracle in my own womb and feel a deep ache, because I will probably never know.

"Oh, my goodness! Look at you two little angels."

I glance up at Mom's words to find Gabe standing at the entrance of the family room with his mother and children. He looks hot as always despite not getting enough sleep. He left my bed before dawn to be there when his kids woke up. Since it is Christmas morning, they would have woken up extra early.

My heart expands at the sight of him, though we've only been apart for a few hours. Being with Gabe for the last few weeks has filled me with happiness. It's allowed hope about the future to sneak in under my defenses.

On this magical morning, even his job doesn't seem so scary. After all, it's not the same as being a cop, on the streets every day, facing unknown dangers. Gabe has been trying to convince me of this for the last couple of weeks, explaining the importance of training and logistics and *preparing* for all possible scenarios that reduces the risk of danger.

There's the occasional unhinged stalker, or distraught citizen seeking revenge for a perceived wrong, or a kidnapper looking for a share of what's not theirs to take. These events are highly unlikely, because the sheer presence of bodyguards makes it so. Most of the time, it's crowd control from overzealous fans or someone who wants their complaints to be heard. When I asked about the weapons, he said they're simply precautions for the unexpected. "Prepare for anything."

Despite my optimism, I'm not being naïve. We still have issues to work through if we're going to make it this time. And I need to tell Gabe about one of the biggest hurdles we'll have to get over before we get in too much deeper, though I fear it might already be too late for that. Because I love him and he loves me. Though neither one of us has voiced it yet, I'm sure of it. He says it to me with every look. I feel it in my heart with every touch.

I have to avoid looking at Gabe in front of his mother so my expression doesn't give anything away. I'm not sure what, if anything, he's told her.

Eager to finally meet Leo, I head toward them, only to falter when I meet Teresa's unsmiling gaze. She is definitely one of those issues we'll need to resolve.

I smile politely at her. "Merry Christmas, Teresa. Gabe." Without waiting for a response, I crouch on my heels in front of the children.

They look so much like Gabe. Leo is a miniature of his father in khaki pants and a button-down shirt, though he does look a bit more serious than a child should. When Gabe was younger, he was much like Rafe still is—carefree and fun.

"Hi, Arianna. Who is this handsome boy you brought with you?" I ask, trying to break the ice.

Ari doesn't say anything, possibly because of the thumb in her mouth. She appears to have just woken up from a much-needed nap after the early morning excitement of Christmas—and having to sit through church. She's dressed in a white sweater dress with gold threads woven through it, white tights, and sparkly gold shoes, with a gold ribbon holding back her hair. Her eyes perk up with curiosity when she spies Alex over my shoulder, playing by himself with the new Beyblades toy Brent gave him for Christmas.

I look at Leo to see if he'll introduce himself, but he stares at me warily.

"You must be Leo," I greet him with a friendly smile.

He peers up at his father, who gives him a nod of encouragement.

"This is Stevie, Ari's swim teacher." Gabe runs a hand reassuringly over Leo's head. He looks over his shoulder when one of the guards calls his name. "I'll be right back." He's gone before I can stop him.

I look around for reinforcements just as Mom and Teresa leave the kitchen. Everyone else is scattered around the house doing their own thing for now.

I turn back to Leo who answers me with no hint of friendliness. "Yeah, I'm Leo. And thanks to your dumb swimming lessons, Ari wants everyone to call her Ariel now. She thinks she's the Little Mermaid."

I'm taken aback by his hostile tone. Though I saw him once when he came to the pool at the end of one Ari's lessons, this is the first time I'm meeting him. He didn't look happy to be there, and he left the pool area by the time the lesson ended. He's refused to take lessons, insisting he already knows how to swim. Gabe didn't want to push the issue, deciding to try again in a few weeks.

Not sure if this is his normal attitude or has something to do with me personally, I decide it's best to ignore it. Rather than channeling the cheery preschool teacher vibe I use around kids I don't know, I reply more sincerely, "I'm so happy to meet you, Leo. Are you both having a nice Christmas so far?"

"Only if you think sitting in boring church is nice."

I choke back a laugh, afraid he would think I was laughing at him. He reminds me of Gabe when he's grumpy, right down to the furrowed brows.

"I definitely don't think that," I say with a sympathetic grimace. He doesn't respond, looking over my shoulder at Alex.

"Come on. I'll introduce you to Alex. He'll be so excited to meet you." I stand and head for my godson who is oblivious to everything but his new toy. Only when I call his name does he look up.

His face lights up when he sees Leo. His uncle Brent and new uncle Luc don't have a lot of time in the midst of football season to spend with him. In our family, he's mostly surrounded by women and two teenage girls. He jumps up and trots past me to the kids who are slow to follow.

Turning back to the trio, I say, "Alex, this is Leo and Arianna."

"Hi." Alex waves and smiles at both of them. Ari only stares at him with wide eyes, her thumb barely hanging on between her parted lips.

"Honey," I say to Alex. "Why don't you show Leo your presents and play with him for a bit? Unless you'd both like some hot chocolate first?"

Leo shakes his head.

"No, I'm good." Alex turns to Leo, excited to have a boy his own age to play with. "Leo, you want to see the Beyblade I got?"

Leo's seriousness fades. He sneaks a peek at his Nonna to see if she's paying attention—she's not—and pulls out a toy from his pocket, one he'd apparently snuck into church. "I got a Beyblade too!"

"Oh cool! I don't have that one yet..." The two boys head to the Beyblade stadium Alex has been practicing on, the apparently more experienced Leo giving him pointers.

"Hi, Leo!" Bobbie wanders into the family room with Daphne and goes to Leo to give him a high five. "Hi, Ari." She waves before sitting on the sofa with Daphne, their heads together as they giggle over something on her new iPad.

When I look down at Ari to ask if she wants to get a snack, her thumb is firmly back in her mouth and big fat tears have welled in her eyes. Concerned, I pick her up. "What's the matter, sweetheart?"

Taking her thumb out, she says in a sad, trembly voice, "Evwyone has a fwend 'cept me." A tear from each eye rolls down her rosy cheeks.

"Oh, honey. *I'm* your friend. You have me." I smile at the adorable girl with her dark curls and rosy cheeks. I tried not to fall in love with her, but failed miserably by the end of the first lesson.

Her eyes widen at the novel thought, then the sun shines through her beaming smile. She grabs my cheeks, scrunches her face, and gives me one of her special nose kisses.

The sensation of being watched is strong. I glance toward the kitchen to see Teresa staring at me, her expression softer than it's ever been. But maybe it's because she's looking at her granddaughter. Ari catches sight of her Nonna holding a plate of Christmas cookies and wiggles to be let down. She starts for her grandmother but turns back to ask, "Can you take my picture in my Awiel costume? Santa got it for me."

"Absolutely. I can't wait to see you wearing it. I love *The Little Mermaid.*"

"Me too. She's my favorite princess," she declares before scampering off. I've noticed her adorable lisp has lessened, coming out only when she's upset, as does the thumb.

Gabe was also watching us and comes to me, his tender gaze on me.

"You're a natural with kids, Stevie. You're going to be a great mother one day."

The pain in my heart throbs. I look away before he can see what I'm not ready to share yet. I want the happiness that I started the day with to continue for as long as possible.

"You're glowing, my friend," Andi says as we sit by the pond later that afternoon. The bench creaks with age as she shifts to face me. "I only need one guess why, but tell me anyway."

I side-eye her. "Since you're Miss Know-It-All, why don't you tell me?"

Her full pouty lips stretch into a grin. "It's a certain tall, dark, and handsome Italian sex god. And he must be a sex god to have you looking like that."

I widen my eyes, intentionally misunderstanding. "Oh, you mean Rafe?" I wave my hand in blasé dismissal, knowing very well she means Gabe. "*Pfft*. He's not my type."

"Shut up." Andi laughs and bumps my shoulder. "I'm talking about the other Italian god. You and Gabe seem to be good. I'm happy for you."

I sigh, the cold making my breath visible. "Don't jump the...gun." I grimace. "No pun intended. I'm still trying to decide if I can handle his job. I'm enjoying whatever this is for now."

"And then? Don't get me wrong," she adds quickly, taking my gloved hand with her mittened one. "I'm glad you're grabbing happiness where you can, but I hope you can find a way to work through your issues and have your happily ever after. You deserve it."

"So do you, sweetie." I squeeze her hand.

Andi smiles. "I am happy. I have Alex and I'm doing what I love."

"And doing it amazingly well. You're killing it."

"It helped to have the photo of Joey and Luc go viral, with everyone wondering who the gorgeous woman on his arm was."

"And who designed the sexy gown that fit her like a glove," I add. Joey went as Luc's date to a gala a couple of months ago. It was Charlie's idea to make Brent jealous.

"The boutique's foot traffic and requests for custom designs have really picked up since then. I had to hire another woman at the store so I have time to make them."

"See? Killing it. And as a single mom to the best little boy."

"I couldn't do it without your help. You taking him with you to Florida is such a gift for both of us. For Alex, so he's not sitting in the back at the store while I work, and for me, so I don't feel guilty for not having time or money to take him anywhere."

"You can thank Luc and Niko for that."

Somehow, the vacation Luc planned for Daphne to spend time with their aunt and uncle has turned into a family vacation for the rest of us as well. Joey is going with Charlie to accompany Daphne and attend the game. When Daphne asked if Bobbie could come too, Luc invited me and Mom as well—and Alex, since he and Andi are part of the family.

Andi's hold on my hand has tightened. I glance at her, but she's staring out over the almost frozen pond.

"Everything okay?" I ask.

She blinks and looks at me. "What? Oh, yeah, everything's great. Didn't we just talk about that? But we didn't finish talking about you and Gabe."

Okay, that's an obvious change in topic to avoid talking about whatever is on her mind. Maybe it's just nervousness at Alex going on a trip without her. I don't push, since I don't want to talk about what's on my mind either. I never told Andi anything more than what the rest of my family knows. She was in labor at a rest stop bathroom when I met her, and by the time I got to know her well enough to trust her, it never seemed the right time. Then the time to say anything had passed.

"Nothing more to say."

She gives me a sympathetic smile. "Okay, I won't push. But I'll say this—I wasn't here ten years ago when you were with Gabe, but the way he looks at you now...I don't think you have anything to worry about."

I hug her. "Thanks, Andi." Releasing her, I ask, "Ready to go back in? I've had enough of this freezing fresh air."

I stand and pull her up. We head back to the house, arm in arm.

Friends who know when to back off and when to push, and are there when you need them, are the best kind of friends.

27

Stevie

"**W**HAT'S THIS?" I ASK Gabe that night when he hands me a large box—wrapped perfectly with a pretty bow on top. I almost drop it at the unexpected weight. "Whoa. You have bricks in here or something?"

"All your questions will be answered if you open it," he says dryly when I place the box on the desk and stare at it. "I promise there's nothing in there that's going to jump out and bite. Go on," he urges, leaning against the desk and crossing his arms.

I tear my gaze away from his biceps that make my mouth water with the urge to bite him. Swallowing, I eye the box like there's a cobra hidden inside, afraid it might be something more personal than what I've given him. We didn't talk about exchanging gifts, but I was prepared with a couple of gifts. The first was a popular hardcover romance book about a princess and an ex-SEAL-turned-bodyguard—except I'd exchanged the book jacket with one that Bobbie helped me make. I used one of the photos I took of him, looking all broody and sexy, for the cover, and she added a background and text to make it look like a real romance book cover. The look of horror in the split second before he read the title was worth the teasing from my baby sister.

"*Gabe's Babe* by Stephanie Anne?" He couldn't stop laughing as he pulled me against him with an arm around my shoulders. He turned the book over to see the back cover. "Where's the blurb? I want to know what it's about and how it ends."

"It's a cliffhanger," I told him. "And the sequel is only going to be published if the model agrees to another photo shoot."

"Only if it's a private shoot," he responded, squeezing my ass before flipping through the book. His eyes widened when his gaze landed on a particularly spicy passage. "I'm going to need to read this."

"Why don't you leave it here and we can read it together?" I suggested, running a finger down his chest. "Maybe try out a scene or two?"

His eyes darkened to midnight. "Oh yeah? You have any book-marked already?" He placed the book on the desk and lifted me by the back of my thighs. Instead of wrapping my legs around him, I wriggled down.

"I'm not telling. You'll have to read the book with me to find that scene. Until then, here's your real present."

I handed him the actual present, a coupon for a portrait session for his family, just in case he showed up with a gift for me. It feels a bit impersonal considering our relationship, but I couldn't think of anything else that wasn't even more so. He'd accepted it with sincere enthusiasm, telling me his mother had mentioned making an appointment at a chain studio at the mall.

A coupon to take photos appears insignificant to the large present I'm unwrapping. I carefully tear away the gift wrap to reveal a cardboard box. He hands me a pocket knife to cut open the packing tape. Opening the flaps, I breathe a sigh of relief at the stack of books I find inside. On top is a folded piece of paper. I take it out and open it to read the description of an online course about opening a swimming school and a receipt of payment attached.

"I'll email you the link to the class," Gabe says. "You're doing an amazing job with Ari and you mentioned maybe looking for a job as an instructor." He shrugs and looks away, running a hand through his hair. Because it's so rare to see, it takes a few seconds to realize he's unsure of how I'll react to the gift.

"Thank you." I put the paper down and cup his jaw, pulling him forward so I can kiss him. "How do you know me better than I know myself?" I stare into his relieved eyes, the corners crinkling as he smiles. I do love teaching Ari how to swim. Taking on more students and making it a business has crossed my mind. The thought didn't fill me with dread as the restaurant idea had, probably because giving lessons was closer to fulfilling my dream of being a teacher and making a difference, albeit in a pool instead of a classroom.

"Check out the rest," he says, turning me and staying glued to my back as I pull the books out one at a time to read the titles. There's one book about being a swim teacher and the rest are all about photography careers...fashion, portrait, wedding. There's even a book on setting up my own studio.

"Thank you, Gabe. These are perfect. But did you buy every book on the subject you could find?" I tease.

He shrugs. "I think you have real talent for either career and you should explore your options." He pulls a business card out of his shirt pocket. "This is also part of the present."

I take the card and read the name on it. "Peter Chester Photography. What's this for?"

"Peter is a fashion photographer who also does celebrity portraits. I met him through one of my clients. I told him about you and showed him a few of your photos—"

"You showed—? How did—? The ones you asked me to send you," I realize. He'd looked through more of my photos one night and marked a few for me to send to him. "That's why you wanted them?"

"Babe, if you can do that without any formal training, I can't wait to see what you'll do with a little mentoring." He smooths his hand over my head, his eyes glowing with pride. "And Peter has offered to do that for you. You can meet him after the New Year and decide if it's something you want to pursue."

"Gabe. I don't know what to say." His faith in me is overwhelming. My eyes mist. "Thank you." I step between his legs and kiss him. Instead of deepening the kiss, he pulls back and reaches into the inside pocket of his sport coat. In his hands is a square, flat jewelry box. There's no wrapping, only a ribbon tied around it with a curlicue bow, slightly flattened from his pocket.

My relief at the thoughtful but practical gift of books evaporates. My heart pounds. Anxiety rushes through me, and I back out of his space, hands behind my back. "Gabe, you've already given me more than enough. I didn't get you—"

"Stevie, take it. Open it and see before you say no." He holds out the gift and gives it a little shake, prompting me to take it.

I do so with great reluctance and untie the ribbon. Keeping my eyes on him, I slowly open the box and remove the cover. Only then do I lower my gaze. My breath rushes out with relief at the simple charm bangle nestled inside.

I don't know what I'd been expecting, but I was sure it was going to be something that symbolized a commitment. Like the promise ring he gave me on the one-year anniversary of our first date. It was inexpensive and made of silver, but I'd cherished it. It's probably still in the shoebox of things from our three years together, somewhere in the dark recesses of my closet.

My thoughts and emotions are in so much chaos, I can't figure out if I'm relieved or disappointed. I take out the silver bangle and take a closer look at the charms. Only then am I able to breathe easy. A camera, a mermaid, and a photo frame with the inscription *Capture the Magic*. I put it on and hold up my wrist, jangling the charms.

"Do you like it?"

Are those nerves I detect? He's watching me carefully for my reaction, the way he did when he gave me the promise ring.

I smile and return to his embrace. His worried look transforms into relief.

All the gifts are incredibly meaningful because of the thought he put into them and show how well he knows me. They create an excitement within me, making me realize how much he believes in me. That he not only thinks I have the potential to make a career out of either, but has taken steps to help me make it happen...God, I love him.

I. Love. Him.

I've never stopped loving him. There's never been anyone but him for me. Not even close.

"It's perfect." I press a kiss to his mouth that has curved into a smile. "*You're* perfect," I murmur, then give him another kiss. "Thank you."

When I meet his mouth again, I keep it there as he grabs my face and kisses me like he hasn't seen me for a month. When we come up for air, he scoops me into his arms and carries me to my bed. Once there, it's fast and it's hot.

He kisses me like he can't get enough of me. I'm lost in him and have no idea when our clothes fall away.

All I know is him. His hard body above mine.

His supple flesh under my hands.

His arms around me, holding me close.

His mouth worshiping my body.

And his thick length pistoning into me until I'm biting his shoulder to stop myself from screaming his name in ecstasy.

"Ah, fuck!" He drives in deep one more time and holds himself there. "I love you, Stevie," he says, his voice rough with passion and so much more. He holds my gaze, the truth of his words shining in his eyes. The emotions swimming in them go straight to my soul and I clench around him and fall apart.

His mouth covers mine in time to muffle my cries. He swells inside me for a moment before releasing himself with strong pulses.

"I love you," he groans into my mouth. "So. Fucking. Much." Each word is punctuated by a shallow thrust and hard kiss.

Much too soon, I come down from the highest peak of my life with a hard landing. I'm very conscious of the fact that I did not say the words back to him. His face is buried in my neck, his breathing still not back to normal, so I know he hasn't fallen asleep yet.

With his weight on top of me and his cock still half-hard inside me, I want nothing more than to say what he's waiting to hear. There would be no truer words, because of course I'm in love with this man. Even more than I was at eighteen—something I never thought would be possible considering how much I loved him back then.

And yet, I can't return the words and give him hope for our future without telling him everything. He needs to know what I did before allowing himself to fully commit to me.

Though I knew this moment was coming, I was hoping it would wait until Victor had been caught. I didn't want to distract him from his job. Yet leaving him hanging after he bares his heart is likely to be just as distracting.

But like a coward, I put it off for just a little longer. Before I can stop myself, I ask, "Will you tell me what happened with Camilla?"

28

Gabe

A QUESTION ABOUT MY ex-wife is not the response I expect to my declaration of love, one I hadn't intended to make, especially during sex. But what I felt in that moment transcended the physical act and the words couldn't be contained.

I push away the hurt at her lack of response so I don't repeat the mistakes of our past. I will try to listen and understand her fears, because fear is the only reason she would ask me about Camilla in this moment.

Maybe telling her everything will let her know she has nothing to fear from my first marriage.

"It's not a pretty story," I finally say, gently pulling out of her and rolling onto my back beside her. She pulls the covers up and lies back down next to me.

After a moment during which we both silently stare at the ceiling, I begin.

"I met Camilla during my SEAL training in Coronado. I'm not proud of it, but I took advantage of what she was offering, because she was there and it was easy. I was too beat from the intense training to make an effort for any kind of relationship. Not that

I was ready for one," I add. "I was still trying to recover from my last one."

Stevie inhales sharply. When I look at her, she's biting her lip. I take her hand to entwine with mine, placing a kiss on her fingers in apology for the unintentional dig. I fold my other arm behind my head before continuing.

"A few months later, she tells me she's pregnant despite precautions. She said she was going to return to Brazil because her visa was about to expire. The thought of her leaving the country and hardly ever seeing my child was not something I could live with. So against my better judgement, I offered to marry her—after making sure the baby was mine."

I shake my head at my naïveté. "I thought I could make it work with her, learn to love her and build a life with her. I should have known better when an image of you popped into my head as I was saying my vows to her."

Stevie's breath hitches, and she lets out a soft cry, but I can't look at her while I tell the sordid tale.

"But I had hope in the beginning. She was the perfect wife and mother—or so I thought. Guys on my team would talk about their wives complaining about the long absences from home. I thought I was lucky to have a wife who was content with what I did."

When Stevie snatches her hand away, I wince. *Fuck.* I hadn't meant it as another jab at her. I continue quickly, wanting to get this over with.

"Unfortunately, the act didn't last long. She hated being stuck at home with a baby. My mother came a few times and stayed as long as she could to help with Leo, and I tried to give Camilla everything she asked for. But I couldn't change the fact that I had to leave them for weeks, sometimes months at a time, while I was off training or deployed.

"She was so miserable, I offered her a divorce, but she didn't want one. In hindsight, I realize why. At the time, I was relieved, and we were fine for a while after that, especially when she asked if Leo could spend a couple of months with my parents instead of them coming to stay with us. I could see he had become a handful, going through what I thought was just the terrible twos, so I agreed. Then I find out she's pregnant again but hadn't told me. When I confronted her with the test result I found, she said she didn't tell me because she didn't plan to keep the baby. Said Leo was already too much for her to handle, and she didn't want another child."

Stevie sits up now to face me, folding her legs under her. A quick glance shows her wide eyes focused on me, waiting for me to continue. I stare back up at the ceiling while I tell the rest.

"She wanted an abortion, though I begged her not to get one."

I'd tried to explain to her that I would support her decision if her health or that of the baby was an issue. As guilty as I feel for thinking it, I would even have understood and supported her if she'd wanted one when she was pregnant with Leo. After all, we had hardly known each other, but she'd never mentioned it then.

All I could do was explain to her it went against my beliefs when she was healthy and we had every resource available to bring our baby into this world. I even promised to leave the SEALs once my contract was up and take a more stable position in the Navy so I would be around more.

"Intellectually, I knew it was her body, her decision, but emotionally...I couldn't accept it. I don't think I could have forgiven her if she'd gone through with it, because it was my baby too."

Stevie makes a sound. Of shock? Horror? She's turned away from me so I can't be sure.

Restless at the emotions that roil at the painful memories, I leave the bed, pulling on my boxer briefs before I start to pace. Stevie shifts to sit against the headboard, pulling her knees to her chest and wrapping her arms around them. Her blank expression as she stares blindly across the room gives me no clue as to how she's taking all this.

"In the end, she agreed to keep the baby with two conditions. If I wanted a divorce, we couldn't get one until her citizenship was final. And I had to buy a house away from military housing, which she hated living in. So I scraped up some money for a down payment and bought a house. As soon as we moved, all the complaining stopped. I should have known something was wrong, but I thought it was because she was happy with the house."

My pride is unwilling to tell her of what a blind fool I'd been, but I inhale deeply then admit, "Turns out she wanted to be away from military housing because it allowed her privacy to be with her lover."

Rafe is the only other person I've told of Camilla's infidelity. When I did, he revealed she had come on to him once when he'd visited to see the kids and check up on them for me while I was deployed. She claimed to not realize it wasn't me when he'd rebuffed her advances. He hadn't brought it up at the time, not wanting to create issues, because I'd told him things were going well between me and Camilla. He gave her the benefit of the doubt, figuring she was drunk and missing me.

"When I found out about the affair, I couldn't do it anymore, not even for the sake of the kids. If she wasn't even trying, there was no point. I asked for a divorce, and she threatened to leave the country with Leo and Ari unless I kept my promise for her citizenship to be final. Even told me I could have sole custody of them afterward. I thought she was just saying that to make me agree."

It never occurred to me she might have planned this, even when I found out she'd been overstaying on an expired visa. I felt like an idiot when I realized citizenship had been her end goal and I was the means. The kids were collateral damage. I don't know if she'd ever felt anything for them because they were simply pawns to get what she wanted. Or if she had to work at keeping an emotional distance from them, knowing she was going to leave them, and that's why she'd left them with babysitters so often.

I'm not naïve enough to think that children aren't abandoned by a parent all too often. I just never expected the mother of my children to do it. I'll never tell my children their mother had written them off without a thought.

"Turns out she meant it. Claimed they were better off with me. I'm grateful she gave me sole custody, though I told her she could maintain contact with the kids and visit whenever she wanted. She didn't even put up a fight when I told her I was leaving San Diego, and she's made no effort to see the kids once we moved. Never even asked to have them come out to see her."

She's still out in California in the house that I sunk my savings into, living with her new husband. Giving up my equity in the house meant I had nothing to start my business with, but it was worth every penny to have my children with me, especially when I learned how often she left them with a babysitter.

It makes me burn with rage when I found out how little time she spent with them when I wasn't there. My mother tried to warn me when she stayed after Leo's birth, but I thought she was exaggerating because of her expectations of how a child should be raised.

A mix of guilt and anger and regret over the tragedy of it all fills me. I've beaten myself up for a hundred different decisions I could have made, only to keep coming back to the fact I might not have Leo and certainly not Arianna if I'd done things differently.

I return to the present and realize Stevie hasn't said anything since I started. I glance at her to see she's in the same position, but her head is buried in her arms. She's gently rocking. Is she crying?

I rush to her. "Jesus, Stevie. Don't cry."

Despite her resistance, I gather her into my arms. She buries her face against my chest, sobbing, saying *I'm sorry* over and over again.

"Shh, baby. It's all in the past. It's okay. I'm okay." I smooth a hand over her hair and rock her, kissing her temple and leaving my lips pressed there for comfort. I hold her until she finally quiets and falls asleep.

29

Stevie

"**C**AN'T SLEEP?"

I jerk in surprise and glance over my shoulder to see Gabe heading toward me. I'm standing at the end of the finger dock on Firebird Key, Niko's private island, staring out at the ocean. Light from the moon reflects off the water with an unearthly glow. Neither the view nor the rhythmic sound of the waves is as soothing to my tortured soul as I hoped they would be.

This is the first time Gabe and I have been alone since Christmas night. After my crying jag, which he'd attributed to the tragic story of his marriage, I'd fallen asleep in his arms without further conversation. I woke up a few hours later and lay awake, wondering how he and I could go on after what he'd told me.

I don't think I could have forgiven her...

I'd pretended to be sleeping when he left at dawn to see Leo and Arianna before we left for the trip to Florida. We've been busy with travel from home to Marathon on Niko's jet, then the transfer by boat to the island, almost a half mile offshore. While everything has gone smoothly, it was anxiety-inducing, not knowing if Victor was nearby, waiting for his moment.

Shortly after our arrival at Niko's house, the Deverauxs, Luc and Daphne's aunt and uncle, arrived for a tearful reunion with Daphne. She's lived with them as her adoptive parents since she was a toddler, but has been staying with Luc since Victor became a threat.

Once we were settled, Gabe went to Miami to double-check everything for our security at the game and attend meetings with clients and potential recruits to hire. The rest of us spent our time in the sun and water, exploring the five-acre island. It has a luxurious, light-drenched six-bedroom house, a pool, a tennis court, a three-bedroom guest house where Gabe's team is staying, a small private beach protected by a lagoon, a helipad, and the finger dock that I'm standing on with a covered deck to enjoy the perfect sunset views. And those are just the highlights.

It's hard to believe I know someone who owns something so grand—and I'd kissed him once years ago on a casual date that had ended with zero sparks.

It seems the only one who can ignite the spark in me is Gabe. Even so, I stiffen when he comes to stand behind me, wrapping his strong arms around my chest.

"Or have you gotten used to having a certain someone next to you in bed?" he teases, kissing my shoulder before resting his cheek on my head.

I want to snuggle into his warmth and hold on to his fore-arms—exposed by his rolled-up sleeves. I resist the urge, not wanting him to start something I don't want—can't—finish until I tell him everything.

"Or at least for him to wear you out," he suggests, kissing my neck. I hitch my shoulder to block further access.

"Not this week," I reply. Fortunately, with Alex sharing the room with me, Gabe won't be able to join me in bed. He's staying with his team in the guest house. Joey and Charlie both offered to take Alex since Brent and Luc didn't come with us, as they have to practice and travel with the team.

I refused their offer with the excuse that I promised Andi he'd stay with me, allowing me to continue being a coward while we're here. I'll have to find another way when we go home, but that's a problem for future me. This one right here has enough to worry about.

"I'll have to scout out a nice dark spot away from the cameras and prying eyes of my team." He sucks on the skin below my ear, making my pulse jump despite my inner turmoil. "Or maybe we can close these curtains here."

The semi-sheer polyester panels had come in handy earlier as we waited for the sun to set. Everyone was looking a little pink despite the sunscreen we've been slathering on ourselves all day.

"We can't. I need to go back to Alex in case he wakes up alone in a strange new place."

My tone and lack of response finally sinks in. He turns me around, holds me gently by the biceps, and asks, "What's the matter?"

"Nothing."

I force a smile, but my gaze skitters away from his concerned one.

"Stevie." His deep voice commands me to look at him, but I shake my head and look out at the waves.

"Babe. Tell me what's wrong. Is it what I told you the other night about Camilla?"

I step away from his hold. "It's been a long day. I'm going to bed." He steps in front of me when I try to walk past him.

"Is it because I told you I lo—?"

"Don't!" I cry out. "Don't say it. I don't deserve your love. If you knew what I'd done, you would hate that you said those words to me." I look down to hide my face. I hadn't meant to let that slip.

He brushes a few strands of hair from my face. I swat his hand away and try to move past him again. He holds my shoulders, a bit more firmly, though his voice is tender when he says, "Stevie, there's nothing you could have done that would make me hate you.

I've loved you since you were fifteen years old. You're the love of my li—"

I jerk away, but he holds on. Tears of anger and frustration and regret spill over. "Don't call me that! I'm not. If you knew what I did, you wouldn't say that. You would hate me...and yourself for saying it."

He frowns. "What are you talking about?"

"Let me go, Gabe!" I don't want to do this now. We have to get through this week. I won't be able to do that with him so close every minute of the day.

My arm practically comes out of its socket when I yank my arm away. I stumble and he grabs me again. The rational part of my mind understands he's trying to prevent me from falling into the water, but the need to get away claws at me with desperation.

Like a trapped animal, I struggle to escape. He's saying something, his voice not penetrating the roar in my ears. I kick and I yank but can't get away, furthering my panic.

"Fuck, Stevie. Please stop!" he finally shouts. "I'll let go but I need you to stop struggling. You're going to fall off the dock. Stop!"

Wary, breathing hard, I do as he says, but am ready to run as soon as he lets go. When he does as promised, I take off at breakneck speed, leaving him staring after me in frozen shock.

30

Gabe

I SIT BACK IN the chair as I finish running background checks on several backup dancers one of our clients wants to hire, as well as a couple of potential employees I met with in Miami. It's a task I normally give to our human resources administrator, but I couldn't sleep after my disturbing encounter with Stevie last night. I dozed between tossing and turning all night, finally giving up when an aggravated Morris threw a pillow at me from the other bed.

I worked out instead, then took a swim in the ocean before coming back to work in the den at Niko's guest house. Anything to stay busy instead of wasting time trying to figure out what Stevie meant.

With my thoughts shifting back to her words, I stare at my laptop. There is a way I can try to find out what she's done, if there's a hint of it on record somewhere. I tap my fingers on the edge of the laptop while I debate all the ways it could come back to bite me. It's an invasion of privacy, a breach of trust she may never forgive me for. The thought has my fingers hesitating over the keyboard.

"Fuck." I exhale sharply and snap the laptop shut. It's killing me that she thinks she's done something so terrible that she believes she doesn't deserve love. *My* love.

Whatever awful thing it is, I have no doubt she had a good reason for doing it. And as far as I'm concerned, there's nothing Stevie could have done to make me not love her. *Nothing.* Hell, if she needs to dig up a body and bury it somewhere deeper, I'll do it for her. I'll do whatever it takes to erase the guilt and grief-stricken torment from her eyes.

A knock sounds on the door.

"Come in." I stand as Shep—one of two female bodyguards on this trip—opens the door just enough to stick her head in.

"Hey, boss. We're ready for the briefing before we head out."

"Okay, let's go."

I went over the plan with the team last night, as well as the necessary details regarding the stadium. One last briefing with the team before setting out on a complicated itinerary with a group of nine people is necessary.

I follow her out, putting everything else out of my mind to focus on the job. Everything goes smoothly and as planned by boat, jet, and three SUVs to the VIP entrance of the football stadium in Miami. Once we're in the tunnel, I take my first easy breath, only to have my phone vibrate with an incoming call from Luc.

"Hey, Luc," I say into the phone. "We're at the stadium, heading up—"

"I just got a call from Victor," he interrupts. "The motherfucker is threatening more shit if I don't do what he says."

Luc's rage and fear come over the line while adrenaline pumps through my veins. Finally. Hearing from his father means we're not hiding from a ghost. The possibility he was dead and rotting, hidden away somewhere, has crossed my mind.

I motion for my team to hold up and move a few feet away before asking Luc, "And what does he want you to do? Tell me exactly what he said."

"Either wire twenty million dollars before the game starts or make sure we lose the game."

Sounds like Victor has gone over the edge into insanity, because neither of those is possible. It's less than two hours before the game on a Sunday, not enough time to arrange a wire transfer. And Luc doesn't have a hundred percent control over the game to guarantee a loss, especially since the Firebirds are heavy favorites to win. Miami has been on a losing streak, plagued by injuries.

"Any clue where he was calling from?" I ask, signaling to Morris for his phone. I send a message to our tech guy to see if he can ping Victor's location based on the incoming call to Luc's phone.

"No, I couldn't tell. I don't think I heard anything in the background, but to be honest, I was more focused on what he was saying."

"Okay, did he say anything else?" I continue typing on Morris's phone, this time a message for him to read when I hold the phone up. I want him to get everyone to the suite and then send two men to the stadium's security office to keep an eye on the cameras for any sign of Victor. Despite the risk, I'm hoping he's here and we can catch him with the help of law enforcement. Morris nods after reading my instructions and gets on it.

"He started right in with the threats," Luc is saying. "I tried telling him what he was asking was impossible, especially when the banks are closed. He said if I didn't either wire the money or throw the game, he was as good as dead—and he'd make sure to take as many as he could to hell with him."

"Good as dead? What the fuck does that mean?" But I can guess. Someone else is involved and threatening *him*.

"I don't know. He hung up. And I don't care if he's dead. But, Christ, Gabe, keep everyone safe. Take them back to the island—"

"No, they're safer staying put for now. It'll give us time to find Victor if he's nearby and for me to call in backup for the return trip."

"Maybe I shouldn't play. If I'm not playing, he can't blame me for the win."

"That's not going to help. Then he'll expect the money."

Luc's frustration comes through loud and clear. "Fuck! There's no way I can get that to him by the end of the game. And there's no way Coach would let me sit this out without giving a reason."

"You might want to tell him and Niko anyway," I advise. "And maybe Brent, since he's involved through Charlie. You don't want any question of impropriety coming back to bite you in the ass if, by some miracle, Miami wins. He may have recorded the call."

"Right. I wouldn't put it past him."

I check in with my team after ending the call with Luc. Everyone is safely ensconced in the private suite, and men are posted inside, at the entrance, and in the stands in front of the windows, which will stay closed.

Next, I go to the security office and make sure my guys were able to get access to watch the cameras. It's an impossible task with the number of entrances, cameras, and sheer volume of people coming in at once, but it's a base I need to cover, just in case.

Lastly, I head up to check on Charlie and the others. Outside the suite, I run into Niko, who is on his way to see them as well.

"Hey," I greet him with a handshake. "Luc talked to you?"

"Yes, he did. I offered to make arrangements for the money transfer to ease his mind, though I hate to give into threats. Luc agrees giving Victor what he wants is not the way to go. We'll just need to be extra vigilant until we catch the motherfucker."

We enter the suite together. I scan the room until my gaze lands on Stevie, who is pointing out something to an excited Alex.

"Ladies."

Everyone turns to look at Niko as if royalty just graced them with his presence. Having guarded a number of celebrities, I'm used to seeing this type of reaction toward famous people, but Joey and the Hutchinsons have met Niko many times. He's Brent's best friend, business partner, and neighbor. But then, he's also a billionaire who's been on magazine covers as much for his movie star looks as for his successful business enterprises.

"And gentlemen," he adds, nodding to Henri Deveraux and Alex.

"Niko. So good to see you again." Sandra holds her arms out to him for a hug. He gives her one, adding a kiss to both her cheeks.

"You look wonderful, Sandra. Beautiful as ever."

"Always a charmer," she says before introducing him to Daphne and the Deverauxs. Daphne and Bobbie blush and giggle when he kisses the backs of their hands.

"Hello, gorgeous," he greets Joey, kissing her flushed cheek. He does the same to Charlie, adding, "You look positively radiant."

"Thank you. And thank you so much for letting us stay on the island, Niko. Everything is beautiful and perfect."

"It's my pleasure, Charlie. You're welcome anytime."

He turns to Stevie, who gives him a hug. "It's good to see you again, Niko."

While he holds her close, he cups one cheek and places a kiss on the other. "When are we going on a date again, Stevie?"

What the fuck? I straighten away from the wall, ready to pull her out of his arms and tear them off so he can never touch her again.

Her gaze snaps to mine, but she looks away before I can interpret her expression. She scoffs at Niko. "You say that as if you don't already have a legion of women lining up to go out with you."

"No one with your combination of beauty, intelligence, and charm."

"Hey!" Charlie protests.

Niko turns to her with an apology. "Sorry, ladies," he says, including Joey. "But you both are taken."

So is Stevie, I want to shout. That's my woman!

"And who's this?" He steps away from Stevie before my Neanderthal instincts get the better of me.

He's looking at Alex, who is staring up at him with big eyes. The seven-year-old doesn't know about Niko's power or wealth, or care about his good looks, yet is awestruck by his presence. I hate to admit the guy exudes a magnetic charisma.

"Alex is my godson." Stevie puts a hand on the little boy's shoulder.

"Nice to meet you, Alex. I'm Niko." He holds his hand out, which Alex takes shyly for a handshake.

"Okay, I need to head out, but I'll see you all after the game for the ride back to Firebird Key. Enjoy the game."

Niko heads out of the suite, with a chorus of thank yous and goodbyes following him.

"I'll be right outside," I tell the men at the door as I charge out after him.

Niko claps a hand to my shoulder and chuckles before I can set him straight about Stevie. "Relax, my friend. I have no designs on your woman. While seeing her again is a pleasure in itself, the look on your face was a bonus."

Narrowing my eyes at him, I snarl, "And just how many times have you *seen* her?"

Niko laughs. "A gentleman never kisses and tells."

I burn a hole into his back with my furious glare as he walks away.

31

Stevie

I BARELY HEAR THE roar of the crowd as the Firebirds score another touchdown. Despite the private suite and the Firebirds having a runaway game, I am not able to enjoy myself.

Charlie and Joey are cheering on their men and high-fiving each other every time Luc passes the ball to Brent. The quarterback and tight end duo are living up to the hype the Firebirds' marketing team have been touting since Brent's trade was announced in the spring. They had made a great team when they played together briefly for the San Diego Sailors, and they're playing again like the years on separate teams never existed.

I'd seen them play together once when we all went to see Brent. All the while, I'd been afraid of running into Gabe, who was based in San Diego. The last time I'd seen Brent play there, I did a stopover in San Diego on my way home from Japan. Gabe had moved back to Connecticut by then.

I'd ended up staying for a week at Brent's beach house, seeing the sights and going on a date with Niko. It had been a fantasy experience to sit across from a gorgeous, sexy man well on his way to being a billionaire and feel nothing more than friendship. The zing I'd felt at first had been because of his powerful presence, not the sexual spark I expected to feel for someone on magazine covers as sexiest man and most eligible bachelor. Even the zing was nothing in comparison to the lightning bolt I feel at Gabe's touch.

With Alex preferring the company of Bobbie and Daphne, and Mom conversing with the Deverauxs, I continue my brooding. I had hoped being away from home would help me get my mind off Gabe, but that was foolish considering he's part of the security detail. I've been trying to avoid him as much as possible, but he hasn't been doing the same—like last night when he followed me out to the dock.

I knew the moment Gabe said he wouldn't be able to forgive Camilla if she'd had an abortion that it was over between us. God, I wish I hadn't asked him about his ex-wife. Everything had been going so well between us—it even seemed like he'd forgiven me for breaking his heart when he'd declared his love to me. He's not going to forgive me a second time.

Was it only a few days ago that I'd woken up full of hope about our future together?

And now it was over. Or would be as soon as we were back home and I broke things off officially.

"I wish Leo could have come with us, Aunt Stevie," Alex interrupts my depressing thoughts.

"I know, kiddo," I reply, ruffling his hair. I give him a commiserating pout. "Too much time with the girls?"

He rolls his eyes, his expression one of male aggravation. "It was fine until they started talking about which player was the cutest." He makes a gagging sound. "If Leo was here, we could talk about guy stuff."

Stevie laughs. "Like who is the biggest and strongest?"

He shakes his head. "That's no contest. It's Uncle Brent."

His hero worship of my brother has gotten stronger since Brent moved to New York and Alex has seen more of him.

"Yes, I suppose he is now. Remind me to show you pictures of when he was just a scrawny kid."

"He was?" He turns to Mom. "Really, Nanna?"

"Really," she confirms. "But then he started lifting weights all the time."

I recall when he did that. Looking back, it had probably been his way of dealing with how our lives had turned upside down.

When Alex lifts his arm to flex his bicep, Joey offers, "I'll show you some exercises you can do, Alex, using just your body weight. You don't want to use heavy weights until you're a little older."

"Can you show me some now, Aunt Joey?"

He moves away from me and goes to sit with Joey and Charlie. Mom comes over to sit next to me. "Are you feeling okay, honey? You've been awfully quiet."

I force a smile to ease her worry when all I want to do is have her hold me like she did when I was a little girl and tell me everything is going to be fine. But I didn't burden her with my problems when I was a teenager, and I'm not going to do it as an adult.

"I'm good," I answer, keeping my voice light. "How about you? Not too tired after all the traveling?"

My perceptive mother ignores my deflection. "Everything okay with Gabe? You seemed happy again, at least until yesterday."

I hesitate before admitting, "I don't think we're going to work out, Mom," I say quietly, wary of his men standing nearby. Without going into details, I continue, "We talked about the past, and there are some issues I don't think we'll be able to move past."

She takes my hand in both of hers and squeezes. "Don't give up too quickly. It's easy to see how much you two love each other. I won't say love conquers all, but it certainly helps if you're both willing to work through whatever the obstacles are, and if you do it with honesty and an open heart. And maybe with professional counseling—someone who is objective. But if you do that and it still doesn't feel right, don't force it. While Teresa and I would love to see this second chance between you work out, you two know what's right for you. And you know I don't like to interfere in your lives, but I'm here if you ever need someone to talk to."

"Thanks, Mom." I smile and nod. I was considering professional therapy for my fears, something I realize I should have done long ago, but it's too late now. Gabe won't be able to forgive me for what I did when he feels so strongly about what Camilla *might* have done. I'm not sure anyone can help us with that issue.

The rest of the vacation goes off without a hitch. Gabe offered to hire extra security, but Luc and Brent agreed it wasn't necessary. The men who were already there and Niko's built-in security measures on the island made us feel safe enough to enjoy ourselves without worrying any more than we had been before Victor's latest threat.

Luc and Brent received permission to come to the island after the game instead of flying back with the team. It helped that Niko, as an owner of the team, is technically their boss. We watched an early New Year's Eve fireworks display that the generous billionaire arranged, though it was difficult to appreciate them when I was busy keeping my distance from Gabe. From the look on his face, he was not happy with my avoidance of him...Even less so whenever Niko came within a yard of me.

Only when Gabe went home the following day to spend a couple of days with Leo and Arianna was I able to relax and enjoy myself. Luc, Brent, and Joey also returned to get back to work, and the Deverauxs went back to their home in Mississippi.

We spent much of the last day on the water in Niko's cabin cruiser, causing us all to be tired and ready for our beds as we wait for the jet to taxi to the FBO at the airport in Connecticut. Security on the plane is light as the rest of the team escorted us to our flight, then began their overdue days off. Another team is meeting us as we disembark here.

Once the pilot informs us we are free to stand from our seats, we gather our belongings and I take Alex's hand as we head to the front of the plane, following Charlie. One of the bodyguards, Fraser, leads the way and tells me to wait at the galley until he gives me the go ahead.

As I wait for the signal, I hear popping sounds. I instinctively step to the opening, expecting to see fireworks. I yelp in shock when I'm pulled forcefully back.

"Stay down!" Kathy yells, pushing me and Alex behind her.

I hear shouts of "Get down!" and "Take cover!" and realize the sharp cracks are gunshots. I wrap myself around Alex and maneuver our position so we're lying flat. Kathy crouches in front of us, gun in hand and ready for any threat that might come through the doorway.

I squeeze Alex tighter when I hear a sudden barrage of gunfire. Whereas the first shots had sounded far-off, these all seem to come from nearby. That means the security team waiting on the tarmac for us are firing back at whoever had started the gunfight.

Turning my head, I check on Mom and the girls and breathe a sigh of relief. They are also on the ground. Ortiz is in front of them, in the same position as Kathy. He's already calling 9-1-1 with a report of shots fired and their location.

After what seems like forever but is probably not more than thirty seconds, there is nothing but stark silence for a brief moment before I hear the muffled shouts of Gabe's men. Kathy rushes out of the plane, signaling for me to stay put.

"Everyone okay back there?" I ask.

"They're fine." Ortiz stops to listen to his comms earpiece. "They got the shooter. You can sit up, but stay on the ground and away from the windows."

I raise myself off Alex and smile to reassure him, but his eyes are big with excitement, not fear.

"Did they shoot the bad guys?" he asks.

"I think so. We'll have to wait until someone comes in here to let us know for sure."

But when no one appears right away, I ask Ortiz, "Can we go out? I want to check on Charlie."

He holds up his index finger while he listens to his comms. "Everyone's fine in here." He pauses. "I'll tell the pilot," he says as he strides quickly past me to the cockpit. "Who's been hit?" I hear him say.

My entire body and mind freeze at the words. Someone was shot? Oh, God! Charlie!

I have to know if she's okay. I stand, telling Alex, "I'll be right back. Stay here."

I hear Ortiz saying "medevac" when I reach the plane's doorway. A dark-haired bodyguard is lying at an awkward angle on the second step, groaning and breathing hard. My heart stops and I sink to my knees. When I recognize Fraser, a rush of guilty relief courses through me. I look around for Charlie and find her sitting with Luc. They both appear to be fine.

Able to focus on the bodyguard, I ask Kathy, "Is there anything I can do?"

She's holding gauze that's already soaked with blood over the side of his torso with her gloved hands. Items from her essential first aid kit lay scattered on the landing by my feet.

"Get me some towels and the first aid kit from the galley." For a second, I can't move until I process that it isn't Gabe. Her words sink in and I run back inside the plane to rifle through the cabinets and drawers until I find the towels.

"Who's hurt, Stevie?" Mom asks.

"One of the guards," I answer, grabbing the first aid kit and running back to give everything to Kathy. Since Ortiz is there to help her, I fly down the narrow steps to Charlie, who is lying cradled in Luc's arms. Both are on the ground next to one of the SUVs. I look around for Gabe, my heart pounding, but I don't see him. It appears he didn't come to the airport with his security team, thank God.

"Charlie!" I fall to my knees by her side. Afraid to touch her, I run my gaze over her but don't see any blood.

"I'm okay, Stevie," she says without opening her eyes.

"You're sure you didn't hit your head, darling?" Luc asks with concern.

Charlie pulls in a deep breath. "I didn't. But I might have had a small heart attack. Just trying to catch my breath."

"What happened?" I ask.

Charlie's eyes finally open. "Just tumbled down the last couple of steps."

"Fraser got hit and it knocked her off balance," Luc explains.

"He took a bullet meant for me," Charlie says. "A little fall is nothing in comparison. How is he doing?"

Not wanting to worry her, I only say, "They're taking care of him."

"What about Gabe?"

What?

Before I can process her words, Luc asks me, "Can you check on him, Stevie?" He holds Charlie closer. "I don't even want to think about what might have happened if he didn't cover you before the next few bullets came flying at you."

My blood runs cold and my heart goes from double time to quadruple at the words. I just might have an actual heart attack myself, at this rate.

I frantically search for Gabe, expecting him to be lying in a pool of blood. My panicked gaze finds him sitting in the dark shadows by the jet's airstairs, leaning against them. He's facing me, his eyes clenched shut and his mouth tight with pain as Morris cuts away his pants at mid-thigh. I force my legs to walk toward him, feeling like I'm moving in slow motion through invisible sludge.

"You've been shot?" I manage to gasp out. I can't see much in the darkness. Just as well, because I don't think I could handle seeing the injury in technicolor. As it is, I recognize the dark patches on his skin are from smeared blood.

My stomach turns queasy, not at the thought of blood, but at the fact it's *Gabe's* blood. This is what I have always worried about happening to him, and it's happened, as I feared.

"Don't worry," Morris says. "The plated vest took the brunt of the shoulder hit. Looks like this one just grazed him," he continues, tipping his chin at Gabe's leg.

My gaze swings back to Gabe's. "You were shot *twice*?"

"I'm fine," Gabe reassures me. "I doubt I'll even need stitches, which I've told Morris here, but he won't let me get up." He peers closely at me. "You okay, babe?"

Tears swamp my eyes and my mouth trembles at how pale he looks. His face is tight with the pain he is successfully hiding from his voice.

"I'm supposed to be asking you that." I bite my lip in an effort to keep myself from crying.

"I've had a lot worse."

At my gasp, he adds, "And I've made it through. This really is nothing. Just a scratch. Are you okay?" He emphasizes the three words, and I know what he's asking. Am I okay with seeing my worst fear come true—almost worst fear. He's still alive, thank God, and his injuries don't appear too serious. One stiff breeze in the wrong direction and the bullets might have been fatal. My heart clenches at the thought of how close he came to being killed.

So no, I'm not okay. And I can't bear to think of what *worse* he's been through. I've seen the scars on his body. I never asked him about them, preferring to bury my head in the sand and not know how they got there.

I hear the wail of sirens getting closer and turn to see several police cars racing toward us and two ambulances a little further back.

"Any word yet on who was shooting?" Luc calls across to Gabe. "Was it Victor?"

"Yeah, we got him," Gabe answers, then hisses when Morris does something to his thigh wound.

"I hope he's got handcuffs on his hands and legs and a couple of men sitting on him so he doesn't get away," Luc says, his voice hard. There was no love lost between him and his father.

"I don't think that's going to be necessary. My guys confirmed he's dead."

"Oh, fuck yes!" Luc exclaims. He kisses the top of Charlie's head. "It's over, darling."

It hits me suddenly how much danger Charlie has been in all this time, despite Victor's first attempt to hurt her when he ran her off the road. All the security I thought was excessive was necessary, after all.

It's horrible to feel glad that someone was killed, but I inwardly echo Luc's sentiment. If Victor is dead, it really is finally over.

"I hope you guys riddled him with a hundred holes," Charlie says with venom. I don't blame her for her bloodthirsty wish. The man had tried to kill her, Luc, the baby, and anyone else who got in the crossfire. As it was, he succeeded in injuring two men, one of whom was fighting for his life.

"Stevie," Mom calls me from the top of the steps. "Could you please help me down? I'd like to see Charlie."

I unglue my lead feet from the tarmac and help Mom, her limp more pronounced after the long day. The stairs are clear since Fraser was moved to lie flat on the tarmac. Kathy is still holding pressure on his wound.

Daphne, Bobbie, and Alex come down the steps as well, escorted by Ortiz. Thankfully, Kathy positions herself to obstruct the view of the injured guard and his bloody wound. Daphne runs to her brother, who hugs her tightly with his free arm. Charlie puts an arm around the frightened teen as well.

"I'm fine, Mom," Charlie says reassuringly. When she tries to get up, Luc stops her.

"Stay down, darling. Wait for the EMTs check you out."

"I barely scraped my knees," she protests.

"Maybe," Mom says when she reaches her. "But we'll go to the hospital anyway and check everything out to make sure the baby is okay too."

Mom's sensible words, tinged with worry, quiet Charlie, who nods and relaxes back against Luc's chest.

The police cruisers come to a screeching halt on the tarmac. When the officers exit their vehicles with hands on their weapons, Morris stands and holds his hands up as he approaches them, explaining what happened.

When the first gurney from the ambulance arrives, Ortiz directs the two EMTs to help Fraser first. Another set of paramedics come with a second gurney. One of them goes to Gabe to assess his injuries while the second kneels in front of Charlie.

I go to Alex, who is taking everything in, still with more excitement than fear at the sirens and lights and police. I move him further away so he can't see as Fraser is placed on a stretcher.

"Go with him, Shep," Gabe says to Kathy. "Keep me updated on his status. Get in touch with Rafe so he can call his wife and make arrangements to get her to the hospital. I'll be there after I wrap up things here."

Kathy nods and follows her boss's orders, but I eye him incredulously. Gabe is lying on his side now so that the EMT can check the wound on the back of his thigh. I look away from the blood smeared all over his leg and focus on his face.

"Wrap things up? You need to go to the hospital, Gabe," I tell him.

"It's just a graze. Another hour or so isn't going to make a difference."

"The lady is right," said the EMT. "Another hour could mean infection. You need to get this cleaned out and possibly stitched up."

"Don't be foolish, Gabe," Mom says sternly when Gabe appears ready to protest. "Sounds like the danger is over. Go to the hospital."

"Boss, we can take care of things here," Morris says. "I'll keep you updated."

"Fine," he agrees reluctantly, "but have two guys follow Charlie's ambulance to keep an eye on her and Luc. Victor is no longer a threat, but until we know exactly what he's been up to, I want to keep some security in place for them and the Hutchinsons. And I want you to stay with the police and get any information you can on how he got here and if there's any evidence on him of anyone else involved."

"Boss, I got this. Go."

Morris goes to the rest of the team, who have been standing in a protective circle around us, keeping an eye for any further danger.

Charlie is bundled onto a gurney and on her way to the hospital. A third ambulance has arrived to take Gabe.

I take a step to follow as he is about to be loaded into the ambulance, but stop when I realize I'm still holding Alex's hand. It gives me pause, enough time to question myself. Perhaps it's best not to give Gabe mixed messages by going with him if I still plan on breaking things off with him.

If? No, it's *when.* Tonight's events made it clearer than ever. I won't be able to go through something like this, or worse, happening again, leaving me broken, the way Mom was when Dad died. I don't want to be on the other end of the phone call that Fraser's wife is getting tonight, getting a call about Gabe on his way to the hospital for a life-threatening injury.

"Go with Gabe, honey," Mom says. "We'll take care of Alex."

My heart rebels at the thought of not going with him to the hospital, but I shake my head. "No, that's okay. I need to call Andi before she hears anything and panics."

She frowns. I avoid her discerning gaze, afraid to see disapproval. But as long as Gabe remains in danger, so does my heart. And if I want to keep my heart intact, I need to keep it safe.

Still, my delicate organ cracks when I see him in the back of the ambulance just before the doors slam shut.

32

Gabe

"WHAT DID YOU FIND out so far?" I ask Rafe when he arrives at the hospital after talking to the local authorities. I'm mad as hell to be stuck in the emergency room, awaiting discharge. Scans of the shoulder show no internal injuries, but some bullshit policy says I can't leave until a doctor signs off. If someone doesn't come in the next ten minutes, I'm walking out.

"I want to know how the son of a bitch knew we were flying in tonight and into this airport."

"He was tracking the jet's tail number. We found a phone on Victor and were able to get into it. There's one outgoing call to Luc on the day of the game and a couple of incoming calls. They appear to be from burner phones, but we'll see if we can find out where they were sold. It seems he mostly used his phone to track Luc and Charlie's movements."

"How the hell did he do that?"

"Believe it or not, using social media. He set up accounts under a fake name and subscribed to anything that had to do with Luc, Charlie, and the Firebirds—celebrity sightings, gossip, that kind of stuff. His search history showed a gossip site article about Joey and Charlie vacationing on Niko's island. Someone also posted a photo of Charlie and Joey getting on Niko's plane earlier, with the tail number visible."

"And he looked it up on one of the flight tracking sites, saw where we were landing. Fuck!"

"Yeah. We need to talk to our tech guys to make it a little harder to track down this kind of stuff about our clients."

"Or at least flag this type of information online and take it down asap," I say. Neither action would stop a stalker bent on stalking, but it might slow them down. "Victor must have already been in the area in order to get here and find a place to hide. The flight was a little over three hours."

Rafe nodded. "He was either waiting near Luc's to catch someone outside or at the Hutchinsons' house—ready to follow through on the threat from a few days ago."

"Probably," I agree. He was quiet after that call. I hate when a threat goes quiet. It almost always means they're busy stewing and planning.

"We're still tracking down where he's been staying the last few weeks and who's been calling him. That information will give us more clues about what he's been up to and if there's any remaining threat."

I nod and look past Rafe when Brent and Luc come into the room. "You're looking better," Luc says to me. "How are you feeling?"

He shakes my hand while Brent greets Rafe.

"Ready to get back to work," I reply, "but Rafe threatened to call our mother if I don't follow doctor's orders."

Brent grins. "He knows that's the only way to keep your ass out of trouble while you heal."

"How's your guy doing? Fraser?" Luc asks.

"It was touch and go for a little while, but the doctors say he's going to pull through, thank God." His wife came to tell me after the doctor updated her a short while ago. "A bullet got him just below the vest."

"I heard your bullet graze was from a ricochet," Brent says. "Thank fuck it wasn't a direct hit."

"Yeah, seems like he was shooting without aim, just trying to hit anyone."

"Even so, he got too fucking close to Charlie. If you hadn't reacted as fast as you did..." Luc trails off, shaking his head.

"No point in thinking about what didn't happen," I tell him. "She's okay and that's all that matters."

"How did he just happen to be there?" Brent asks.

Rafe explains what he'd learned, adding, "We saw from the security cameras, he was hiding in a van in the parking lot. He waited for someone to exit the plane before jumping out and shooting."

I blame myself for not being prepared for such a scenario. Everyone's safety is my responsibility.

"Is this over now that he's dead?" Luc asks. "Is there anyone else, any associates, we need to worry about?"

Rafe shakes head. "So far, it looks like he was on his own, but we'll keep looking into his debts and finances."

Luc lets out a loud exhale, running his hand over his closely cropped curls. "I should have just given him the money. I have more than Charlie and I will ever need to live comfortably, and we're both willing to work for more if we have to."

"That's not the point," I say. "You did the right thing by saying no because it would always have come to this moment after he bled you dry. You've been giving him money for years, and he always came back for more."

"I had a thought or two of dropping the ball or letting it go through my fingers during the game, to give him what he wanted," Brent admits.

"You and me both," Luc says.

"How's Charlie?" Rafe asks.

"Thanks to Gabe, she just has scrapes and bruises." Luc turns to me with a grateful, earnest look. "You saved her from far worse. I'll never be able to repay you for that, Gabe."

I brush off the gratitude. "That's my job, but if I'd done it better, she wouldn't have suffered even a bruise. I'm just glad she and the baby are okay."

Luc holds out his hand for me to shake. "I want to thank you and your team for everything you've done to keep the family safe these last weeks." He turns to Rafe and shakes his hand as well. "I'll talk to you both about having some kind of permanent protective detail from now on for Charlie and Daphne, but I'd like to have a couple of the guys stay on board until then."

I notice he doesn't mention security for himself. Reggie has always been his bodyguard and driver, and it appears Luc intends for that arrangement to continue. But Reggie was hired for his intimidating size and appearance, as well as for being one of Luc's closest friends, not because of his experience in security. I make a mental note to talk to Luc soon about giving Reggie additional training to deal with more than groupies and overzealous fans, just in case.

"Not a problem," Rafe says.

"Yeah, I'll talk to Joey about getting someone for her as well," Brent says. "I think having someone nearby might give her peace of mind if the paps start bothering her."

"Charlie's being discharged," Luc says, looking at his phone. "Take care, man. I'll talk to you soon." Shaking my hand once more and then Rafe's, Luc leaves.

"Get some rest," Brent tells me as he follows Luc.

"I was planning on heading out too, but looks like you need a ride home," Rafe says. "I thought Stevie would be here by your side."

I can hear the question in Rafe's statement. Unfortunately, I don't have an answer. I'd expected her to ride in the ambulance with me, but she'd watched as the doors closed. I'd like to think it's only because she had to take Alex home. But I know better.

Her absence means she's running away from the relationship that we've spent the past few weeks rebuilding. I can practically feel the breakup coming. Panic sets in at the thought. I have to talk to her before she thinks too much about her fears, whatever they may be.

I only hope it's not too late.

33

Stevie

"**S**TEVIE, ARE YOU OKAY?"

I startle at Rafe's sudden appearance behind me as I sit on the old bench by the pond. I'd come here seeking solace, despite the cold.

At least it's a sunny day, though my thoughts are dark with visions of Gabe bleeding like Fraser was. Gabe still and pale on the stretcher...

Looking at Rafe when he sits next to me, I nod and try to smile but can't quite manage it. My eyes are gritty from lack of sleep. I took Alex directly to Andi so she could see for herself that her son was safe. Then I checked on Charlie when she came home from the hospital. Luc said she was resting and the ultrasound looked good, but she needed to be on the lookout for bleeding, pain, and anything that doesn't feel right.

Good advice, especially the last part. I'd ignored the feeling that something was wrong after I'd taken the abortion pills, resulting in an emergency D & C. And then I'd ignored the pain every month for years because doctors, especially male ones, said period pain was normal. They told me to use a heating pad and take over-the-counter pain medicine. Or they prescribed birth control pills to see if that helped. It didn't.

Unable to sleep, I asked one of the remaining bodyguards about Gabe's status. He said Gabe had been released during the night. His wound required a few stitches and his shoulder was bruised. I was relieved, but I still couldn't sleep. I kept picturing Gabe's bloody leg and imagining the worst if the vest hadn't stopped the bullet.

"How is Fraser?" I ask.

"His surgery went well, but it's going to be a long recovery."

"That's good. I mean, about the surgery." I pause and ask, "Have you seen Gabe?"

He tilts his head and frowns. "Yes. I thought I'd see you with him."

My gaze returns to the frozen pond, the sparkling ice almost blinding in the morning sun. "I had to take Alex home," I say.

"Right," he replies. I can't be sure if his tone is sarcastic or if my guilty conscience is making me imagine it.

After a few moments of silence, he puts a hand around my shoulder and hugs me to his side. "He's fine, Stevie. Don't worry. He barely got a scratch."

Two bullets hit him, never mind that neither one went through him. One wrong move or a slight breeze that redirected the bullet by a degree, and Rafe would likely not be saying that right now.

"Did you know my father knew my mother was the one for him the second he set his eyes on her?"

I'm distracted by the sudden turn in conversation.

"Gabe never believed in that kind of thing until he looked up and saw you in a completely different light one day. Told me you were the one for him, the one he was going to marry. Things somehow got screwed up between you, but I don't think that's changed for him. You're still his 'one.'"

A sudden lump forms in my throat. I stay quiet, afraid if I open my mouth, I might sob uncontrollably.

"Something to think about when you feel scared." He gives my shoulders a gentle squeeze before removing his arm. "You look beat. Talk to Gabe so you can hear for yourself he's fine, and then get some rest."

Forcing down the ball of tears, I nod and attempt a smile but can't manage more than a press of my lips. I stand and walk back up to the house, heading straight for my room and directly into my bathroom to turn on the shower.

I enter the steaming spray and allow the hot water beating down on me to wash away the tension from the rigid muscles of my shoulders and back. I force my mind to go blank, but the floodgates abruptly open. The sobs I held back all night finally release. The force of my tears drown out my fear-filled thoughts.

When I come back to awareness, I'm sitting in the tub, my arms clasped around my knees that are pulled to my chest. I have no idea how long I've been crying. Only the cooled water and a headache throbbing against my temples give some indication that it's been a while.

Getting up slowly, I turn off the shower. Drained by my crying jag, I go through the motions of drying off and pulling on a robe. I fall face down on the bed and wait for sleep to come quickly.

Unfortunately, despite my emotional and physical exhaustion, my mind begins to race. Sighing, I turn onto my back and stare up at the ceiling, my earlier circling thoughts coming back to life.

I've been deceiving myself by thinking I'll be able to work through my fears this time, believing it would be easier than living without him. But what kind of life will it be if I live it in fear every day? He was lucky this time, but what about the next?

And there would be a next time. It is the nature of his job and his own nature to put himself in harm's way to protect others. It is why he'd wanted to be a police officer, why he'd turned to the military, and why he founded a company whose mission it is to protect people.

Gabe shielded Charlie with his own body, for which I'll be forever grateful. But it just highlights for me that it is his job to do the same for every client.

I shudder at the thought. All the fears I had when I rejected his marriage proposal have come back full force, not that they'd ever really gone away.

So much for being older and wiser, because I can't do it. Won't do it. To watch him leave the house every morning, knowing it might be the last time I see him, is no way to go through life. I refuse to live that way.

And if that means not being with him...Well, it has to be easier than having to go through this again—or worse.

At least I won't have to worry about him forgiving me for what I did. I was hoping if I explained to him why I made the decision I did, he'd understand. Better than anyone, he knew the strain I'd been under with the amount of responsibility I had back then, sympathized with me when I talked about our finances, and did what he could to help me. Though he hadn't been in a position to do much about the money problems, just having him there to talk to and be my rock had made it all a little more bearable. Without him to support me, I'd had no one and no other choice than the one I'd made.

But there is no longer any need to even tell him about the pregnancy, about any of it. What's the point in breaking his heart with that when I'll be doing it anyway by breaking up with him? Again.

Although, I don't know if he'll run away like last time. There is a chance he might not let me go without a fight.

In that case, I'll have to make sure he's the one who pushes me away—for good.

34

Gabe

I PLAY WITH MY phone, tempted to call Stevie, who I still haven't heard from since the airport last night. I came home from the hospital, then rested for a few hours until Leo and Ari woke up.

They were concerned when they saw me walk with a slight limp due to the pain in my thigh and wearing a sling for my aching shoulder. I've since taken it off so there is no visible evidence of my injury and to prove to them I am fine. Since I had to say something to explain the injuries, I decided to only tell them that I had a little accident and fell, hurting myself. Ari had sweetly kissed my shoulder to make my "ouchie" feel better, while Leo looked at me with grave concern.

Though I need to talk to Stevie, I spend time with my children first to ease their anxiety. I'll have to deal with Stevie's later.

Understanding their need to be close to me, I played Minecraft with Leo earlier with Ari snuggled up next to me while she watched *The Little Mermaid*. She's now making a mess at one end of the kitchen table with her finger-painting, and Leo plays with his Legos at the other end with an episode of *Beyblades X* playing on the iPad. I sit between them with my laptop, catching up on emails and making changes to the schedule. With Victor out of the picture, we're able to take on another client, even with Fraser's absence.

When I stand to get more coffee, Leo watches me carefully. I smile at him, holding up my mug, silently letting him know my intention. Assured I'm not going anywhere, his gaze returns to his show.

On my way to the coffeepot, I stop at the stove to see what Ma has cooking. A pot of tomato sauce is simmering while she forms meatballs and places them on a baking sheet. Spaghetti and meatballs. The kids' favorite—besides pizza, of course.

"I'm going out after dinner, Ma," I tell her in a low voice.

"Another couple of days of rest before you go gallivanting around won't hurt, Gabriel."

I'm not sure if it's concern for my wounds or because she knows I'm going to see Stevie that is the reason for my mother's acerbic tone.

"As you can see, I'm fine. Just a couple of scratches."

Ma scoffs but says quietly so only I can hear her words over Leo's show, "A scratch doesn't require stitches."

Ironic how Ma holds a grudge against Stevie, yet the two are very similar in their concern for me, though they're handling it differently. But then, their experiences are different since my mother has not lost anyone she loves in the line of duty. Why couldn't I have understood this better ten years ago?

Not that my job was usually dangerous at all. In three years, this is the first time I've had to draw my weapon or had one pointed at me. And now that the company has grown, more and more of my time is spent on business development and administrative work—bringing in clients, hiring new team members, and overseeing the management of the company. The amount of time I work as a bodyguard has decreased by more than half—until recently, when Luc and the entire Hutchinson family needed last-minute protection.

I talked to Stevie about my job and thought she had started to see she didn't have to worry so much. Being shot at undermines all the progress I made and means I'm back to square one.

Stevie is scared again about me getting hurt, which is why I need to see her in person and make her understand this was a rare event. But she had pulled away even before the shooting. There's something else going on, and I need to find out what it is. And I will, right after I eat dinner with the kids and put them to bed.

"Daddy," Leo says, holding on to me tightly when we hug goodnight one last time that evening, "are you coming back home tonight?"

He must have overheard me telling Ma that I was going out after dinner. "Of course I am, T-Rex," I say, pulling back so I can look at my son. He appears distraught, tears glittering in his eyes. "You know I call and tell Nonna to let you know if I'm going to be late or away."

"Mommy sometimes didn't call when she went out and the babysitter would get mad," he says, looking away, his voice small and anxious.

I swallow hard before I can ask, "You remember that?"

He nods, his mouth trembling. "I remember one time the babysitter called the police because she had to leave and Mommy didn't come home. What if you don't come home and the police come?"

I pull my little boy against my chest to hide my own wet eyes from the emotions that rise up every time I remember getting the call while I was deployed. Camilla had been in an accident and someone needed to be with them until my mother or I could get to them. That was when I learned about her lover who had been driving the car, and that she often left them with the babysitter when I was away.

I'd hoped the trauma of that experience—his memories of her—had faded, especially with the help of therapy. He appeared to have adjusted well, but apparently not. Has he been suffering from anxiety all this time and was only now giving voice to his fears since I'd been injured?

More than ever, I'm glad I made the decision to move back home so my children could have the same love and security I had growing up. Gathering my roiling emotions and setting them aside for later, I shift back and look my son in the eyes.

Praying I'm saying the right thing, I tell him, "I won't lie and promise you that nothing will ever happen, but I can promise you I will always try my hardest to come home to you. And you will always have family who loves you and to be with you whenever I can't be." Caressing his head, I add, "I love you and Ari so much. More than anything in the world."

"I know. But I still don't want anything to happen to you." His little boy voice cracks with the effort to not cry.

"Ah, my sweet boy." Cradling him, I move to lie down on the bed next to him. "I'm right here." I want to tell him that I'll always be here, but I don't want to make him promises I can't guarantee. His mother already broke enough promises to him.

While I rub Leo's back and murmur soothing words to him, I make a mental note to get in touch with a child psychologist as soon as possible. I have no idea if I said the right things and want to make sure I don't say anything to him that will make his anxiety worse. Though Arianna doesn't remember any of what happened, it's probably a good idea to have both of them seen by a professional again to see if any residual effects remain from their time with Camilla and her abandonment.

When Leo's breath finally evens out into sleep, I ease up from the bed. Adjusting the covers over him, I press a kiss to his forehead and quietly leave the room, keeping the door open a crack.

Now, for another difficult conversation with someone else I love. But first, I join my parents in the living room. Pop is in his usual recliner, dozing off while Ma sits on the sofa with her customary half glass of after-dinner wine. She turns down the volume of the talent competition show on TV when I take a seat next to her. I recap my conversation with Leo before asking her to keep an ear open, in case Leo awakens.

"I'll be home in a couple of hours, but call me if he wakes up."

"That poor baby has been through so much," Ma comments. "Make sure Stevie is up for dealing with it before you let him get too attached to her."

"Teresa." My father's voice, soft but firm, is a warning to his wife to not interfere.

Of course, she doesn't heed his unspoken words. Her mouth tight, she leans over to set her wineglass on the coffee table with a harsh clink. Straightening, she takes my hand in both of her soft ones. "She's broken your heart once. Who's to say she won't do it again, and this time, the children's too?"

Pressing a reassuring kiss to her forehead, I retrieve my hand from hers and stand. Despite her concerned gaze and lips that have softened enough to tremble with emotion, I say firmly, "I won't live my life worrying about the what-ifs, Ma. That's what Stevie is doing and I need to convince her to live in the here and now."

"Hi, Sandra. Do you mind if I come in and talk to Stevie?"

I'm at the Hutchinsons' front door—I figured throwing pebbles at Stevie's window was not going to work this time. But getting through the formidable force that is the Hutchinson matriarch might be more difficult.

"Does she want to talk to you?" Sandra asks, not opening the door fully.

I half-smile, her protectiveness similar to my mother's. "I don't know. But I'm hoping she'll listen to what I have to say to her."

Not satisfied with my answer, she narrows her eyes at me and crosses her arms over her thick robe.

I'm impatient to go to Stevie, but I ask, "How are you doing, Sandra? Feeling okay after everything that went down last night?"

"I'm feeling incredibly grateful." Her entire being softens, and she opens the door wider to let me in. Once I enter the foyer, she hugs me. "Thank you for saving my Charlie."

I enfold her and give a gentle squeeze. Her delicate form reminds me of how much she's been through. Her usual projection of strength wavers as she lets go for a moment, wilting against me with relief.

"I'm glad I was there, but we got lucky."

She pulls away, frowning. "Yes, sometimes we do get lucky, but being good at your job and reacting quickly puts luck on our side."

"Would you mind telling Stevie that?" I ask with a wry twist of my lips.

She sighs and takes a step back. "Oh Gabe. Be patient with her. She loves you."

"And I love her. Why can't that be enough?"

"Unfortunately, fear is sometimes more powerful."

"So what do I do?"

"Continue showering her with love and patience." She hesitates, opens her mouth to say something but changes her mind.

"What?" I prompt. "You can tell me. I appreciate any advice that can help us."

After a thoughtful pause, she says, "I've told Stevie to consider professional counseling for the two of you if you need someone objective to help you work through whatever issues you're having."

Despite recognizing the value of a professional when it comes to helping Leo, my first instinct is to balk at having a stranger, someone who doesn't know me or understand how much I love her, meddle in my relationship with Stevie. But with Sandra's steady, compassionate gaze on me, I nod. "I'll do whatever it takes."

"Even if it means changing careers?"

The question gives me pause. The company is my livelihood, something I'm proud to have built from scratch with Rafe. My pride and joy, as if it was another child. But it's *not* my child. I have two children at home, and one of them is scared I won't come home. Like Stevie is.

Fuck me. While I recognized where her fear stemmed from, I realize now a part of me felt like she'd been trying to control or manipulate me with it. But she wouldn't do that to me. Just like Leo isn't doing it when he voices his anxiety.

She loved me and couldn't bear the thought of losing me, like she'd lost her father. Like Leo is afraid of losing me. Her fears are visceral, not something she can control with a switch.

It suddenly becomes crystal clear.

I beam at Sandra and clasp her shoulders with excitement, smacking a kiss on each cheek.

"Sandra, who needs an objective stranger when we have you?" Hugging her, I say, "Thank you."

She gives me a puzzled smile. "You're welcome."

Calling a good night over my shoulder, I bound up the stairs—at least the first couple until my thigh protests. I limp the rest of the way to Stevie's door and knock.

When she opens it, I take her in my arms and squeeze her to me, despite my aching shoulder.

"I love you so fucking much," I exclaim, pressing my lips to the top of her head. When she tenses, I realize this is not what she's expecting. Everything is suddenly illuminated in my mind, but she's still in the dark.

My arms loosen around her, unwilling to let her go, but I take a step back. Figuratively and physically. But she surprises me by pulling me back to her and lifting her face to kiss me. Her eyes shine with a mix of emotions, but the one I see so clearly is love.

Despite everything, she still loves me. Unable to resist what she's offering—and asking for in return—I lower my head and meet her soft lips.

She opens her mouth to deepen the kiss, her tongue begging for entrance to mine. Instead, I kiss her upper lip, her lower one, the corner of her mouth, keeping my touch gentle. She tries to follow to recapture my mouth, so I cup her face to hold her still while I shower it with tender kisses. The tip of her nose. Between her brows. Each eyelid. Down her cheek and across her jaw. Until she finally melts into my arms and sighs.

Only then do I take her mouth again, parting her lips to slide my tongue against hers. The kiss stays soft and slow, though my blood flows south and my heart rate picks up into a gallop. Desire and passion are tempered with love. So much love.

We'll get through this. We're going to make it this time.

With that thought, I take my time to remove her clothes with trembling hands, touching and kissing every inch of skin I reveal. She mirrors my actions, and together, we undress each other. I pick her up in my arms and carry her to the bed, careful to put most of her weight on my good arm. I slowly lower her to the mattress and take her in, burning the image into my brain. She's fucking perfect, from her long legs to her curves up to the swirls of dark caramel-colored hair around her head to the expression on her face, her beautiful blue eyes wide and shining with love.

With my gaze on hers, I move over her. She widens her thighs to make room for me, sliding her silky-smooth calves along mine. My cock reaches for the entrance to her sweet tight pussy, but I hold still above her, bracketing my arms along her head. Keeping my eyes open, I lower my mouth to hers again, continuing with the softest of kisses until neither of us can hold back anymore. Our eyes close as the kiss deepens. I lower my body to hers, my erection notching into place between her legs and slipping between her folds without entering her.

In unspoken agreement, we keep our movements slow, soft, gentle. I can't remember ever making love like this before, not even her first time. I'd broken out in a sweat back then, trying to hold myself back.

But tonight, though I'm as desperate to be inside her as I was back then, I want to treasure these moments of being wrapped in each other's arms.

I want to enjoy the sensation of her hands roaming over my back, from the base of my spine to the nape of my neck, leaving a trail of goosebumps in the wake of every tender caress.

I want to savor the taste of her mouth...the touch of her soft skin...the sound of her low hums as our tongues tangle...of the scent of her lavender and vanilla fragrance mixed with that of her growing desire...

My thick length glides against her with ease, her slickness fully lubricating me. As our passion burns hotter, our breathing quickens to quiet panting. Our gentle rocking against each other gains force but not speed. On my next upward stroke, I slip into her. She's so wet, I have to stop myself from sinking in all the way to the hilt. We both groan as her walls cling to my head, grasping for more. Without breaking our kiss, I brace myself on my good leg and move my hips in a slow, undulating motion. With each measured thrust, I reach farther and deeper inside her until I'm fully seated within her. Only then do I release her mouth and a long, low groan of steeped pleasure.

Okay, now I'm sweating. Fuck, she feels so good, squeezing around me with each small circle of her hips. Her fingers knead my ass, encouraging me to go faster, harder, but I keep my movements slow, going longer, deeper, harder on each upward thrust.

When she starts to whimper, begging for more, I roll us halfway over so we're lying on our sides. I take a breast in one hand while the other slides down between us. Both thumbs get busy—one on her nipple, the other on her clit, rubbing, circling, pinching—until she's panting into my mouth. She pushes me onto my back and takes control, driving herself onto my cock to chase her orgasm. I allow her to use me, helping her reach the peak with my thumb on her clit.

As her body tenses with her impending release, I bring her mouth back to mine and lock my lips overs hers. A split second later, her orgasm begins to milk my cock with strong pulses. I resist the urge to roll her onto her back in pursuit of my own release. While I prefer to have her on her back, her legs over my shoulder as I drive into her, I don't want to rip open my stitches and remind her of my injuries.

"Ride me, babe," I tell her, breaking our kiss.

She rises above me, a vision of a siren—no, a sensuous mermaid—her full bare breasts thrust out as she lifts her arms to push her tangled fall of hair away from her face. She keeps her hands buried in her hair as she circles her hips over me, her pace slow, all urgency having left her.

"You're so fucking beautiful," I say.

She opens her eyes and smiles, bringing her hands down to my chest to lean over and kiss me. Before I can trap her mouth with mine, she pushes away and changes her rhythm. It becomes faster, harder. I hold her waist and bend my good leg to support myself so I can meet her hips every time she propels herself over my cock.

"Oh fuck," she cries out. Despite her recent orgasm, she appears to be reaching for another.

"Touch yourself, baby," I encourage her. I'd rather do it myself, but I'm too close. I need her to get herself to the edge fast. Sliding my arm to her back, I pull her down to bring her breast over my mouth. I play with her nipple, sucking, licking, tonguing it. Her hips go into overdrive. It's taking everything I have to hold back my climax, so I hold myself still, my entire body tense.

I'm shaking, sweating, trying not to come before her. She cries out in frustration as her orgasm stays out of reach. Putting my hands on her hips to stop her, I tell her, "Get up here, baby. Sit on my face."

She bites her lip, then does as I ask. "Good girl," I murmur when she crawls up my body to hover over my head. I pull her down over my mouth, keeping my eyes open to watch her grab the headboard with one hand, the other cupping her breast and playing with her nipple. Within moments, she's grinding herself on my mouth as I suck on her clit and flick it hard and fast. She comes in a rush over my face, using the crook of her arm to muffle her cries.

Despite my aching cock that's ready to burst, I don't rush her. I wait for her to come down from her high before helping her move back over my raging erection. I pull her down hard, lifting my hips to meet her. The movement triggers a flutter of pulsing inside her that contracts around my cock. I'm coming even as she bounces over me. I grab her hips to stop her and hold her tight against me. I stay buried deep as I empty myself inside her.

She folds herself over me, and ignoring the wetness that still clings to my lips, takes my mouth with hers in a kiss full of passion and love.

I wrap my arms around her and hold her to me as our kisses become gentler, slower, until we're back to where we started, with soft tender touches of our lips.

"Hi," I murmur, smoothing a hand over her hair, my lips curving into a smile of contentment.

"Hi." The word is barely a whisper. She doesn't smile back.

Before I can roll us onto our sides for some post-coital cuddling, she scrambles off me and stands, making my mouth water at the sight of her perfect ass. Only when she pulls on a robe to cover herself do I ask, "What are you doing? Come back to bed."

She moves to the window and sits in the chair nearby. "We need to talk."

"Yes, we do." I ease myself up and sit against the headboard, putting one hand behind my head. The edges of my mouth tremble with the need to smile in satisfaction when her gaze goes to my biceps, then roams over my bare chest. I pat the mattress next to me. "Come here and let's talk."

She shakes her head. "We shouldn't have done this. I didn't mean for this to happen, to lead you on."

"Lead me on?"

"I can't be with you, Gabe."

I straighten, swinging my legs over the edge of the bed. Her words are what I feared on my way over, but not now, not after we'd made love the way we did.

"Babe, I know you're afraid," I say, pulling on my pants. "I understand, especially after what happened last night. But I don't want you to worry about that anymore. I'm going to stop doing field work, take on an administrative role—"

"No. No, you don't have to do that for me."

I go to her, trying not to limp. The workout in bed has inflamed the wound, making it sore again. But I'd suffer through worse for the divine experience of what just occurred.

"Babe, I'm doing it for us. For you and me, for the kids. Leo—"

"No, you can't. At least not for me. I can't ask you to do it for me. You'd come to resent me, not being able to do what you love."

"I love you more. Don't you know that by now?" I shake my head at my stupidity. "No, of course you don't. I've never proven it to you."

Her voice pitches higher, almost desperate. "You don't need to prove anything to me. I know you love me. I love you too."

My heart stumbles at finally hearing the words.

"Stevie," I breathe, overcome. I drop to one knee, intending to wrap my arms around her hips and put my head in her lap. But she jumps up, almost knocking me back as she rushes past me.

"No. Please, Gabe. Don't. Don't do that again."

I look at her in shock until I realize what she means. I jump to my feet, wincing at the pain when I forget to use my uninjured leg to push off the floor.

"That's not what I was doing, I swear. I know you're not ready for that yet. We'll take our time. I'll wait however long you need. As long as I get to be with you."

She still looks panicked, shaking her head. "No. No, I don't want you to wait for me. Please don't—"

Desperation and my own panic make my voice sharp when I say, "What do you want from me? I'm trying to prove to you that I'm worth the risk, giving you what you need. Meet me halfway. Or even part of the way. Please," I beg.

"Stop, Gabe. Don't."

"Stevie, I've known you were the one for me, my soulmate, since I was seventeen years old. I forgot that ten years ago when I stormed out. I was an insensitive idiot, a selfish asshole." I run a hand through my hair, feeling ashamed of my stupidity for proposing when she was just eighteen and scared, and then leaving her. Looking back, what I did was an immature gesture of *I'll show you how dangerous my job can be.*

"I'm sorry. I should have said that a long time ago. I'm sorry, baby."

"If you knew what I did, you wouldn't want me. Trust me." Her voice is thick with tears, her eyes shimmering with them. I want to go to her, comfort her, but she's closed off, her arms crossed tightly in front of her.

"What are you talking about? There's nothing that would make me not want you." I come to a stop in front of her, holding my palms up to let her know I won't touch her. "Whatever it is, I will always love you, Stevie. Always."

Her tears overflow, forming tracks down her tormented face. I ache to touch her, hold her, but I drop my arms, my fingers curling into helpless fists, unable to bear her backing away from me.

"Don't cry, babe. You're killing me. Just tell me what it is. I can handle it."

"You said you wouldn't have forgiven Camilla if she'd had an abortion."

She takes a shuddering breath as I look on in confusion. What does Camilla have to do with—?

"Well, I did."

I stare at her, brows furrowed, when she doesn't continue. Did what? Then her words sink in, my brain connecting her two statements. My knees almost give out as my hearts skips a few beats before it restarts, thudding hard. I stumble back, the backs of my legs hitting the mattress. I sink onto the bed. Does she mean—? I shake my head, trying to focus on what she's saying.

"I wasn't going to tell you. I didn't want to hurt you unnecessarily. But then you said you love me and I knew we couldn't move forward until I told you what I did. And now that you know..." She hitches one shoulder. "You won't be able to forgive me for it."

"What?" Her words are scrambled, not making any sense.

"I had an abortion while you were in bootcamp," she says baldly, her direct words finally coming through loud and clear.

Oh fuck. I grab my head and bend over, elbows on knees. *Oh fuck. What did I do?*

"I understand if you can't forgive me," she continues, her voice devoid of emotion, "but I felt it was the only choice I had at the time."

I can't think clearly. Until I can, I can't continue this conversation. I stand to dress quickly while she watches in sad resignation.

"I'm not running away, if that's what you're thinking." Hoping? Why would she want that, unless she's looking for an excuse to end this without the guilt of being the one to break things off again? I shake my head to clear it. It doesn't help. "I just need to process this for a minute. Give me some time, okay?"

She nods, but her expression indicates she's sure I'm not coming back. I don't even know what I'm feeling right now, except that I'm devastated that she had to go through that without me because of my actions. I press a kiss to her forehead on my way out, making sure she knows I love her. But I say the words anyway, in case I need to make it clear.

"I love you, Stevie."

35

Gabe

"**Y**OU OKAY, BRO?"

I glance over at Brent as he comes out his penthouse overlooking Central Park. Sounds from the party inside become muffled again when he closes the glass doors and comes to stand beside me at the metal balustrade of the terrace. He invited a bunch of us over for a guys' night after the Firebirds' last regular season game, which they won, earning them a first-round bye. Joey went to Luc and Charlie's for a girls' night.

Luc and some other Firebirds teammates are inside where it is much warmer. Despite the outdoor firepit, I'm freezing my ass off but can't bring myself to join the fun and games inside. My mind is on Stevie, as it has been for most of the past week.

I haven't called her since her revelation because I'm still trying to take it in. I don't want to talk to her until I know what to say. One wrong word could send her running again, this time for good. But my thoughts won't stop bouncing around long enough for me to get any clarity.

I take the bottle of beer Brent hands me and clink it with his before taking a long swig. My gaze goes back to the view of the city lights surrounding the mostly dark rectangle of the park.

"Sometimes, I still can't believe you're a big fucking deal with all the glitz and glamour and girls—well, just one girl now—but, damn, look at all this." I gesture with the bottle to include the large terrace and the larger penthouse behind us. "You done good, Hutch."

"You haven't done so badly yourself, D'Angelo. Badass Navy SEAL and guardian of the rich and famous."

"Hm." I shrug off the compliment. "You ever wonder how things might have been different for your family if your father and RJ were still alive?"

Brent turns serious and stares out into the night. "I used to, all the time, but it was useless. I had to stop or it would have driven me fucking nuts. Why?" he asks, swiveling to face me, leaning a hip against the railing.

I hitch one shoulder, avoiding his gaze. I know better than to underestimate what lies beneath his carefree, playboy image...Well, no longer a playboy now that he's with Joey.

"Just thinking about the paths we take in life, the choices we make, and how different life would be today if we had taken that other path, picked the other option."

"Are you talking about joining the SEALs?"

"Among other things."

"Like Stevie," he guesses. "I always wondered why you two broke up."

I take another drink of beer before facing him and answering. "I asked her to marry me when she graduated high school. She said no."

"She said no?" He hoots with laughter.

I glare at him.

"Sorry, man." He grins, not looking sorry at all. "It's just good to know I'm not the only one who can't get a girl to say yes."

The corner of my mouth ticks up in amusement. "How many times have you proposed to Joey?"

He's not laughing now. His grin turns into a scowl. "Too many fucking times, no matter how often I tell her I've had enough time to know I'm sure it's what I want. Who would have thought such a sweet girl could be so damned stubborn?" he grumbles.

I shake my head. "I'm just amazed you have the capacity to keep asking after getting rejected so often." I sigh. "I wish I had handled it better when Stevie said no. Instead, I flew off the handle and told her to get—" I wince and don't complete the sentence, forgetting for a moment that Brent is her brother first, my friend second, no matter how close we are.

"Jesus, Gabe." He abruptly straightens and glares at me, his back up in defense of his sister. "What was she, eighteen? She was still young, and pretty fucking smart to say no."

"You can't say anything I haven't already told myself. That path right there, that decision, is one that changed the course of my life—and hers—and set things into motion that I might regret for the rest of my life."

"What do you mean?"

I don't respond right away, my thoughts starting their tornadic activity that I can't slow down and make sense of. Finally, I only say, "If Stevie had accepted my proposal, I wouldn't have enlisted and joined the SEALs. I wouldn't have met and married—and divorced—Camilla. But that would mean no Leo and Ari." I can't imagine a world without them, yet the path I'm on now is a world without the child Stevie and I created together.

What would I do differently, knowing what I know now? Any one decision I changed would alter who I am today—and who would be in my life.

What if I had stayed? Would our relationship—our love—have lasted under the pressure of a baby, my job, her fears? As mature as Stevie was back then, she was young, like Brent said. I was also young and clearly immature.

This circular thought pattern makes me want to avoid thinking about the topic altogether. Which means I have yet to get in the right frame of mind to go back to her to talk about it. Not wanting her to get the wrong idea, I've been texting her every morning and every night for the past week with short, simple messages that require no response. I'm not looking to have this conversation over text, only to let her know I'm still here, trying to get my head on straight.

"I had no idea you proposed to her. But then, it seems I'm the last one my sisters tell anything to." He scowls.

Probably because he takes his role as man of the house seriously, one he took on when he was fourteen. He thought it meant he had to threaten anyone that messed with his sisters. We used to tease him about how he scared all the boys away from Stevie—until me, because I told him she was it for me, the love of my life.

It made sense he might not know, but did she tell anyone else in her family? Her friends? About anything?

I would feel worse than I already do if she went through the ordeal all alone. Based on how we used to talk about having a big family, the decision couldn't have been an easy one.

It's not my place to reveal to him what happened, so I stay quiet.

"Hey! Why the hell are you guys standing out in the fucking cold?" Luc comes out and joins us at the railing, standing beside me. He glances between me and Brent and raises his brows. "I can leave if you two are having a moment here."

"Fuck off," I tell him. Our relationship has evolved into an easy friendship since the shooting.

"Let's ask the expert here," Brent says. "How did you get Charlie to say yes to you the first time you proposed?"

I don't need to wonder if Luc and Charlie are getting married for the sake of the baby, like when I asked Camilla. They clearly love each other.

Luc grins. "Actually, I got her to say yes both times I proposed. Maybe you should get your girls pregnant."

"Not funny, asshole." Brent scowls again.

No, the idea of getting Stevie pregnant isn't funny at all.

"I can't believe both of you are with my sisters and I have to listen to this kind of shit now."

Luc laughs. "Hey, you asked."

When Brent looks like he's actually contemplating it, Luc reaches across in front of me and smacks Brent's chest to bring him back to reality.

"I was kidding. You know Charlie wouldn't marry me just because of that. And Joey wouldn't either. Despite her tender heart, that girl has a backbone of steel."

"That's what I said before." Brent grins and says with pride, "It's one of the things I love most about her, when it's not driving me bat-shit crazy."

"Gabe, you taking the leap too?" Before I can answer Luc, he says, "Shit, that means we'll all be brothers-in-law. How about that?"

"Gabe still needs to learn to hang on to Stevie before he can propose," Brent says. "Not that Luc asked for my blessing before he asked Charlie to marry him, nor would I have given it to him if he had..." He pauses to mock glare at Luc. "But I give you my permission, Gabe. I still remember when you told me you were going to marry her one day." His eyes narrow as he figures out the timing. "Apparently, you'd already been dating a year when you said that. Better get it right this time and don't fucking hurt her." He punches my bicep lightly, but there's a warning note beneath the joking tone. "Now let's go inside. My fingers are frozen and I'm pretty sure my balls are about to freeze too."

Despite the cold, I take my time following the two men inside. Brent is right. I need to get it right this time.

36

Stevie

"**E**ARTH TO STEVIE."

"Sorry, what?" I snap out of my thoughts and focus on the faces looking at me with varying degrees of humor. While the guys are gathered at Brent and Joey's place uptown, the women are at the other end of Manhattan at Luc and Charlie's to make plans for her bridal shower and wedding.

Charlie was supposed to have come to Connecticut for the weekend to pack up the rest of her stuff now that she's officially moved in with Luc. But she started spotting a few days ago, so her doctor put her on modified bed rest.

"You just agreed to a fluorescent color scheme for the brides-maids' dresses. Yours is orange."

"Over my dead body," I deadpan.

Charlie pouts. "It's my wedding and you already agreed. Everyone here heard you say yes when I asked if it was okay with you." She looks around at the others to back her up.

Andi and Joey can't hold back their laughter. Even Mom is smiling, which clues me in to the fact that no such conversation has taken place. As deep into my thoughts as I was, I could have just as easily agreed to going naked without realizing it.

"Ha ha. Very funny," I say, scowling.

"I know. I'm a riot," Charlie replies, smirking back at me.

"Okay, girls. Do you think you can act your age now so we can get through this list?" Andi asks from beside me.

"Yes, *Mother*," Charlie answers with mock contrition.

"Joey, I thought I was organized and detail-oriented, but your lists are a mile long."

"Are you complimenting her, Stevie, or are you whining?"

"Charlie, don't start again." Joey bumps her shoulder against Charlie's in rebuke. "Stevie's right. I did go a little overboard with the lists, but between the two showers and the wedding itself, I didn't want to miss anything," she explains.

I do my best to stay tuned in to the discussions of showers and weddings, but my mind insists on going back to my last night with Gabe. I didn't intend to make love with him, but the way he'd held me tight, looked at me with such love...and having him with me, alive and in one piece...

Anticipating that he'd come to see me as soon as he could, I was prepared to tell him about the abortion. Believing he would walk away once I did, I wanted one last time with him.

And I don't regret it for a second. His lovemaking was so tender and loving. I can still feel his strong arms around my body, holding me close as he moved inside me.

I'd felt every inch of him, every bare inch, and hadn't been able to bring myself to stop him to put on a condom. It wasn't really required since I'm also on birth control in the rare chance I become pregnant. The doctor who finally believed my pelvic pain was not normal performed tests and discovered intrauterine scarring, making pregnancy unlikely. However, it's not impossible, though the doctor warned me of the risk of miscarriages. But even before that diagnosis, I'd used two forms of birth control, never wanting to be in the situation of having to make that kind of decision again.

By finally telling Gabe about the abortion, it appears I've accomplished what I set out to do—pushed him away. Despite his short daily texts—simple messages like *have a good day* or *I love you*—he's made no effort to see me or finish our conversation about what I revealed.

"Are you okay, Stevie?"

I'm forced out of my thoughts when I feel a hand on my shoulder. Everyone is looking at me with concern, but it's Andi who is gently rubbing my shoulder. When I blink, a tear runs down my cheek and I realize why they are all looking at me that way.

"I think Gabe and I are over," I blurt out. "Again."

"Oh, honey," Mom says, taking my hand. "I'm so sorry."

"What happened?" asks Charlie. "I thought you two had found your way back to each other and were happy together."

A part of me wants to tell them everything. About the details of the breakup ten years ago, the subsequent abortion, the likelihood of infertility. But I can't drop all that on them when this is supposed to be a happy occasion for Charlie—one that is in painful contrast to my situation a decade ago. I don't want to ruin it for her or make anyone feel like they have to tiptoe around me.

"Is it because he was shot on the job?" Andi asks with gentle concern.

Before I can answer, Charlie says with much less tact, "Because he was shot? The other night was scary, but Gabe could be an accountant and still die crossing the street, or get hit by a drunk driver, or..." She makes a circling motion with her outstretched hand. "What was the name of that contractor who worked on the house and kept asking you out? The poor guy died of a brain aneurysm last year, about a year after getting married."

I hadn't heard about that and feel a pang. He'd been a nice man, handsome enough, and a little bit older. I'd been tempted to give in to his persistent efforts, thinking it would be better to be with someone I didn't love because it would hurt less if anything happened to him. I'd been ashamed of my selfish thoughts. He'd seemed like a good man who deserved more than I could give him, so I'd refused him every time he asked me out.

I hope the woman he'd eventually married had loved him whole-heartedly, the way I never could have, before he'd died. But what that poor woman must be going through now that she'd lost him. And that's exactly what I've always wanted to avoid.

Charlie has a point, but the risk is much higher in Gabe's field of work. While he said he was going to change his role, I don't want him to do that for me. If we get back together, I want him to be to do what he loves.

"Charlie," Mom says, frowning at her, "an accident or un-expected health issue is quite different from putting yourself in harm's way every day." She turns to me. "But what your sister is saying so inelegantly is that you can't live your life in fear of something that may never happen. You'll miss out on so much good if you live that way."

Mom takes my hand in hers, her mouth turned down in sorrow and guilt. "I'm sorry I didn't realize you were still struggling with what happened, sweetheart. If I had known, I would have made sure you continued your therapy."

"Mom, it's not your fault. You couldn't have known since I never said anything. Besides," I say, shrugging, "I didn't feel like therapy was helping anyway."

"Sometimes you need to try a few times with different people," Joey says, her voice gentle and sympathetic. "I didn't find the right one for me until my third try. She really helped me deal with my father's abandonment and my mother's death."

The thought of baring my soul to strangers over and over until I find the one who can help sounds daunting.

"Maybe the one you recommended for Luc can help," Charlie says to Joey. "She's been amazing for him. Without her, he would not have been ready for what we have now. And if I had your fears, Stevie, I would do everything possible to figure out how to work through them, because I could never give up having Luc in my life, even if, God forbid, I knew we only had a few years instead of a lifetime together." Charlie looked at Mom. "Would you have walked away from Dad if you knew it was going to end the way it did?"

Mom shakes her head. "Never, but I didn't go through the childhood trauma of losing someone the way you girls did." She raises a hand when Charlie is about to interrupt. "Each of you have dealt with it in your own ways. Brent had his nightmares and was driven to succeed because he felt the burden of taking care of us. Georgie left at the first opportunity and, I hate to say it, likely married a little too impulsively."

She turns to me. "Stevie's afraid to take a risk and let herself love. Even you, Charlie, though you appear to have adjusted with no issues, have a strong need for a tight-knit family that is at odds with your need for independence." She smiles gently at my sister, who looks pensive at hearing Mom's observation.

"I loved your dad from the moment I laid eyes on him, and it just grew stronger every day until I loved him with every fiber of my being. Until he was a part of me. I may have found happiness with someone else who was safer, but the kind of love we had comes once in a lifetime, and if I had let him go because I was afraid every time he walked out the door to go fight fires, I would have missed out on the very best part of living."

"So you were scared? When he left for work?" I ask.

"Every single time."

"Did Dad know?"

"Yes, he knew, though I never told him." She smiles, remembering. "Why do you think he never left without giving me a kiss, even if we were in the middle of a fight?"

"I thought it was just because you guys were sappy," Charlie quips, wrinkling her nose.

"But, Mom, how did it not break you to watch him walk away each time, knowing it might be the last time you see him alive?" I ask.

"Because that's not what I was thinking about when he walked out."

"What were you thinking?"

Mom brushes a hand over her my hair. "I was thinking about how lucky I was to have this man who loved me, shared a life with me, gave me a house full of wonderful kids."

I shake my head, unable to fathom that kind of thinking. "But it had to hurt that much worse because you'd given yourself, your heart, so completely."

"It nearly broke me when he and RJ died. But I believe that it would have hurt so much worse if I'd let that kind of love go, always wondering what might have been."

"It's the things you don't do that you'll regret, more than the things you do," Charlie says, with Joey chiming in on the last few words.

I remember Mom saying something like that to us, more than once, while growing up. Apparently, those two had been listening.

Mom smiles. "Exactly. My heart might have been safe from pain and loss, but it wouldn't have been whole, not without your father. And RJ. My sweet, beautiful boy." She rubs a hand over her heart as if to ease the pain it is feeling, similar to how I often do when thinking about the baby I'll never have.

She squeezes my hand gently. "You don't want to go through that loss again, of losing someone you loved, so you think it's better to not to love or have that person in your life. But I can't imagine a life without your father and brother, of the joy of loving them and of them loving me in return. A lifetime wouldn't have been enough, but your dad and I had eighteen wonderful years as husband and wife. And I cherish the memories of all of RJ's firsts—his first smile, first word, first step..."

She smiles, her gaze turned inward. "First touchdown, first girlfriend...So many of them." Focusing on us again, she asks, "Do you know how many mothers don't get even that much, for one reason or another? And I have five more beautiful children your father gave me. He lives on in each of you. In the color of your eyes and Georgie's, in Brent's nose and smile, in Charlie's blond hair and taste in music. Even in Bobbie, when she moves her head a certain way. And the memories. Ah, the times we had."

When Mom's eyes stare off into the distance at something only she can see, Charlie breaks in. "Ew. Stop that, Mom! I can guess what you're picturing." Despite her words, she swipes her fingers under her eyes to remove the tears.

Mom laughs. "You don't know how close we came to one of you walking in on us, with so many of you in the house. It was almost impossible to get any privacy. I remember once, you and Georgie must have been about three, when..."

I watch Mom as she recalls the funny moments of raising five children in a three-bedroom house with a husband who couldn't keep his hands off her. Not that she says it in so many words, but I remember Dad always touching Mom in some small way. A hand around her waist when they stood next to each other, a kiss on her hand when she passed him a plate at dinner, a lingering pat on the butt when he kissed her before he left for work. As an adolescent, I had been embarrassed to witness my parents sharing these intimate moments. As an adult, I can only wonder how she's able to survive with only the memories.

I can't imagine feeling anything but grief and torment if I lost Gabe that way. And if I haven't made him hate me with my confession, can I force myself to stay with him, despite my fears, and pretend every day that I'm okay as he kisses me goodbye each morning?

"Brent better propose again, very soon. I'm ready to say yes," Joey says, her eyes shining with tears. "Or maybe I'll propose to him. I'm wasting time, being so silly and stubborn, telling myself it's for his sake when, really, I'm just scared he'll change his mind."

"Sweetheart, you could wait until you're old and gray and he'll never change his mind. My son is as crazy in love with you as his father was with me."

Joey's tears overflow. "Then I'm the luckiest woman in the world."

Charlie takes Joey's hand and snuggles against her side. "Mom, tell us about some more of your memories of RJ and Dad."

Seeing Mom laugh at another memory she shares, I begin to feel the faintest tingle of hope.

It's the things you don't *do that you'll regret more...*Or to paraphrase, the *risks* you don't take...

Maybe I can do this, because what I feel for Gabe, what we have between us, shouldn't be taken for granted or thrown away. And wasting the time I could have with him for fear of losing him too soon would rob me of our cherished moments together—in whatever time we're given.

Isn't loving him and being loved by him worth every risk?

37

Stevie

I AWAKEN SEVERAL HOURS later, in the early morning, to sounds of panicked voices. Rushing out of bed, I open the door of the guest room and look over the stair railing to see Luc carrying Charlie out of the elevator on the first floor. For a second, I think I've intruded on a romantic moment, with Charlie dressed in a silky nightgown and robe and Luc with his shirt half buttoned, but then I hear Luc's shout.

"Reg! Are you here?"

A voice comes out of a cell phone one of them is holding. "I'm almost there, boss. Sixty seconds."

"Luc! What's happening? What's wrong with Charlie?" I call as I run down the stairs.

Luc tilts his head to look up at me. "She's bleeding and cramping. I'm taking her to the emergency room."

"Oh, God! Charlie!"

"It's okay, Stevie."

My legs almost fold in relief when I hear her voice, albeit tight with pain.

"Should I...? I want to come with you."

"Sorry, Stevie," Luc says. "I'm not waiting. Ask Ortiz to make arrangements to bring you to the hospital."

"Of course. Okay." I reach the front door at the same as Luc and Charlie. "I'll get it." I slip past them and open it. "Charlie." I put a hand on my sister's head.

"Don't worry. It's okay."

Despite her calming words, I see the worry in her eyes. Luc is beyond that, his eyes wild with fear.

"It has to be okay. I'm not losing you. I just found you." He holds her closer to his heart before he carefully goes down the steps just as Reggie screeches the SUV to a stop. Ortiz opens the back door for Luc.

From the light of the streetlamp, I see Charlie trying to reassure Luc, cupping his cheek and saying, "It'll be fine, you'll see."

"God, I hope so," he says, before gently lowering her into the back seat. He and Ortiz exchange a few words while he fastens her seatbelt, then runs around to the other side.

When the SUV takes off, Ortiz lets me know he's called his replacement in early, and he'll drive us as soon as he gets here. Nodding, I whirl back into the house to get dressed.

"I heard a commotion. What's going on?" Mom asks from the landing upstairs, leaning on her cane.

I start up the stairs. "Charlie started bleeding, so Luc is taking her to the hospital. Ortiz is going to drive us to the hospital. Do you want me to help you get dressed?"

Mom shakes her head. "You go on and get ready. I'll be fine."

I head to my guest room while calling Brent to let him and Joey know what's going on. I debate calling Andi, who went home instead of staying over. I don't want to wake her when there's nothing she can do. She has to get Alex to school and open the shop. Deciding to text her when I have more information, I get dressed.

As soon as I'm ready, I go to the front door to wait for Mom and Ortiz. I can see the sky through the windows of the multi-story foyer, lightening with the sunrise.

"Bobbie and DeeDee are going to be mad we didn't take them," I note when Mom steps off the elevator.

"Probably," she agrees, "but there's no need to worry them until we know exactly what's going on. I'll wait to call Georgie, too, once we know."

My phone dings with an incoming text. "Ortiz is ready for us outside."

Twenty minutes later, Mom and I are directed to a private waiting area for VIP patients of the maternity ward. Brent and Joey join us a little while later, but it is almost an hour before Luc comes in to give us an update. He looks haggard and scared. Mom puts an arm around him while he fills us in on the condition of Charlie and the baby.

"The baby seems to be fine, but Charlie's blood pressure is high. They've managed to stop the bleeding. They might have to deliver the baby, but since her lungs haven't completed developed, they want to try to keep her inside as long as possible. They also want to keep an eye on Charlie's blood pressure. I said that, didn't I? Sorry." He runs a hand back and forth over his short curls a few times. "They're hoping complete bed rest will help and they're going to keep her here, at least for a couple of days, to monitor both of them."

"Did they say why she started bleeding?" Mom asks.

Luc presses his fingers to his eyes. I'm not sure if it's due to stress or to prevent us from seeing his tears.

"It's likely from the fall in Miami and something about the placenta." He looks at us, his eyes red. "I'm sorry. I don't remember exactly what the doctor said."

Mom rubs his back. "It's okay, sweetheart. Charlie's getting the best medical care possible, and they'll make sure she and the baby are just fine."

I don't know how Mom can be so calm and positive with her daughter lying in a hospital bed. It's all I can do to not go into a dark room and huddle into a ball and never come out. Despite our differences and sibling bickering, I love my sister. If anything happened to her...

Turning to the windows, I squeeze my eyes shut in an effort to stem the welling tears, not only for Luc's sake, but because I'm afraid that once I start, I won't be able to stop. Between the terrifying ordeal last week and memories of the terror I'd felt ten years ago when I was bleeding and in pain, I'm not handling this as well as Mom is.

Despite all the suffering I witnessed during my travels and talking to people who survived immeasurable loss, I still can't understand why bad things happen to good people or how anyone can keep going after such a tragedy.

I mentally slap myself. Nothing bad is going to happen to Charlie or the baby!

Forcing myself to stay positive, I keep a vigil with my family throughout the day. Ortiz dropped off Bobbie and Daphne when they insisted on coming after waking up and hearing the news. Since the Firebirds have a bye week during the first-round of playoffs, Coach has given Luc and Brent permission to miss practice. Not that anything was going to pry Luc away from Charlie's side. The rest of us were allowed to see her in small groups but had to keep the visits shorts, though she insisted seeing everyone is helping her to stay calm.

While the others catch naps in the waiting room seating, I spend my time alternating between desperate prayers and trying to keep my mind blank, unable to fathom another tragedy befalling our family.

Less than twenty-four hours after Charlie was admitted into the hospital, she gives birth by emergency C-section to a tiny, three-pound baby girl who is rushed into the NICU, while another team of doctors work on Charlie.

38

Stevie

"**Y**OU OKAY?"

I see Gabe from the corner of my eye as he comes to stand beside me in front of the NICU observation window. I can't take my eyes off the tiny human being, about the size of Bobbie's old American Girl doll.

My niece, Evangeline Joy Saint. She has needles sticking into her and tubes coming out of her. Her little chest rising and falling quickly, she's breathing hard with her barely developed lungs as she fights to stay alive.

Thank God Charlie is doing much better, though she too has needles and tubes going in and out of her. She lost a lot of blood, but she is stable now and resting. Her blood pressure has come down too, so the doctors are confident she will have a complete recovery.

The family had a few minutes with her after the delivery, but she soon fell asleep due to exhaustion and painkillers. Knowing Charlie, she'll be loudly insisting on coming to the NICU as soon as she wakes up.

Overwhelmed by the close calls and overtired from another sleepless night, I can only nod in answer to Gabe's question. In my fatigued state, and in his presence, I'm unable to stop my thoughts from traveling down the dangerous path of "what might have been."

Looking at all the equipment helping her fight the battle for life, not to mention the best team of doctors money could afford, I don't know what would have happened if I'd decided to go through with the pregnancy and something like this happened. Being able to afford even the basics for a healthy baby had felt daunting at the time.

I know I made the best—the only—decision I could under the circumstances. While I regret having to make the decision, I can't regret the decision itself. And yet, grief for the child that would never be, for a child I may never have, makes my heart throb with pain.

"Hey." He puts a finger under my chin and urges me to face him.

I blink away my tears, but not before he sees them. He pulls me into his chest. "She'll be fine," he reassures me.

I'm not sure which "she" Gabe is referring to, but it doesn't matter. Charlie and the baby both need to be fine. But they aren't the only reasons I'm so emotional.

In the arms of the man with whom I'd dreamed of having a large family, the tears can't be stopped. They flow silently down my cheeks, soaking his shirt.

"Hey," he says, hugging me tighter. "It's going to be okay. Don't cry, my love."

I am filled with unbearable sadness, and I need to unburden myself of some of it. "I was...I was thinking...of our...our baby," I gasp out between the choking tears...tears I never shed when it happened.

"Oh, Christ, Stevie. Don't. Don't do that." Gabe holds me impossibly tighter, one hand cupping my head. I feel his kisses on the top of my head, my temple, drifting down to my cheeks. He cups my jaw with both hands and leans back to peer at me. Noting the nurses looking at us curiously, I duck my head. He tucks me against his side, keeping an arm around my shoulders, and walks me to the elevators.

I keep my head bowed and pressed to Gabe's shoulder to hide from the curious stares. It isn't until he tells me to sit that I look up. He's brought me to the hospital chapel. There is one person sitting in the front row of folding chairs before a simple nondenominational altar. He takes one look at us and rushes out.

Gabe sits and urges me onto his lap. I don't resist, burying my face against his chest. He circles his arms around me and holds me close, murmuring words I can't make out through my tears. I try to stop them, but the well from which they are spewing is deep. They appear to have been stored up for years and there seems to be no end in sight.

"I'm sorry, Stevie. I'm sorry. Please, baby. Don't cry."

After long minutes, Gabe's words finally penetrate. "Why are you sorry? You didn't do anything," I choke out. I take a breath to add the word "wrong," but he starts talking.

"Exactly. That's the problem. I didn't do anything except run away. I didn't stay and fight for you or wait until you were ready. And I was selfish for applying to the academy without talking to you first."

I shake my head. "No. I pushed you away," I whisper hoarsely. "I was the one who gave you the ultimatum, and it wasn't fair to you. You were always clear about your plans and I wouldn't accept it. I was in denial, thinking you'd change your mind."

"And I'd always known how you felt."

We sit in silence, our respective guilt a heavy blanket weighing us down. After long moments, I hear Gabe sigh.

"Stevie, can we talk about what you said the other night? I should have stayed and talked to you, but I just had to process, you know? It was a bombshell revelation. I'm sorry it took so long. Will you tell me what happened? When you found out you were pregnant?"

As much as I don't want to go back to those painful days, it is time to tell him all of it. It might be the only way we can both move on. To what and in which direction, I don't know.

I move off his lap to sit next to him and stare at the altar. Taking a deep breath, I begin. "I didn't know I was pregnant when we broke up. As depressed as I was, it wasn't until a few weeks later that I realized I had missed a period or two. When I confirmed with a home test, I went to your house, not knowing you had left. I thought you were just staying away and avoiding me. Your mother was there."

I huff out a short sarcastic laugh. "To say she wasn't happy to see me is an understatement. She blamed me for you enlisting with the Navy when we broke up and leaving for Illinois soon after to wait for bootcamp to start. And it had only recently started, so the only way to get in touch with you was to wait a month for the one allowed phone call or to mail a letter, which might not get to you for a couple of weeks.

"She didn't want to tell me how to get in touch with you. She was afraid I might upset you and distract you, causing you to get hurt." I shake my head. "I don't blame her. She had every right to be angry at me for knocking you off your chosen path and onto an even more dangerous one."

"You didn't force me to do anything, and it wasn't your fault," Gabe asserts with force. "I should have—"

I swivel in my seat and raise a hand to his mouth. "Please let me finish this." He holds my wrist and purses his lips against my fingers. I'm not sure if it's meant as an affectionate gesture or to prevent himself from talking.

I lower my hand, which he enfolds in his. "I want you to know," I continue, "that I did come to you when I found out. But when I learned you were gone, I had to figure out what to do. Your mother gave me your address, but I couldn't wait two or three weeks on the off-chance you might reply—or even open my letter. I was probably almost two months pregnant and needed to make a decision soon. But I was so scared and had no one I could turn to. Mom was still recovering from her stroke, and my sisters were too young to help me through this. My closest friends had moved away to college, and we were already drifting apart. And Brent was stressed enough with college and football and managing our finances."

A heavy weight descends on my shoulders as I remember how overwhelmed and alone I felt. "I was already trying to take care of everyone. I didn't know how I was going to take care of a baby too. We were barely scraping by as it was. Dad's benefits were going toward medical bills and the mortgage, and I was working as many hours as I could at the pool. Charlie, Georgie, and Joey were helping out with part-time jobs, but they also had school. I tried to figure out what to do, but kept coming back to the only possible answer. Any other option meant telling my mother, but I couldn't add to her stress. She already suffered one stroke. I didn't want to risk her having another one."

My throat tightens with more tears. "I thought about all the times we talked about having a big family and what we'd name our first-born and which one of us it would look like..."

His hand tightens around mine for a moment before he realizes and releases it. I forcibly swallow the growing lump so I can continue. "But there was no way I could keep it. To have the baby and be out of work, even for a few weeks...There were so many medical bills and so much work to do. I was already tired. I didn't know how I would manage it all while pregnant or with a newborn."

I pause and note Gabe's hands are closed into tight fists on his lap. He stares at them blindly. I'm not sure what he is thinking or feeling. Anger? Guilt? Loss?

"I really felt like I had no choice," I avow. "It wasn't easy and it wasn't what I wanted to do, believe me. I waited as long as I possibly could to make the decision, maybe too long. I'm not sure exactly how far along I was since I didn't go to the doctor to find out."

When I taste salt on my lips, I realize the tears are flowing again. Wiping my cheeks, I continue. "Luckily, my insurance covered abortion. I don't know what I would have done if it hadn't, since I didn't have that kind of money saved up. I went to a clinic for the pills, and they worked the way they were supposed to. I was told bleeding was normal for a couple of weeks after, but I didn't realize the cramping after the first few days was not. I was in so much pain and developed a fever, I finally ended up driving myself to the hospital. It turns out I had an incomplete abortion that became septic. They had to do a D & C since I hadn't...it hadn't completely..."

"Oh, Jesus. Oh, fuck." Gabe bows forward, his fists rising to press against his tightly shut eyes.

Just thinking about that day brought back all the emotions I'd felt—scared, helpless, in horrific pain, and terrified I was going to die.

My throat starts to close again with more tears as I form the words to tell him the rest, but they won't come out. I can't. Not now. It's too much all at once. All I'm able to push past the lump that makes my voice crack is, "Do you hate me for what I did? Can you forgive me?"

His words about Camilla's intent haunt me. Afraid of what I'll see in his eyes now that he knows what I did, I keep my head down and eyes closed. I jolt when his hands cup my face. My eyes spring open to see tears swimming in the deep blue ocean of his. He puts his forehead against mine and whispers, "I could never hate you. But you have every reason to hate me. I'm the one who needs to ask for your forgiveness for putting you in that position and leaving you to deal with it on your own. I'm—"

His voice breaks with tortured emotion. He swallows audibly and tries again. "I'm so fucking sorry, Stevie. Sorry I took off, sorry for not understanding your fears, for not considering you might have been pregnant."

I had never considered it either since we'd been careful to use protection. As much as I wanted a big family with Gabe, I had not wanted to start one at eighteen when I had so many other responsibilities.

He pauses, searching for the right words. "I wish you'd confided in someone who could have helped you, been there for you, kept you safe." He releases my face to push the heels of his palms against his brows. "Fuck! It should have been me." Clasping my head again, he screws his eyes shut again and presses his lips to my forehead, leaving them there for a long moment. When he leans back, his eyes are dark and turbulent.

"I was supposed to be that person. I'm sorry I wasn't there for you. It kills me that you had to go through that alone."

"I didn't want to burden anyone else. We were all going through so much already."

"So were you," he says, his voice and expression fierce. "It's not fair to you to take care of everyone and not accept any support in return. You took on a lot at a young age, did so much for your mother and your siblings, but you never asked anyone for help when you needed it. I've always loved that you are a strong, caring, unselfish person, but I wish you had opened up to someone—*anyone*—with your troubles."

He enfolds me in his arms again and shudders. "I came so close to losing you forever. I wish—" He brushes away his word with a shake of his head. "It doesn't matter. What happened can't be changed, and you made the best decision for you at the time."

I pull back in shock. "But you said you wouldn't be able to forgive Camilla when—"

"Is that why you've been so distant? Sweetheart, her situation was completely different from yours. She wasn't eighteen, broke, or alone." His voice hardens. "And if she'd been honest about why she didn't want the baby, that she was just counting the days until she could divorce me, I might have reacted differently."

We sit in silence, both of us lost in our thoughts, until I finally gather the courage to ask, "Gabe, do you want more children?"

"I'd love to have—" He breaks off when I start to pull out of his embrace. "Or not," he course corrects, sensing my distress. "Whatever you want. As long as I have you in my life."

"What if I can't have any kids?" I ask in a small voice, unable to look at him.

"Then we don't," he says simply. "Or we explore other options if you want." His brows furrow. "But why can't you?"

Saving the details for later, I say, "I had an infection that caused severe uterine scarring. It would take a miracle for me to have a baby now."

"But you insisted on me suiting up—except the last time."

"I can probably still get pregnant, but it comes with a lot of risk. I allowed one slip since I'm on birth control. After the terror and pain I went through after the botched abortion, I'm terrified of going through it again with a miscarriage."

"We'll do whatever keeps you safe, my love." He runs a hand over my hair, then rests it at my nape. "Does this mean we're back together?" he asks, his voice soft, a little uncertain and a lot hopeful. "Now that you're back in my life, I don't think I could handle it if you were missing from it again. I believe, more than ever, that you and I are meant to be together."

"Oh, Gabe. I don't know." Not wanting to disappoint him or lead him on with false hope, I caution, "I have some issues I need to work on. But I think I'd like to try, if you're willing to be patient."

He gathers me in his arms again and whispers against my temple. "Sweetheart, if being a SEAL—and a parent—has taught me anything, it's patience."

I give him a tentative smile, feeling a little of the hope and optimism I woke up with on Christmas morning.

39

Gabe

I WHISTLE AS I walk into the kitchen at home and sniff appreciatively at the delicious aroma that assails my nose. My gaze automatically goes to the stove to see what's cooking. Ma is standing there, as expected. My mood dims when I recall what she said to Stevie when she came here looking for me ten years ago.

We'll talk about what happened, but I've already forgiven her because I have no doubt she would have done everything she could to help Stevie in my absence had she known about the pregnancy. Without hesitation.

She'd loved Stevie before we started dating and approved of her when we did. I need to ensure Ma makes her peace with Stevie and treats her with love and respect. Otherwise, I will have to start looking for a new place to live. Although...I probably should anyway. I'm a grown-ass man with children of my own. I can't live with my parents forever. I'd much rather be living with Stevie as soon as possible. We've spent enough nights apart.

But a serious conversation about that will have to wait. Leo and Arianna rush into the kitchen to wrap themselves around me.

"Daddy!"

"Hi, Dad!"

"Hey, my little monsters. What have you been up to? Being good for Nonna?"

They loudly insist they have been and talk over each other about their day. I limp across the kitchen as Ari clings to my leg. I ignore the dull ache that the pull of the healing stitches causes. On my way to the sink to wash my hands, I kiss my mother on the cheek she already has tilted toward me.

"Smells great, Ma."

"Not that I'm complaining, mind you, but what are you doing home so early?" Ma asks, holding out a spoon for me to try the ribollita.

I take a taste and smack my lips. It reminds me of when Sandra had done the same with this exact dish. Had it only been two months ago?

"I gave Stevie a ride home from the hospital. Thought I'd stop by for lunch with these two little monkeys since I was nearby."

She opens her mouth to say something but changes her mind after a glance at Leo and Ari, who are listening with big ears. All she says is "Hmph" through tightly pressed lips. I narrow my eyes at her response. Okay, looks like I'll need to have that conversation with her sooner rather than later.

I shake Ari off me with a laugh and ruffle Leo's hair. "Okay, that's enough. Go play in the other room. I'll be there in a few minutes."

"And tell Nonno it's almost time for lunch," Ma says. "Make sure he doesn't fall asleep."

Pop's medications make him sleepy at all hours of the day, so he's often nodding off in his recliner. Because Leo and Ari have been raised mostly by Ma the last three years, they immediately do as they are told. My annoyance with her eases as I watch them scamper off.

My heart full of gratitude, I turn back to Ma. I take the spoon from her and have another taste.

"Mmm. Do you know the last time I had this, Stevie made it?"

"Oh, really?"

She turns her face away, but I bet her expression is as sour as her voice. My next words are meant not only to tease her, but also to set the stage for what we're about to discuss.

"It was as good as yours. Seems she still remembers it from when you taught her."

"Really?" she says again, slightly less sour, maybe even a little pleased.

"I'd like to invite her here for dinner tomorrow night." I'm not wasting another minute, which means getting the kids used to seeing her more often. I figure a casual family dinner that includes her mother and sister is a good start.

"Really?" She turns to me in surprise.

How many ways are there to say one word? When she realizes she is repeating herself, she gives me a narrow-eyed look that dares me to comment on it. I grin at her, eyebrow raised.

Her expression tightens with disapproval. "Are you sure it's a good idea for those two?" She tips her chin toward the family room.

Keeping my tone even, I ask, "Why wouldn't it be?"

She crosses her arms. "I'm afraid she's going to hurt you again...and this time, those two babies too." Her voice turns hard. "She did it once already, and it seems she's playing hot and cold already."

"What are you talking about?"

"Word travels."

"Rafe," I growl. "Since when did he become a gossip?"

Ma continues, ignoring my question. "I know how much you loved that girl back in the day. She broke your heart so badly that you weren't thinking clearly afterward."

"How do you know I didn't break up with her?" I challenge.

"Because you were ready to marry that girl."

"Okay, Ma. You have to stop calling her 'that girl.' And I'm still ready to marry her. In fact, I intend to as soon as I can convince her."

"You shouldn't have to convince her," she grumbles, her voice sour again. "And why would you risk heartbreak like that all over again?"

"Because we're older, wiser, and learning to communicate with each other. We have already started working through the issues we had before. Besides, I'm asking her to risk her heart too." I clasp my mother's shoulders and turn her to face me. I take a fortifying breath and ask, "Do you know why she broke up with me in the first place?"

Ma shakes her head. "You refused to talk about it to anyone, and I didn't ask when I saw her since I figured she wouldn't tell the truth anyway."

"She didn't want to marry me back then because she was terrified something would happen to me in the line of duty. Like her father. And yet, I went behind her back and applied to the police academy."

She gasps in disappointment. "Gabe, how could you do that to her? It's a valid concern, especially for a young girl. I wasn't crazy about you joining the force either when you mentioned it."

I nod. "The difference is that her anxiety is trauma-based. I didn't understand that back then." When I called the child psychologist the kids saw three years ago, I asked him about what to do about Leo's anxieties until his appointment, which was scheduled for next week. He'd mentioned that phrase, so I did some reading to help me understand what that meant and realized it applied to Stevie as well.

"Well, of course it is," she says like it's a no-brainer.

"There's one more thing, Ma. And I'm only telling you so you're more sensitive about the topic and keep your opinions to yourself around Stevie. I don't want you giving off this angry, distrustful vibe when she you see her. And no judgement."

Ma wanted more kids after me and Rafe, but it didn't happen. Because of it, she's made her opinion clear about those who choose to have abortions for reasons other than the extreme exceptions. She crosses her arms again and stares at me, already on the defensive.

I look in the direction of the family room to make sure Leo and Ari are still engrossed in their activities. I take a deep breath and exhale, knowing I'm going to devastate her with my words.

"Neither of us knew it at the time, but she was pregnant when I enlisted and left."

Ma's hand goes to her chest and her mouth gapes. "No." She shakes her head and looks at me. "But she never said when she came looking for you. She didn't tell me." The shock turns to distrust again and her eyes narrow. "How do you know she's not making all that up now? If she's telling the truth, why did I never see her pregnant?"

"If you saw her this morning, crying her heart out..." I stop, knowing this will break her heart even more, but I can't have her questioning Stevie at a later date about this. "With me gone and her family struggling with everything else that was going on with them, she felt she had no choice but to get an abortion." When Ma's face pales, I enfold her in my arms.

"Oh, Lord, forgive me. I'm so sorry, Gabe," she chokes out through her tears.

"Ma, I'm not blaming you. You didn't know. Ultimately, it was my fault for pushing her away and taking off in a tantrum when she turned down my proposal. I was humiliated, and I was angry she couldn't get past her phobia about something happening to me if I became a cop. I told her to get out of my life, Ma, and refused to talk to her before I left."

"Oh, Gabe. That poor girl," she says, then shakes her head, smiling wryly at me despite the tears still falling. "There I go again, calling her 'that girl'"

I chuckle. "At least you added a qualifier this time."

"To be eighteen and to have go through all that alone, with all the other burdens she was shouldering. And to think I practically cut the entire family out of my life after you left. That's how angry I was. I blamed her completely for making you go so far away and putting you in harm's way."

I kiss her cheek and let her go. "You can understand her fears. She's not to blame for my actions. I take full responsibility for them. I was immature and impulsive. We can't change the past, but I need you to make peace with Stevie. I plan to get us back on the path we were meant to be on. *Together.* I still love her, Ma. Just like you were it for Pop, she's the one for me...my soulmate and the girl I want to marry."

Ma comes back to me and places her palms on my jaw. "Then I hope you do. And I wish the two of you all the happiness in the world. You both deserve it, especially that poor—" She laughs sheepishly and corrects herself, "Especially Stevie."

40

Stevie

Despite the cold January temperature, I'm sweating as I arrive for my first dinner at the D'Angelo home in over ten years. My palms are so damp, I'm afraid the baking dish I'm holding onto for dear life is going to slip out of my hands. My nerves ease a bit when Gabe opens the door. His welcoming smile encompasses Mom and Bobbi, then turns tender as his gaze lands on me. He ushers us in. "Come on in, ladies. Let me take your coats."

Mom hands him hers and heads down the hall, eager to see Teresa and the kids. Bobbie puts the tin of cookies I baked on top of the tiramisu I'm holding so she can take her jacket off. Instead of taking the containers from me so I can do the same, she rushes after Mom. I appreciate the opportunity to have a minute alone with Gabe, but she could at least have taken the desserts with her.

I start down the hall so I can put them down, but Gabe holds me back with a hand on my hip. Instead of helping me out, he cups my face. "Hi, babe," he whispers against my mouth before kissing me deeply. I sigh into his mouth, the tension I've been holding since his invitation to dinner melting away.

In the next instant, it all comes rushing back, and I'm tight as a bowstring when Teresa's voice cuts through the bliss.

"There you are."

I jerk away, almost dropping the sweets I spent hours making. The sight of Gabe's mother coming down the hallway toward me has me taking a step back, ready to run out into the below-freezing temperatures of a New England winter. It may be warmer than the reception I'm about to get from Teresa.

Gabe's hands on my shoulders as he stands at my back prevent me from following through on the urge.

"Steady, sweetheart," he murmurs, pressing his lips to my temple. "It's going to be fine. Don't worry."

Easy for him to say. I paste on the polite smile I usually give his mother whenever I see her and hold out the desserts like an offering. She doesn't take them or say anything. Afraid of what I'll find in her eyes, I focus on her unsmiling mouth—and see it tremble. My gaze snaps up to meet hers. Her face transforms with the biggest smile she's ever bestowed upon me, even as her eyes overflow with tears.

I look over my shoulder at Gabe, bewildered, unsure of what to do. He just smiles and comes around to take the containers from my hands, a split second before his mother wraps me in her arms and sways side to side.

"Welcome, Stevie! It's been a long time since you've come to the house."

Uh, yeah. Because you basically told me I'd ruined your son's life and hate me.

I try to grab the back of Gabe's shirt as he walks away, but my upper arms are trapped by Teresa's strong grip around me. He winks at me and continues to the kitchen, leaving me alone with his mother, who seems to be suffering from selective memory loss. Even when she used to like me, she never greeted me with this much profuse enthusiasm.

"Stevie!"

I'm saved by Arianna, who comes running to squeeze herself between us, forcing Teresa to take a step back and let go of me. Able to breathe again, I smile at Ari and lean over to hug her. With love and affection. The way her Nonna just hugged me. The realization makes my eyes prick with tears and I stand. Teresa is wiping her face with her apron, and my heart softens.

"Happy birthday, Teresa." I take her hand and squeeze it, giving her a smile—a real one—to let her know all is forgiven. More tears roll down her cheeks, but she's still smiling—less rabidly, thank God.

"Thank you, my dear. I'm so glad you came. Please come in."

She leads me back the way she came, Ari taking my hand and chattering with her usual bubbly personality. I notice Anthony, Gabe's father, sitting in the same recliner he always sat in when I used to come over. Where my father was a big, blond, gregarious man who loved to laugh, Anthony is his almost complete opposite, becoming even quieter after my dad's death. They'd been best friends and firehouse brothers for over fifteen years.

Rafe sits on the sofa nearby, talking to him. For a surreal second, it feels like I've gone back in time and everything is the way it once was.

Except it's not. I'm here in the present, and though Dad and RJ aren't with us, it feels right to be here again.

I meet Gabe's warm, loving gaze across the room and know it's all going to be fine, just like he said.

I meet Leo's hostile stare across the dining table and wonder if it can really be fine if one of Gabe's children hates me. But then, Teresa hated me for ten years. The thought filling me with hope, I smile at the serious little boy. His suspicious gaze slides away from me to his father. Though Gabe included Mom and Bobbi in the invitation to dinner to ease his kids into the knowledge of our relationship, Leo is not fooled. I'd like to think it's because this is the first time his father has brought a woman home. But he looked at me with the same mistrust the first time he saw me at the pool, and again when we met at Christmas.

Determined to make progress with him tonight, I came prepared.

"Hey, Leo," I say softly, not wanting to interrupt the conversations around us. His gaze, more suspicious than ever, swivels back to me.

"Your dad tells me you like Legos. Since you were too young to see the Lego movies when they came out, do you want to see them with Alex when I take him? There's a theater near his house doing a Lego movie marathon." It's a good thing Andi won't be coming. I don't want him to think this is an activity with mothers and sons and that I am trying to replace his mother. But I do want him to see me with Alex, who loves me and thinks I am fun.

"I wanna go!" Ari yells into the silence that fell while I was speaking.

Shit. I should have asked when I was alone with Leo—or at least away from Ari's big ears. I suppose I could take her too, but I want to give more of my time and attention to Leo during the outing.

Her big blue eyes stare at me, begging me to include her. Unable to say no, I'm about to agree when Gabe's stern voice stops me.

"Arianna. She was talking to Leo."

Her eyes are welling with tears before he finishes speaking. Unsure what to do, literally stuck in the middle, I look at Teresa. I'm surprised she doesn't speak up and tell me what to do. She only quirks her brow at me, asking me silently how I'm going to handle this.

Turning back to Ari, I ask, "Wouldn't you rather have a girls-only spa day with me and Bobbie?"

Charlie would chew me out for promoting gender stereotypes. She used to hate being relegated to playing with dolls with me and

Georgie when she'd much rather have been playing ball with our brothers. Yet from what I've seen, I'm sure Ari would prefer an at-home spa day. She only wants to go so as not to be left out.

"Okay, but I want a playdate with Alex too," she demands.

Rafe chuckles. I bite my lip so I don't laugh, but I turn my head to look at Gabe and raise my eyebrows. His eyes narrow, not finding it amusing that his daughter already has her first crush. As sweet and charming as my godson is, it's not a surprise Ari is drawn to him. He'll be kind to her, but his mind is usually on Minecraft, Beyblades, and Legos...and sometimes sports.

I glance at Leo, who is staring at me with mistrust. Is that a step up from hostility?

Holding his gaze, I say, "Alex would love to have a playdate with you and *Leo*." I wink at him so he knows who Alex really wants to play with.

I'm rewarded with a twitch of Leo's lips before he purses them and looks away. My gaze meets Teresa's. She smiles and nods in approval. Gabe takes my hand under the table and holds it on his thigh, caressing my palm. The tingles that spread from there to the rest of my body are highly inappropriate while I sit at the table with parents and children. Rafe catches my eye and winks knowingly at me when those tingles gather between my legs, making me squirm.

Unable to take the sensation any longer without wanting to drag his hand between my legs so his thumb can continue the motion on a different part of my body, I turn my hand over so my palm lies flat on his thigh.

As we continue with dinner, my fingertips scrape over the fabric covering his bunching muscles. I don't even realize I'm doing it until he places his hand on top of mine and captures my fingers. I look at him in surprise, only to find his eyes blazing with desire.

I'd turned him on without meaning to, unintentionally getting payback. Unable to torture his thigh, I lick the corner of my lip, making it appear to anyone looking as if I'm wiping away a crumb with my tongue. He narrows his eyes at me in warning and puts my hand back on my own thigh.

I glance down at his lap and smirk at the bulge that's grown behind his zipper.

41

Stevie

"WELL, THAT WENT MUCH better than I expected," I say later as we lie in my bed. Gabe came over after he put the kids to bed so we could finish what we started at dinner. I stayed much later at his house than I anticipated. It was almost like old times, except we're with a new generation in our family. We played Uno and Candy Land after helping Teresa clean up after dessert. She raved about my tiramisu, telling me it was better than hers. Feeling the need to make up to me for some reason, she may have been laying it on a bit thick. I haven't had as anything as phenomenal as hers, even in Italy.

"Mm-hm. Told ya," Gabe mumbles, his face buried in my neck as he lies behind me. He sounds like he's ready to drop into sleep. A long yet gentle round of sex can have that effect, I suppose.

But I'm revved up after a successful evening. "What was that all about?" I ask.

"What was all what about?"

When I turn over to face him, he falls to his back, his forearm covering his eyes. My gaze runs over the tuft of hair at his armpit, over his rounded hard biceps, to the forearm resting on his forehead. The pose highlights his sexy mouth, which had been doing sinful things to me not long ago.

Unable to resist, I nip his luscious lower lip, holding it between my teeth. He grunts and slaps my ass in retaliation. I giggle and release him, running my tongue over the abused lip and sucking it to soothe the hurt. He keeps his palm on me, rubbing it over my buttocks.

"Baby, I can be ready again in thirty seconds flat if you do that to my cock."

"What? Bite it?" I tease.

I squeal when he pinches me softly.

"Bite me there and you're asking for a few more of these." Another slap, this one not as light as the first. It's his words more than the prickle of a sting that has me squirming against his leg.

He lifts his forearm to peer at me. His mouth curves into a grin. "You like that idea, do you?"

I stick my tongue out at him, embarrassed. Sex when we were young and inexperienced was exciting enough for us to never have the need to explore. Nor did we have the time or privacy. And if I could only have sex with Gabe the same way every time for the rest of my life, I'd be perfectly happy, because no one ever made me come harder than him, even when he had little experience. Still, I wouldn't mind exploring a little light play with him. Being with him as a grown woman and feeling safe and comfortable enough to discover different ways to turn each other on...

"Hm," he murmurs, eyes closed again. "Be a good girl, and—"

"Don't you mean bad girl?" I tease, crossing my arms on his chest and resting my chin on my forearm.

"—And *maybe*," he continues, "I'll make you come after turning your ass a pretty shade of pink." He peeks at me from under his elbow, his lips curving into a smug smile. "Almost like the color your cheeks are turning."

I'm over my embarrassment. My face is flushed because the thought of him doing that to me is making me wet and achy. I need to ease the ache. Since his leg is between mine, there's only one thing to do, I guess. I squeeze my thighs around his muscular one and start to ride him in a slow trot.

"What do you think you're doing, you bad girl?"

I moan, increasing the pace and pressure, loving the feel of his skin and muscle against my clit. He lowers his arm again, smoothing a hand over my head and down my body. My spine arches into his touch, loving the feel of his rough, callused hands wandering over my back and thighs.

"Fuck," he groans. "I need to find a place to live for us. One with soundproof walls."

I freeze, not sure I heard him correctly. "What?"

"I'm imagining you dripping wet, begging for release, until I finally finish you off with a handful of spanks on your pussy. I can almost hear you scream my name when you come."

I lose my train of thought at his words. I'm already wet, making a mess on his thigh, but the images he evokes in that deep sexy voice of his has me dripping, just like he imagined.

"You are insatiable, and I fucking love it," he growls.

Without warning, he flips us over and spears into me with one hard thrust. I cry out, forgetting to be quiet. It's impossible to hold in the intense pleasure of his hot, hard length filling me to overflow.

This bout of lovemaking is hard and intense, sexual rather than sensual. He pushes deep into me, over and over, stopping only to reposition me. He lifts my legs so that my knees are at my shoulders. Just as I'm ready to explode from his powerful thrusts, he stops again, pulling out.

"No! Keep going!" I pant.

Instead, he lifts me like I weigh nothing and flips me over, dragging my hips to his as he kneels behind me.

"Hold on, baby," is all the warning I get before he's inside me again. Good thing I wasn't on all fours, or I would have fallen flat on my face at the force of his entry. I brace my hands against the headboard. Within moments, I'm on the cusp of an orgasm again.

Sensing it, he curves an arm around me to hold me steady while he continues driving into me. Suddenly, I feel a sting on my ass. Before it can fully sink in that he spanked me, I'm coming. I remember to turn my mouth into the pillow in the nick of time, muffling my short scream.

Gabe follows me into orgasmic bliss, using my shoulder to silence his long groan. We stay like that, his strong body curved over mine, until he catches his breath enough to slide off me. The arm still around my waist tightens around me to pull my back against his damp chest. I snuggle against him. I'm the one ready to fall into sleep this time.

"Ah, fuck me. How does it keep getting better?"

"I don't know, but I can't fuck you again. Not tonight." I giggle at my own joke.

He smacks my thigh with just his fingers. "If I had any energy left, I'd love to prove you wrong, but I can barely even lift my hand."

Unfortunately, I need to clean up before I can go to sleep. We didn't use a condom, but I'm still protected by birth control. I make a move to slip out of bed, but his arm tightens around me.

"Where are you going?"

"Bathroom. I need to wash up."

He kisses my shoulder. "Stay right there."

Despite his lack of energy, he crawls over me, giving me a kiss on the forehead before he rolls off the bed to stand. I watch him—more specifically, his taut buttocks—as he walks into the bathroom. Something he said earlier niggles at the edges of my thoughts, but it slips away again when he comes out a minute later with a wet washcloth and a dry hand towel. On the way back to the bed, he stops to pull out one of my sleep shirts from my dresser.

I hold out my hand for the washcloth, but he hands me the shirt instead and sits by my legs.

"I got you, babe."

Our gazes meet and we both laugh. It helps ease the bit of embarrassment I feel at him cleaning me up between my legs and thighs. The old song title was one he'd often say to me. Sometimes it was when he pulled out his wallet before I could pay for something. Other times, it was when he held me as I cried out my stress and frustration. And when he wanted to make me laugh, he'd sing the song to me. It eventually became our song, the lyrics apropos of our young—idealistic—love.

When he's done, he gets back into bed with me and holds me close against his chest. His sigh of deep satisfaction warms me.

"What were you saying before?" he asks after he settles in. "About it going better than you expected?"

It takes a second before I'm able to pivot my thoughts to his mother. "Your mother was so sweet to me. I expected her to stare daggers at me all night." I gasp in dismay when I realize why. I lift up on my elbow, causing him to grunt when I disrupt his comfortable position. "How much did you tell her?"

"Not the details, but I explained why we broke up and told her not to blame you for me leaving and enlisting. I also told her you were pregnant and why you got the abortion." He holds my head to his chest when I try to lift it in protest. "Instead of fawning all over you, she would have stared daggers at you all evening. Tell me, which would you have preferred?"

"I suppose you have a point." I absently play with the coarse hairs on his chest. "I can't believe she's not upset with me."

"She understands." He kisses the top of my head and captures my hand, which has ventured farther out to explore the strands around his nipple.

"I'm not sure if I'll tell my mother. I don't want her to feel bad when there's nothing she could have done."

"If my mother knows, you may want to tell yours. Ma won't say anything, but it'll always be a secret between them. I think your mom would be more hurt if she somehow found out later."

"You're right." I sigh, not looking forward to the conversation. Shaking it off for now, I lean up on my elbow, careful to keep it from digging into him again, and grin at him. "You've come a long way, oh wise one. Is it being a SEAL that gave you so much wisdom?"

"If it was, then I'm thankful for it." He pauses, caressing a thumb over my cheek. "It's more likely experiencing life. I have to believe everything happened the way it did for a reason."

I frown, not sure if I agree.

"As painful as it was," he continues, "maybe we were meant to take that fork in the road first before walking on this path. Everything that happened led us here." He kisses me before adding, "And right here is pretty fucking perfect. Which brings me to what I really wanted to talk to you about. It's official. I won't be doing any more protection work."

Distressed at his pronouncement, I scramble to my knees, my legs folded under me. "Gabe, no. You don't have to—"

He sits up as well. "I want to. Rafe and I have been talking for weeks about hiring an operations manager. Since I'm already doing most of it, in addition to the security work, I'll take on that role full time instead of hiring someone who will need time to get up to speed. Rafe will take care of any business that's longer than a day trip. And I've had an idea for increasing revenue on the training end that I'll finally have the time to execute. There will still be some long days, but less overnight travel. I want to be home every night to put the kids to bed—then join you in ours."

Ours.

I need to find a place for us to live. I didn't mishear him when he said that earlier.

He tenderly tucks a strand of hair behind my ear. "See? This works out for all of us."

I stayed quiet, allowing Gabe to finish, but it's my turn now. I cup his perfectly chiseled jaw, his long past five o'clock shadow rough against my palm. This is everything I wanted ten years ago, and yet I tell him, "I can't ask that of you. It's not fair." When he is about to interrupt, I kiss him. "No, wait. My turn." I smile in reassurance at his worried expression. "You should do what you love to do when you go to work. Mom and Charlie said some things the other night that gave me a new perspective. And I'm going to start therapy soon to help me deal with everything that's happened since my dad died."

He takes my hands from his face, kissing each palm and holding them firmly. "I think that's a good idea if it will help you process your grief and trauma. In fact, I'm restarting Leo's sessions." He looks away and swallows before continuing. "He asked me something after the shooting, and it made me realize nothing is more important than the happiness of my family."

"What did he ask you?"

"He asked if I was coming back home that night and what would happen to him and Arianna if I didn't. He'd been going through exactly what you wanted to avoid, except he didn't have the option of walking away to avoid living with that anxiety every day." He buries his face in my neck, his voice tight when he continues. "It hurt so bad to know my little boy was carrying that inside him for years. How can I put him through that every night?" He lifts head to look into my tear-filled eyes. "How can I do that to you?"

I stare at him, searching for the truth of his words in his deep blue eyes.

He stares back unflinchingly. "The only job I've ever wanted was to protect people. And there is no one more important in the world for me to protect than my family. That's my number one job."

I nod, believing him. Or at least I believe that he believes what he's saying. I still have reservations. It can't be this easy, can it?

He settles back against the headboard, holding his arm out for me to settle in next to him. "Besides," he says, pulling the covers over our legs, "I'll still be protecting other people by training others how to do it right. And I'll continue to supervise and help plan and coordinate big events. I don't need to be in the field, standing in front of someone, to protect them."

"But you hate sitting at a desk," I argue. I remember that being his biggest objection to a "regular" job.

He huffs out a self-deprecating laugh. "I was an idiot for thinking carrying around a gun meant nonstop excitement. Some of my employees are former cops who talked about the hours of administrative shit they had to do after every incident." Shaking his head, he continues, "Standing guard for hours in front of a door is not exactly exciting either. It made me realize it's not sitting at a desk that I dislike so much. It's the drudgery of routine, doing the same thing every single day."

His eyes light up in excitement. "The best part is, I'll be working from the compound most days. Rafe and I agreed to give up the office space in Midtown since we hardly use it. We'll use the funds instead to speed along the construction of our new admin building. I can't work out of a trailer. But I can work on my laptop from anywhere, even home...Very convenient for midday quickies."

Beyond the beaming smile, the love and tenderness shining from his eyes tells me he means it when he says, "I'm excited about these changes and the opportunity to take the company in a new direction. To diversify it. So you see?" He picks up my hand and kisses the palm. "I'm not giving anything up that matters by changing my role. I'm gaining a strong and secure and happy family."

This time, I believe his earnest conviction. I shift to straddle him, my sleep shirt riding up my thighs. I loop my arms around his neck to clasp the back of his head and take his mouth in a kiss full of urgency and gratitude, hope and happiness. And most of all...love.

Epilogue

T HE LAST FEW WEEKS have flown by. It's been like a ride on a roller coaster, one with unpredictable twists and turns, not steep, scary dips. Exhilarating but nerve-wracking. Although, my long overdue visit to see Georgie after a call out of the blue could be considered a very scary dip. Thinking of how ill she looked fills me with profound sadness and regret for accepting her excuses instead of forcing the issue to see her long before now. Once I did everything I could to help her for the time being, I came home to focus on building a future—and a family—with Gabe.

Whether I'll be able to have a baby is still uncertain, but spending time at the hospital in the NICU with Evangeline has given me the chance to talk to new mothers who had challenging pregnancies. Watching them take their thriving newborns home has given me hope. I'll pursue my medical options once I'm certain the two children I already have—not of my body, but of my heart—feel secure with my presence in their lives.

Though Leo is not as openly effusive about me as Ari is, he and I have bonded over endless hours of blasting away at pixels without understanding the objective—on my part, at least—of Minecraft. It was during those times that a few words about the game eventually became longer conversations, during which we got to know one another.

I would sometimes tell him about things I saw while traveling, like the lions on the safari I went on in Africa.

"Were you scared?" he asked.

"I was a little nervous, but I'm glad I went. It was really cool to see them and the cubs playing in their natural habitat instead of a zoo."

Another time, I told him that my father had been best friends with his Nonno, which intrigued him.

"What happened to your dad?"

Not sure how much I should say, but not wanting to lie, I decided on honesty. "He died when I was in middle school." Then I confessed I was going to therapy because I still felt sad about it.

"Yeah, I'm going too." He said it casually with his eyes on his screen.

"I just started," I say, staying equally nonchalant. "I find it hard to talk about stuff with someone I don't really know. Does it get easier?"

He shrugged. "Yeah, I guess."

It was hard not to react when one day he said, "I know you're my dad's girlfriend."

Keeping my voice light, I replied, "Oh yeah? Well, did you know I was his girlfriend in high school?"

That got a reaction out of him. His eyes were big as he stared at me. "Really? Then why didn't you guys get married?"

By then, I had talked to his therapist, who said to always be honest, but don't offer more than he asks. "If he's ready to know more, he'll ask."

I kept my gaze steady on his and said, "We were too young."

"But didn't you love him?"

"I did, very much. And I love him even more now. But we wanted different things and didn't know how to compromise."

His brows furrowed, so much like his father's.

"It's like if you want to do one thing on your playdate with Alex, but he wants to do something else. Instead of figuring how both of you can do what you want together, you do what you want by yourself, and Alex does what he wants by himself."

"That's not a playdate then."

"Exactly," I said, proud of myself for how I explained it in a way he could understand.

"So Mom and Dad divorced because they wanted to do different things."

My moment of triumph didn't last long as I ventured onto that minefield. Cautiously, I answered, "Maybe. You would have to ask your dad about that."

I warned Gabe that Leo might ask him questions. When Leo didn't bring it up, Gabe did. They had a meaningful conversation about it, and it seemed to be a turning point in Leo's sense of security.

Between the time I spent with him doing what he likes, playdates with Alex, frequent family dinners, and eventually, bedtimes...it paid off. He not only asked for swim lessons of his own accord, he also asked if I could teach him how to take photos with my camera.

Only slightly less challenging had been my conversations with my mother and Teresa. Mom and I cried buckets and Teresa hugged and rocked me when I told them, separately, about the abortion and possibility of infertility. Guilt flowed between us, even as we insisted the other had nothing to be guilty about. I assured them it was the right choice and I don't regret it. My only regret is not going to the hospital sooner when I suspected something wasn't right.

But with the help of my therapist, I've learned to stop the useless thoughts of "what if" and "I should have." Wishing things had been different doesn't change what actually was, or is.

And when Mom called me brave and strong, two words I've never used to describe myself, it immediately made me feel like I had been—and still am.

Teresa shocked me because her response to my possibly not being able to give her more grandchildren was pragmatism. "Medical science is a marvel these days," she said. "I'll find specialists who can help you. And don't worry about the cost of the surgery to remove the scarring or the IVF if you need it. We'll figure it out," she adds.

I didn't tell her it was being on an operating table again with my feet in stirrups that scares me more than the cost. I still get anxiety every time I go to see my gynecologist. But with the help of my therapist, and after talking to Gabe, I've made an appointment with the specialist to see what she has to say.

Starting therapy has helped more than I ever thought it could. I like the woman that Joey's former college professor recommended. She's helped me process losing Dad and RJ in a way I hadn't been able to as a twelve-year-old who had been forced into a caretaker role once Bobbie was born.

She's given me tools to help me cope if I start to feel anxious, though I hardly do anymore. With everything out in the open between me and Gabe, we're communicating more honestly.

As for my career, I met with the photographer Gabe put me in contact with. I felt awful for refusing his generous offer to mentor me, but after learning he spent much of his time in the studio and hired assistants to edit the photos to give them his signature look, I realized that's not the kind of photography I want to do. I don't want to learn photo editing software or how to set up lights. I just want to work with my camera settings and natural light and capture whatever catches my eye.

But I'm looking into photography for live events like weddings or children's sporting events—as long as I'm not the one who has to do the touchups. And Bobbi wants to help me make photo books with some of my travel photos. "Otherwise they'll never see the light of day," she said.

However, the idea of becoming a swim instructor—maybe even starting my own business—is more appealing every time I consider it. Whenever I teach Ari and Leo something new and they beam with pride, it reminds me of why I wanted to be a teacher. This could be the next best thing, or even better, because I don't want to go back to college for four years to get a degree.

I want to have time for Leo and Ari—and any future children Gabe and I have. With the risk of miscarriage and perinatal issues still high even after surgery to remove the scarring, I don't know if I want to go through with that option. He and I discussed surrogacy and adoption if I decide not to undergo surgery to remove the scarring or if it doesn't work.

For now, I'm focusing on the present, which is holding hands with Gabe as we finish our tour of a house that hasn't yet come on the market. Leo and Ari ran around, marveling at the size of their potential bedrooms, which they've already claimed. They are especially excited about the playroom off the kitchen, the in-ground pool, and the home theater in the finished basement.

"Well? What do you think?"

"It's a wonderful house, but..." I hesitate, not sure if there's more to the question.

"What's the matter, babe?"

I bite my lip. His gaze goes to my mouth, then meets mine, the excitement in his eyes dimming.

"You don't like it? I know it needs a little updating, but—"

"The house is perfect. The kids love it and—"

"But you don't?" He takes my hands, his frown clearing. "That's okay. We'll keep looking."

I laugh, some of the tension easing. "No, that's not it. It's just...you haven't actually said who will be living here. You told the kids you wanted to show them something, and Ari asked if I could come too."

His eyes widen and his mouth drops open, then he smiles sheepishly. "Okay, yeah. I see how that looks. But, babe, I was asking *them* to come with *us*. You are the first person I wanted to show this to when I heard the owners were going to put the house on the market." He cups my face and leans in for a soft kiss. "Because I'm tired of not being able to sleep next to you all night, every night.

I want the space and privacy of our own house where we can live together...as a family."

"Are Leo and Ari okay with this? Did you talk to them about it?"

"Yes, they both approve." He kisses me again. "You asking me that is why I love you so much."

I loop my arms around his neck and raise my brows. "Oh yeah? Is that the only reason?"

He tugs me closer so I'm plastered against him from chest to thigh. "One of many, many reasons."

Lowering his head, he takes my mouth in a tender kiss that soon turns passionate. I forget everything as his tongue slides against mine, his—

"Did you ask her yet, Daddy? Did you? What did she say?"

I break away, but Gabe doesn't let go of me. We face Ari, who is bouncing with excitement, clapping her hands. Leo comes up next to her, grinning broadly.

"Yes, he—"

"No, I haven't." He laughs. "Pipe down for a second so I can."

Didn't he just ask me to move in with them? Confused, I turn to Gabe, but he steps away and takes my hand, then drops to one knee. When I stumble back in shock, he holds on to my hand to steady me. With his other, he reaches into his jeans pocket and pulls out a box. A ring box.

I gasp, unable to believe how quickly we've come to this point. I cover my open mouth with one hand, tears blurring my vision.

"Stephanie Anne Hutchinson, I knew you were the girl I was going to marry when I was seventeen years old. Life may have taken us on a detour, but we are back on the path we were meant to be on—together. I don't want to wait any longer to make you my wife. Will you make me the happiest man on earth and marry me and join our family?"

I glance at his—our—children, who are watching us with rapt attention. They appear to be holding their breaths. I hope not, because I have a question of my own before I can respond to his.

I drop to both knees in front of him and whisper, "Did you make sure they're okay with this? It's a lot. Moving into a new house...me moving in...and now this?"

He cups the back of my head and kisses my forehead. "I already talked to them, babe. Don't worry."

I need to hear it from them. Well, from Leo. Ari's feelings about this are practically vibrating from her. I hold out my free hand to them. Ari runs over immediately to grab it. Leo follows a bit more slowly and stands next to his father.

"Leo, if you're not ready for this, I understand."

"I am, Stevie. It's okay. I want you to marry my dad and be in this family."

"Then I'd be honored to join your family. I love you all so much." With tears overflowing, I free my hand from Gabe's and hold out my arm to the little boy. He readily comes to me and I hug him close. Ari throws her arms around me. I laugh and cry and try not to tip over, but I didn't need to worry about that, because Gabe puts his arms protectively around the three of us, holding on tight.

"Is that a yes, my love?"

"Yes! Of course I'll marry you."

He sits back and takes the ring out of the box.

"Then let's get this on you. I've waited over a decade to do this."

Letting go of Ari, I hold my shaking hand out to him. I can barely see what the ring looks like through the tears, though the diamond sparkles as he slides it onto my finger. And I can clearly see Gabe's love shining even brighter.

Keeping my hand in his, he brings it to his mouth for a kiss and says, "Together. Forever."

"Forever. And no more waiting."

"Does that mean we can fly to Vegas today and I can call you my wife by tomorrow?" He stands and helps me up.

I grimace. "I would love to, but can you imagine what your mother would have to say about that? No, let's do this right. I want my mother and Brent to walk me down the aisle, and Leo and Alex to be ring bearers, and..." I pause for dramatic effect, knowing Ari is waiting for her name to be mentioned. "And Ari to be our flower girl."

Her expression goes from breathless anticipation to boundless joy as she squeals and claps her hands.

"I'm going to be a flower girl, *and* I'm going to get a mommy," she screams. She runs around, unable to contain her happiness.

My gaze meets Leo's. He shakes his head and rolls his eyes at his sister's antics. But he's smiling as he looks from me to his father, who holds me close.

Remembering Charlie's wish for a double wedding, I consider it for a half second. That was in June. Much too far in the future. I don't want to waste a minute more than we already have.

Author's Note

TRIGGER WARNINGS:
Ready To Risk contains profanity, several steamy scenes, and the sensitive topics of gun violence, abortion, pregnancy loss, infertility, and preterm labor. Also, child abandonment and tragic loss of family members in the past.

AUTHOR'S NOTE:
Abortion is a sensitive and controversial topic, one not often found in romance novels. I had no intention of including it when I wrote the first draft. As a pantser, I start every book with a glimmer of an idea and NO outline to guide me, simply writing down what my characters reveal to me. That is how Stevie's story came about, her experience flowing onto the page without conscious thought. With every rewrite, I wrestled with the decision to keep it or to revise it and stay within the norms of romance novels. In the end, I opted to keep it as part of Stevie's story, as it is for millions of real women.

What's Next?

I hope you enjoyed Stevie and Gabe's story as much as I did writing it.

Reviews are so important for new indie authors like me. It would mean the world to me if you took a quick moment to leave a review on <u>Amazon</u> and/or <u>Goodreads</u>, and of course, any other platform.

The Ready For Love series continues in Ready To Trust, featuring another couple with appearances by the Hutchinson siblings. In the meantime, be sure to stay updated by signing up for my newsletter at: <u>http://www.shefaliprem.com</u>

My (not very frequent) newsletter will also have information about giveaways and sneak peeks of upcoming titles in the Ready For Love series that will include more of the Hutchinsons and their friends. Please visit my website for book blurbs and links to order the books as they are released.

<u>READY FOR LOVE SERIES:</u>
Ready to Play (Brent & Joey)
Ready to Live (Charlie & Luc)
Ready to Risk (Stevie & Gabe)
Ready to Trust – Early 2026
Ready to Fight – Mid 2026
Ready to Hope – Late 2026/Early 2027

Acknowledgements

A HUGE THANKS ONCE again to my editor Kristen Tate for your endless patience and your knowledge and expertise. It allows me to write freely, because I know you'll be coming up behind me to clean up the mess I make.

A special thank you to my beta readers who helped me work through the sensitive issues in this story.

My heartfelt gratitude goes to my ARC reviewers who post their beautiful reviews and help spread the word about my books. You put a smile on my face and make my day, every time! Your kind words and enthusiasm keep me going when I wonder why I stay up nights to write instead of getting much-needed sleep!

I also want to thank every reader who has taken a chance on one of my books when you have so many others to choose from. I hope I've made it worth your while with Stevie and Gabe's story.

Thank you to the indie authors and bookstagrammers who cheer me on and engage with me online so I don't feel like I'm posting into the void.

And last, but definitely not least, I couldn't do this without my family. Sure, as my dedication says, they don't understand my obsession with romance books, but they encourage me to do what I love.

About the author

S HEFALI PREM IS A South Asian-American who has lived on both coasts and traveled to—or at least passed through—almost every state in the US. She loves to read and write heartfelt emotional romances with a lot of heat and a guaranteed happily-ever-after.

Sign up at to be notified of bonus content, upcoming releases, sneak peeks, and giveaways. And don't forget to follow her on social media. Get all the social media links:

https://linktr.ee/shefalipremromance

Scan Me

www.ingramcontent.com/pod-product-compliance
Lightning Source LLC
Chambersburg PA
CBHW050027120726
47903CB00006B/1940